This book belongs to...

First Printing 2010 (E. R. Hardcastle) as *The Recruit Adventure*. Re-printed in 2018 (E. Rachael Hardcastle) as *Heaven & Eternity*, part of *Finding Pandora: The Complete Collection* - ISBN: 978-1-9999688-0-9

I

Published by Curious Cat Books,
West Yorkshire, UK
www.rachaelhardcastle.com

Map designed with Inkarnate. The map is not to scale and is for entertainment purposes only.

Typesetting: Requiem, FoglihtenNo04, Aline, Old Cupboard, Old Almanac, Times New Roman. All fonts are free for commercial use.

Cover design: Rachael Hardcastle. All images are free for commercial use under the CCO License.
Copy-editing and proofreading by Curious Cat Books.
Interior formatting and design by Curious Cat Books.

OF HEAVENS & WILD FLOWERS

Harvest Fields
Mousique
Manaia Forest
Pouki's Cabin
Casper's Cabin
Orc Pit
Drakonta
Highman's Point
Wolf Territory
Recruit Lair
Haeylo City

Volcanic Ruins
Demonic Territory
Marshland
Petrified Forest
The Land Bridge
The Depths
Queen's Port
Entit Sehde Palace
Rulecast Tower
The Edge
Abandoned Dwarf Mine
The Valley
Recruit HQ
Enzo
Enzo Beach
Drakontan Mountains
Barren Fishtail
Tribal Settlement
Mirror Of The Soul

ONE

Arriette Monroe ripped back the ugly off-white curtains in the infirmary's waiting room. She grumbled and slumped on her back to gaze out at the constellations of twinkling stairs against the Recruit lair's midnight canvas.

Those fabricated specs of silver enticed a second glance; she imagined worlds besides Haeylo with little more to worry about than a day's housework, because now she'd found and taken shelter with the Recruit—the organisation responsible for the protection of their delicate planet—hard work and arduous choices would hunt her.

After stretching her legs, she yawned and checked the time. A full day had passed since Baby A's tragedy, and briefly, Arriette lost herself. She remembered the angel's face twisting in agony as the waiting room door swung open; Arriette startled as a tall, broad man strolled in. He knelt beside her makeshift bed to place a comforting palm on her cheek.

"Tobias, how is she?"

"She's going to be fine," he whispered.

Tobias Shallow, their group's dreamer, was a scale

two on the Haeyloian Power Scale. Despite how intimidating that sheer unused power was, Tobias was also Arriette's crush and her first since Kalvin Avery, the man she thought she had loved wholeheartedly, until she met Tobias. Their eyes locked—her khaki with his hazel—and she sighed against his warmth.

His mousey hair had grown since they met and now hung in shaggier locks across his hazel eyes. He blew a loose strand away and kissed the back of Arriette's hand.

"Tabitha said she's on the ward now and you can visit if you want to."

"Isn't she sleeping?" Arriette sighed—she wished *she* had been sleeping, but she couldn't switch her mind off.

"Casper's been to see her, so she's awake."

Tabitha Hope had rushed Baby A to the lair's infirmary. Years of study as a retainer had filled Tabitha's eidetic memory with medical research and practices, so Arriette trusted her more than anyone to care for her best friend.

She handed Tobias a bag she'd been using as a pillow and sat upright. Inside, she'd stuffed some spare clothes and snacks. Many of the other chairs in the room were occupied by sleeping supes: a sorcerer awaiting the birth of his first child; an elderly shape-shifting woman; a nurse of Arriette's age who, by the constant huffing and groaning, regretted agreeing to work this double shift.

Arriette nodded at them as she left the room, hand-in-hand with Tobias, and grateful for his grounding palm cupping hers.

"You look exhausted," he said. "Why don't you stay longer and rest. I've got this."

"No. It's been a lousy few days, but you already let me rest too long."

Determined not to waste time, they strode along a narrow white corridor that smelled of chemicals, but was shiny and clean. Arriette could see her wild brunette hair reflected in the tiles like a ruffled lion's mane. On this floor, thankfully, there were few passers-by except for the occasional retainer.

"At least she'll make a full recovery. I don't understand how she didn't—"

Tobias cut in. "Doesn't matter. It's not our business. When she's ready, she'll explain how this happened. We should give her time."

Arriette nodded, mostly to herself. "Yeah, you're right."

She slipped into her spare clothes before psyching herself up to see the group's time-travelling angel for the first time since her miscarriage. The clothes were not her style and to her, a luxury. Sebastian Sky was the first sorcerer Arriette had ever met, and he'd paid for them as thanks for the group's efforts so far. Having always provided for herself at Rosewood Cottage, Arriette felt guilty for allowing it, especially since Sebastian was so much younger than her. Afterwards, he'd also given her a full tour of the underground lair, including the town hall and infirmary.

She'd remembered most of his directions.

From her purchases, Arriette wore a white short-sleeved shirt and cream cotton trousers. Her hair was dishevelled and dull and her khaki eyes sat upon puffy grey bags. Around her shoulders, she wrapped a charcoal-coloured cardigan.

"Are you coming?" she asked Tobias.

"I'll wait here," he insisted, so she slid into the room alone and anxious, thankful for the warmth of the soft material as the window's breeze tousled her hair.

Although now medicated, exhausted, and wired to magically-powered machines, Baby A was still beautiful. Her stunning sapphire eyes were bright and her short, golden hair perfectly straight.

"Arriette! I'm glad you're finally here. Are you alright? Hey, Recruit fashion looks *good* on you!" She winked.

Arriette cleared her throat, self-conscious in her unfamiliar attire. "I'm... fine; I fell asleep in the waiting room."

Baby A rolled her eyes. "Liar."

"Alright, so I sat and worried about you. Sue me."

The distraught angel ran a delicate hand across her stomach. "I'm in much less pain. Tabitha promises my blood will fade the scar."

"How do you feel?"

"Lost, actually. I'm mourning someone I never met."

The Recruit's retainers, including Tabitha Hope, said the cause hadn't been determined, but Tabitha had narrowed it down. Most likely, she explained, to the werewolf attack in Manaia Forest or even the strain of catching her friend as she fell from the sky.

Arriette couldn't remember her complaining of any discomfort, though, but her healing angelic blood likely masked the symptoms.

Arriette stared at her feet. "It happened so suddenly."

"If I knew I was pregnant I'd have told you," Baby A said, taking hold of Arriette's hand. "I swear."

Thanks to the qualities of her blood, Baby A's recovery would be smooth. Retaining doctors had already asked her to be a donor for other supes in need. Reluctant to supply even the smallest sample (and given how humans were almost extinct so there was a higher demand for transfusions) most angels didn't want to be taken advantage of. Baby A had agreed to donate a one-off volume, once released, as a thank you. And Arriette had been asked but refused. She needed her strength and couldn't afford to feel weary with an approaching orc army and the missing member of their group, Pouki Hallidae, still to find.

Arriette sat in the chair beside her bed.

"How could I miss something *this* serious?" Baby A asked. "Though, perhaps it's for the best. Timing wise, I mean."

"There is never going to be an ideal time now Pandora's box is back on the Recruit's radar." She cleared her throat. "I hate to ask but do you know who—"

"It's not important. Not *possible*, even. The Recruit don't need a petty dispute."

Arriette sighed. "I think it's obvious who the father is, though. It's awkward—"

"It shouldn't be. It's in the past now, *right*?"

Arriette had already considered who the father of Baby A's child was likely to be. Her conclusion didn't inspire any confidence in her crush, and over-thinking this would distract her from her many important duties, or eventually destroy the relationships she held so dear. Baby A was right that it *shouldn't* matter. But to Arriette, it did.

"You need to go," Baby A said.

Saddened, Arriette shook her head frantically. "I won't leave you here. This place is creepy and it *smells*. I can stay with you and the others—."

"I'm safe here and it's so clean I could eat off the floor. It's quiet. I can rest. I *need* to." When Arriette didn't move, Baby A shooed her. "What are you waiting for?"

"I guess even this place needs protecting now. Let me know if there's anything you need."

"Go!"

The girls hugged as tight as Baby A could comfortably manage before Arriette left her to sleep.

She braced herself when she collided with Tobias in the corridor.

He raised an eyebrow. "Everything alright?" he asked when she'd closed the door. "You weren't in there long."

"I didn't need to be. Ooh, I can't *believe* you didn't tell me, Tobias!" She suddenly lowered her voice. "How could you knock her up and keep it a secret?"

He startled, then scowled. "How is this *my* fault?"

Arriette scoffed at his ignorance. "I'm sorry, I had no idea women could make a baby *alone*. Given *our* situation," she said and slapped her hands between their chests, "I thought you'd have said something to *me* at the very least."

"Uh, it's complicated, Arriette."

With a snort, she replied, "Understatement of the century!"

"Well what did you expect would happen here?"

Arriette scowled, taken aback. Did he mean in the hospital, or between them?

"Perhaps that you'd have the decency to admit you got my best friend pregnant? Eww, what is it with my boyfriends and my friends? I'm destined to be alone, I know it." She smacked her palm against her head and took off down the corridor. "Perhaps it's me? I'm just a monster magnet. Oh, and she's not coming with us anyway, not after what you've done."

Tobias stomped along behind. "You really believe Baby A and I are an item, don't you?" He chortled in disbelief, and seeing Arriette's fierce expression, gripped her by the wrist and pulled her aside.

"Wait, I'm not a criminal, Arriette, and I wouldn't—"

Arriette shoved him away... hard. "*How* could you even suggest that?"

"Because of those!" Tobias gestured at the claws protruding from Arriette's knuckles and shifted to hold her by the shoulders instead. "I see how you're glaring at me, too. Do you hate me?"

"This is just my face. And you don't need to manhandle me," she said, swinging one arm to separate them. "I can be convinced through responsible discussion."

"Really? Because your tiger paws suggest otherwise."

His strength quickly made it impossible for her to use them when he pinned both hands to her butt and forced the weight of his chest against her. Arriette went face-first to the wall, and he held her still for a moment, keeping his distance from her Shape-Shifted weapons.

"Sometimes it's like you haven't changed at all. Not since day one. So say what you're thinking aloud, Arry!"

"I'm thinking that I've asked you repeatedly not to call me Arry! *It's Arriette!*"

His eyes were alight. "What went on between Baby A and me has absolutely nothing to do with you. Any of you. That situation ended long before you and I met. What you're suggesting is impossible because Baby A and I never, well, our relationship wasn't physical. But... I *am* the father. I think. Oh, I don't know!"

She squirmed but still couldn't gain enough freedom. "Get off me!"

"I mean it," he said, squeezing her tighter. "This

whole thing is a huge mistake. It doesn't add up."

Arriette thrashed until he let go. They stood, teeth barred at one another, for a few silent seconds.

"You're so *difficult*," Tobias growled.

She rubbed her wrists, careful not to catch her unmoving claws. "When I have to be. If you're going to threaten me, opt for a more subtle method."

"*I'm* threatening *you*?"

"There's a witness!"

Arriette gestured behind Tobias as two thin sandals, a long white robe and an equally lengthy beard appeared in the corridor. Casper was Arriette's shape-shifting mentor and the current leader of the Recruit. He stood with his arms folded, frowning at Tobias's scrunched fists through a mass of white facial hair. However small and insignificant he'd become to infiltrate their conversation, Arriette had grown to love Casper for his honest, calming nature.

And she couldn't blame him for lingering by Baby A's ward as a literal fly on the wall. They were all worried about her.

He admired the claws she'd inherited from his power, then adjusted the robes he'd quickly re-dressed in following his first proper shift since the city.

"Arriette is never to be harmed, Tobias."

She offered half a smile, still flustered. "At least there's one gentleman in this building."

The dreamer's fists relaxed and his shoulders loosened. His eyes, however, never left Arriette's, and were narrow with fury.

"Are you going to let her get away with that?"

"What? Telling the truth?" she spat.

He shook his fist at her. "I'm not finished yet, Arriette. Test your gifts, I *dare* you. I know you want to;

there's no hiding it these days."

Casper slid between them. "That's enough! Distance yourselves. In my presence, men do not hit women."

"How about when you've gone?" Tobias mumbled, but he backed off at the old man's command. "She's not a woman, Casper, she's a vicious weapon. You said it yourself. Look at those claws. They materialised from a mere accusation! Did you hear her suggestion that Baby A and I were... or that I..."

Arriette retracted her claws and groaned as her hands throbbed. "Ugh, there. Remember what happened to the last person who defied me, Tobias, hmm? I swept her up and threw her in the trash. I'm not the only weapon around here," she hissed, nodding at the shape-shifter. "You wouldn't want to end up like Harriet, *would* you?"

"And *you* stop winding him up!" Casper demanded. "I did what I had to with Harriet. Our relationship had always been... rocky." She flinched but didn't back down. "You are both much more sensible, or so I thought."

"Go on and dig your claws in me, Arriette. I'll make it easy. If you can manage to produce them again, that is."

She strained as her fingernails grew this time, leaving her knuckles to rest. He was right, she had zero control and if she swiped now, she'd probably take off his head.

Despite her doubt, she uttered, *"Try me."*

Casper shoved Tobias further down the corridor away from the ward. "You leave me no choice. I can't risk taking you out there if you're going to squabble. The orc army is getting closer. I'd planned to hand leadership over soon, Arriette, but now I'm not sure you wouldn't assassinate your own boyfriend."

"He's not—"

"She's not—"

"Doesn't matter," Casper groaned. "I have enough to worry about at the moment, and so does poor Baby A, without you two being at each other's throats."

Arriette protested. "I can't leave anyway because I won't abandon her when she needs me the most, nor Pouki now he's missing."

"Oh just go, Arriette. Baby A's safer without you."

Arriette scoffed and threw him a rude gesture. She'd mastered two of her now five gifts including the everlast pendant she'd chosen from the Indalo store in less than a month, which was a Haeyloian record because few possessed more than two abilities. To top that success, she'd been one of the best and only friends Tobias Shallow had ever known.

Had she been wrong to trust him? To care for him?

Casper sighed. "He didn't mean that. He's just tired and worried about his friend's recovery. *Right*, Tobias?"

Tobias glared at his feet and shrugged. Whether he'd meant it or not, Arriette was hurt.

"I'll take your silence as an apology." She mumbled.

"Do with it what you will," he replied."

"Just be careful around me. I don't want to kill you, too when you practically said it yourself, Tobias; I'm good at murdering my loved ones."

TWO

It took a few profound, courageous breaths for Arriette to calm the adrenaline in her system. She could be planning the orc army's defeat instead of dealing with their unexpected love triangle.

The orcs had been patrolling the only entrance to the Recruit's underground lair—at least the only *working* entrance, which was beneath the waterfall and through the tunnel to the Indalo passageway. For now, they were trapped and Pouki hadn't re-emerged yet; Arriette *knew* the orcs were responsible for his kidnap. He'd never leave without a word, especially at such a crucial time.

The Recruit's first priority would be to find the wormhole and figure out how to get it to work again. Then her friends and everyone else seeking shelter in the lair could exit safely. Arriette could look for Pouki.

With Baby A now in the infirmary, they'd need a stand-in time-traveller to assist; although Arriette did possess the gift, she hadn't trained to use it. Nobody could replace the trusted and respected angel they all loved anyway—it felt like... *cheating*.

As if on cue, Tobias poked his head around the corner and cleared his throat. "We need to make a plan, Arriette."

"Storming off is your cue to leave me alone, Tobias, and I have a plan, thank you." She was in no mood to be pestered.

"It looks like you're panicking from where *I* stand."

Arriette thumbed her aching temples. "Well, go stand somewhere else then!" she growled. "Susan, Scarlett and Coyote died in vain if we don't respond to Charles's message. He was clearly warning us about Falkon Lou's involvement—he tried to prevent it. He owes me for returning Rihaana. He'll send help if I ask."

Thanks to Arriette and her friends, Charles and his daughter Rihaana Melovich were happily reunited. Arriette assumed they'd jump at the chance to repay their debts. As a first-class everlast, Charles could afford to settle *all* his debts (and then some!). If only they could break free of the lair and send word to him somehow.

Arriette teased his handwritten words on the end of her tongue, remembering that he'd quoted William Blake's Auguries of Innocence with '*God appears and God is light, to those poor souls who dwell in night,*'" to indicate their enemy was a day-walker. So Arriette thought it originally referred to an apocalyptic event, caused by an unexpected form of evil. Not an orc, demon or a vampyr, but a creature unafraid of the daylight. Someone the Recruit had no advantage over.

Someone like the everlast, Falkon Lou.

"We already figured out the poem thing," he said. "So what's the problem? This isn't about responding to Charles. You want to go outside the lair for some other reason. I can practically see the cogs turning."

"I don't need to justify anything to anyone."

In Drakonta, when visiting her mother, Arriette met a creature named Coyote. He looked like an orc—bribed to hide his true identity by the powerful everlast they were now so afraid of. Burned to his skin was the everlast symbol for immortality—Infinity's figure eight—which looked a lot like Arriette's Dagaz dreaming rune, but less jagged.

The Recruit now believed Falkon to be the cause of Susan and Scarlett's deaths. Like Arriette, Falkon Lou had also been reunited with his ideal everlast pendant (or his *Mirror of the Soul,* as it was often called). His newfound power was now focused on finding Pandora's box to rule Haeylo's government *and* the Underworld, so he could eventually prevent the human race from taking back their planet. In exchange for providing the Underworld with human slaves, Falkon had roped every orc messenger he could find into the hunt, resulting in smaller armies like the one the Recruit now faced, roaming the surface on behalf of horned demonic masters who couldn't handle the sunlight.

To distract Arriette from this plan (and to punish Coyote), he'd sent the confused shape-shifter to the Underworld as an orc, and they'd brainwashed him before dispatching him in search of the Recruit. Arriette could only deem their orc problem to be the result of Falkon's orders or, since *she'd* pushed him through the mirrored entrance, Coyote's capture and successful torture.

Perhaps both.

She'd sent Coyote back to the Underworld to avenge his family. Was this Arriette's fault? Had *she* triggered this nightmare? If Falkon succeeded in finding Pandora's box before they did, *'darkness is coming'* would no longer be a message. It would be Haeylo's reality.

"We can't leave Pouki out there. We should go after him." Arriette shoved Tobias aside, hating that she still shuddered at any skin-to-skin contact. It blew around the butterflies in her stomach, sent electric bolts through her veins and furiously thumped her heart against her chest—this physical reaction to his presence gave her love for him away.

He scurried to block her path. "You can't just waltz out there. There are orcs swarming the river bank trying to get in here. You'd have to be crazy. That's why we're searching for that old wormhole, remember? We can evacuate *away* from their patrols."

"And away from Pouki? How many times do I have to tell you all that I'm not walking away without him."

He sighed. "You're too reckless for your own good. Pouki wouldn't want you to risk your life for his."

"I guess this is why *I'm* the next in line for leadership and you're not," she mocked, then shook her head at the mere suggestion of abandoning their friend.

"Wow. Cheap shot."

She groaned and combed her sweaty fingers through her hair. "I've already killed three good guys, Tobias. I can't condemn Pouki to meet the same fate. Sometimes we have to make sacrifices for the ones we love. I'd do the same for you." She swallowed hard. "For any of you, I mean. We have to act foolishly and recklessly. It's *my* responsibility, not yours. If Pouki is still alive then I'm going out there to rescue him. To do that, I need to leave now."

Tobias called out for Casper. He hadn't been far away; he trusted neither of them to behave, but hoped they'd put these petty disputes to rest on their own.

When will you both learn?

Arriette heard shuffling footsteps at the end of the corridor and squinted beneath the luminous lighting to focus on his brilliant white robes.

"She's leaving, Casper." He turned to face Arriette

and announced, "You're not being as brave as you think."

Casper squeezed Arriette's shoulder but resisted the urge to hug her. The sadness he'd seen at the waterfall had crept back into her lonesome gaze. "None of what's happening to us down here is your fault."

"For you to have to justify that only confirms that it is," she moaned. "Have we discovered the official cause of Scarlett's death, other than just a 'hex'?"

"Not yet. Her body is still in our morgue."

"There's a morgue here?" Arriette shuddered. "*Creepy.*"

"Necessary," Casper said blandly.

"There's your reason for me to stay, Tobias. Happy?"

"Not really," he grumbled, "because Scarlett's death isn't going to lead us to Pouki."

"It might indicate who or *what* else could be waiting."

Arriette elbowed him in the ribs and barged past towards Baby A's room. It was close to the main stairwell, leading to the exit.

Casper hurried along behind her, his speed restricted by his clothing. He came to a sudden halt at the sight of the Paulei Leigh, sitting alone on a chair outside the angel's ward.

"What are you doing here? Are you alright?"

He stared blankly into a rippling cup of lemon tea, and startled when he saw the determination in Arriette's scowl.

"I have nowhere else to be right now," he replied. "Is everything OK... here?"

She offered a weak smile and nudged him gently. "I'm worried about Baby A too, that's all. They're taking good care of her. She's in high spirits, and Tabitha is here."

"Thank you," he said. "I can't help but wonder... if I'd thought to read you all as you entered the lair, I might have been able to—"

"Telepathy wouldn't have changed the outcome," she assured him, then placed her hands defiantly on her hips. "I think it's time we finished what these orcs started. Do me a favour?" She whipped her wrist. "Round up the troops."

Paulei dumped his empty cup in the trash. "Sounds like the beginning of a plan!"

It only took half an hour for her friends to gather in the waiting room. Paulei began showing each of them to their seats, whilst Arriette bit her nails in her own. She didn't want it to come to this. Casper had said no to war when the group first arrived at the lair. Given the proximity of their enemies, she could find no other alternative.

"That's everyone," said Paulei, offering a thumbs up. He perched on the edge of a coffee table beside her.

Arriette tugged Casper's arm. "Before I visit Scarlett's body, should we have a history lesson, even if it's painful for you?"

Casper nodded. He stood, arms folded by the door, but didn't seem to want to run from the truth.

"I think it's time, too." He patted her back and addressed his friends with a clear, projecting voice. "As your next leader, it's Arriette's responsibility to ensure our safety. Without us standing in the way, Haeylo will be crushed by what I predict to be a dark future plagued with evil and led by a wicked, power-happy everlast. As far as we know, the orc army at the river bank can't get in here."

Arriette turned to Sebastian. "It's protected by magic?"

A unanimous hum of agreement filled the room and Sebastian confirmed verbally. They were safe in the lair... for now, but they couldn't hide forever.

"Good, then we have some time. Because at the moment, there's a secret weighing heavily on the Recruit and Arriette can't do her job if you're all blind to it."

She cast a sideways glance at Tobias. He avoided her gaze, instead following Casper's movements as he took a few nervous steps, swallowing hard.

"This goes against all my instincts, and the rules I am so accustomed to following." He closed his eyes as he said, "I am not who you once believed me to be."

The room fell silent. Everyone was confused, intrigued, impatient. Their leader hadn't lied, though, because Casper was the first ever Recruit member to be appointed. The creator himself had given him the gift of morphing into another form. Arriette felt guilty asking him to reveal his origin story now when Zïnnyi ordered him never to do so, but the strength and integrity of the group mattered more.

The air was thick with tension.

Breaths caught.

Arriette's fingers fumbled in her lap as she scanned concerned faces. The first supe she found was Tabitha Hope, who'd read Casper's diary. She already knew most of what was about to be revealed. Arriette could see she was anxious to leave thinking Baby A would need her help, so she sat juddering her legs and checking the clock.

Beside her sat Joy Johnas. Her chocolate eyes were narrow and urgent, whereas Sebastian Sky sat quietly, sipping a cup of water with one hand and tapping a pencil with the other. He seemed out of place and hid behind the netting from his purple sorcerer's hat, which he'd tucked his auburn hair up into. He stared at Casper expectantly.

By the way the elderly shape-shifter was preparing for the speech, Arriette understood this was a *huge* moment in the Recruit's history.

Finally, he clarified, "My real name is Andrew Kaines, born on the planet Earth."

There was an audible gasp, but no questions.

"In the year 2140, I was killed during the apocalypse and because of my greed and selfishness, Zïnnyi instructed me to protect Haeylo until a new saviour—a woman— could take over my role. It was *I* who signed the contract to build Haeylo. It was *my* original species, humans, who ruined Earth.

"Zïnnyi never fully explained what I should expect from my life. I was reborn until my duties were fulfilled, and it is only recently and quite by accident that I stumbled upon Haeylo's saviour. That means it is almost time for me to retire."

After Scarlett Evermay had been mauled by werewolves in Manaia Forest, Harriet Foley, the wiccan author Arriette admired for so long, was exterminated by Casper simply for challenging Arriette's decisions. This only confirmed *how much* he believed in her. He'd murdered one of his own to ensure Arriette didn't bail.

A mild chatter filled the room.

The noise irritated Arriette but she bit her tongue. They were entitled to their honest reactions. Casper would have to repeat this if word didn't spread too quickly to Baby A, vampyr Dion, and Tobias's human hunting buddy Reiko Port as they would now be in Haeylo's city, no doubt worrying about everyone else. But it wasn't a shock to everyone. Simply, a reminder.

The door creaked open behind Casper, demanding

silence, and Jet Carter scurried in. He'd been researching the wormhole's details from the Indalo store for Arriette, so she ushered him to a seat. Sebastian caught him up. The colour drained from his face.

"Arriette needs to get you all out of here," Casper said. "We can't wait around to die."

Arriette frowned and span to face him. She flung up her arms. "Uhm, who said anything about dying?"

Confused, he said, "We will... if you don't find the wormhole and learn how to safely re-activate it. You need to make it to Haeylo's city, find Charles Melovich, and tell him we all agree Falkon Lou is to blame."

"He knows," Tobias voiced from the back, arousing Arriette's senses and sending a shiver down her spine.

"I found some information that can help us find the wormhole," Jet added.

"Then there's no time to waste."

Sebastian raised a shaking hand, but didn't wait to be selected. "You can't just announce something like that and not allow us to respond."

Arriette rolled her eyes. "There will be time for that later. You all should leave without me and head to the city. Casper can explain when you're safe. I can't abandon Pouki," said Arriette before anyone else could interject. "He could be injured or dead! We're weak without our friends, and our fighting force is in the city with the Guard. The lair-dwellers are scared and they're untrained. If you don't get them out first, they'll be wiped out," she said, exhausted by their determination to abandon one of the most experienced members of their group.

"Are you ordering us to leave you here, Arriette?"

She shrugged. "Casper said there was supposed to be a ceremony or a crowning. That hasn't happened yet, so

I'm not the leader and cannot order you to do anything. Though, I strongly suggest it." Her eyes pleaded with Casper not to demand she go too.

"Well, Zïnnyi instructed me to find and nominate the HPS gifts to form an army against evil. I did that. Technically..."

She sighed. This was all happening so suddenly, and she wasn't ready to leave this visitor's room as the Recruit's next leader.

"Casper, you were gone for so long. The Recruit is not going to be whole until I'm crowned and this frantic search for Pandora's box is over. There's a reason you were asked to *sign over* the responsibility. You can't throw it casually my way. Let me do this... *please*."

Casper wiped away a tear whilst trying to regain some dignity. Arriette had never seen him cry but was sure Andrew Kaines did so often, especially after being convinced by Zïnnyi to stay away from his wife and children. But he knew a lot about the Recruit and their capabilities; things Arriette needed to learn first. Quitting now left them all at a disadvantage.

"We don't have time for this," Joy said. "Our determination is what makes us stronger, with or without Zïnnyi's blessing. Why are we sat discussing politics when we should be out there fighting a war? For all we know, Falkon already has Pandora's box. Who cares who leads us, as long as we're being gallantly led to victory?"

"You don't want to evacuate?" he asked.

Joy shook her head. "The lair is my home. I want to defend it from those who don't deserve this Eden."

This riled objections and arguments. Casper gestured for everyone to calm down. There was logic to Joy's suggestion that they should stay and fight. This sanctuary was the only haven he knew of, warded against any breed of demon, werewolf, vampyr or, it seemed, selfish everlasts. But was remaining a wise move? Dying would mean leaving the rest of Haeylo helpless.

"I don't know what to do," Casper admitted. "Some of you won't wish to fight beside me anyway."

Arriette tutted, knowing everyone in the room would give their lives for their cause, no matter his history.

Tobias must have been thinking the same, because he stood and announced, "We're with you, Casper. No matter what."

He raised his head, and Arriette swore she saw a single tear fall. "I needed you to believe in me as your friend, not just a leader. It's the only way I could keep you alive all these years, Tobias."

He sighed. "Casper, we're not stupid. We *all* know our place in this. We've known for a long time, and you've told us the legends of Andrew Kaines."

"You know about it, not how our relationships... our *family*... came to be."

"I do! I got shot and you saved me."

Casper closed his eyes. "*I* shot you."

Tobias narrowed his eyes as he snapped, "You *what?*"

Ashamed, Casper pulled out a chair and slowly sank into it, making his frame as small as he felt. "Our creator said the powers would be individually assigned and instinct could help me to identify who I needed. When I saw you, you *sparkled*. So I shot you and gave you the test. You passed."

"That dream we all experienced—we knew it was some kind of test, sure, but... you just stole my life from me? I was happy as a hunter, but you could have explained your mission. I'm a decent guy, I'd have given it thought. I'd have joined you anyway."

Paulei placed a hand on Tobias's shoulder, suggesting he should sit down. "He's telling the truth. I see it in his memories. The guilt is still fresh, and he's sorry."

Casper offered Paulei half a smile as he added, "But I don't regret it because I never had a choice."

Arriette bit her tongue. Neither did she.

"You're a good man, Tobias, and I couldn't risk you turning me down. I needed you to believe staying with me was the only way."

"The way to what?"

Casper pointed his bony finger directly at Arriette.

She blushed and replied in a whisper, "There's always a choice, Casper."

Before Casper could further justify his actions, Tobias stormed out and slammed the door.

Arriette asked Casper to confirm he'd been training Reiko as their potions expert (or the potions master) and he nodded once. He knew each tree, shortcut, bog and blade of grass by his cabin as though they were one soul. He'd steered Reiko home for miles and diverted the tribal hunter toward his future. Since then, he'd been practising cooking and herbal remedies, programming potion mixing into Reiko from day one of his arrival.

Reiko had sparkled too.

Their angel was found at the riverside as a child with nothing but a picture and two lungs of water. Casper went on to tell everyone how he hadn't been involved with Baby A's background, but the second he laid eyes on her and by the way she shimmered, he realised her potential.

"It was as if Zìnnyi brought her to me."

Casper kept her safe from harm. He trained Baby A

until she became the vibrant personality they loved, all the while thinking her family would come to take her home. They never did, and Casper was... *relieved.*

Lucky for him, Baby A loved him too much to be angry, or so he prayed.

"I'm a whole other story, then," Arriette uttered.

Casper blinked through tears. He took her hand.

"When you turned up on my doorstep in Tobias's arms, I was *thankful.* You were strong, fast, brave. You staked a vampyr and survived two of their attacks! It's unheard of. You fought off a specially trained Retaining guard from the city, repaired a relationship between an influential high-ranking everlast and his daughter—you hold all the qualities of a leader. You were given to me... to us... as a gift." Casper held up both hands then. "I promise, I had *nothing* to do with Kalvin."

"You gave me the powers to do something about my situation, though."

"Yes, because I knew you were important!" He stood suddenly, causing Arriette to jump back a few steps in awe of his enthusiasm. "I couldn't just allow you to disappear. That's why I insisted we share our blood with you and have you stay in our care until you learned to use your powers. Unleashing a creation like you upon this world, untrained and unsupervised, would have been dangerous and reckless. I didn't lie to you, Arriette, I just saw how you shone, and I needed you."

Arriette said nothing until Casper's desperate eyes broke contact. Surely, he wouldn't lie to them all again?

"I believe you," she said. "So now what?"

THREE

Outside the lair, the orc army marched on, defended by sickles, battle axes and maces. The orcs' target would eventually be Haeylo's city if they succeeded in destroying the Recruit's underground lair. Without the Recruit to back them up, the Guard wouldn't stand a chance. Shape-shifting spies kept a cautious eye on their movement from high above the treetops, and sent scouts regularly to report to Casper and Arriette.

Arriette returned from a short break to get a drink of cool water, to find Joy at the front of the visitor's room where her friends were mulling over what they'd learned recently from their current leader and the last scout.

"Nobody quite knows where we should go from here," said Joy, turning to face her. "They haven't broken through yet, but they're braving the water."

"Not good. Not good at all." Arriette slammed her cup down. "But this lair is filled with supes dominating the HPS. I think maybe you should take the map and find the wormhole with Jet. Speak to people as you go; hear their passion for this place. They won't evacuate easily, but if they feel the same way you do, we have a chance.

"I'm not searching for the wormhole so we can abandon the lair, but for *Pouki*. He's out there all alone and somebody, even if not me, needs to find him!" Arriette added. "Now go, please. Jet, Joy, and Paulei, we're relying on you. The rest of us will prepare for the inevitable. Tell everyone not willing to stay to gather what they can carry to leave as soon as Jet's party return with good news. I won't hold them responsible; I understand they need to protect their families."

"Do you *really* think they'll get through the magical wards?" Tobias asked nobody in particular.

"They won't stop trying," Arriette said. "Casper, can I talk to you in private, please?"

The waiting room was now in a frenzy. Once she'd ushered Casper down the corridor and through into the stairwell, she clunked the door behind them and in unison, they sighed with relief. The clang of the door and their footsteps on the metal walkway echoed through the floors.

"You're not going to crown me."

Casper didn't reply, but he wasn't pleased with the statement. She waited for his unusually angry eyes to simmer; this wasn't an accusation from her, but a realisation.

"Not yet."

Arriette had shown leadership, power and authority. She'd made some difficult decisions under pressure and managed to organise the group so far. When she asked why, it was justified.

"Do you think it's necessary?"

"It's what you wanted." She quieted. "Isn't it?"

"It was." He rubbed his eyes and smoothed his palms across his face, exhausted. "I mean... it *is*."

"Then crown me now. If you really want us to leave here, I'll find Pouki and lead everyone to the city; you needn't question my devotion. They can be safe there behind the huge city walls. I can come back then and—"

Casper took her hand in his. "I never questioned *you*."

She gripped the stairwell railing, frustrated by the delay. "So what are you waiting for? Our people are out there *right now* preparing for a war. All you have to do is get your selected powers together, Casper. That's what Charles wanted when he told Scarlett *'eleven'*. He wanted us to get on with this. *My* Recruit are needed. Soon our planet will swarm with whatever crawled from Pandora's box. That filth has bred and grown over the past one hundred years and Falkon is leading it! Orcs are reacting to Coyote returning to the Underworld, but I think with careful tactics we can still defeat whatever breaks through no matter what he told them under torture."

Casper's fists clenched. "I just don't want to leave you."

"I don't under—"

"I've been the leader of the Recruit since I can remember. My family are barely visible or audible in my memory. All I have left are my followers and our little kingdom."

"You won't lose me. Baby A said I'm alive and well in the future, though she wouldn't tell me how this ends." She flung her arms up in protest. "We *must* win, Casper. If a war isn't initiated then we're no closer to being triumphant. I'm just trying to give things a nudge."

"The war has already been initiated by those orcs," he said, "but if you remembered Earth like I do, with its stunning blue skies and landscapes, you might not be so quick to take the first step towards destruction. This has been my mission for so long. To fix what *my* humans broke. If I crown you leader, you'll suffer a consequence, and I can't be here to help you or to witness your new lives."

She reached for him. "Casper, I'm not going to die."

"No." He pulled away from her touch. "But *I* will. If you become the leader, I'll lose everything that's meant anything to me since 2140. If you inherit the responsibilities, in doing so, you'll remove mine."

"Physically?"

"Physically," he said.

She chewed her lower lip for a second, then said, "So you don't really want me to take over?"

"You'll be a *wonderful* leader, but... I'm scared. I couldn't admit that in there, but that fear is festering."

Arriette already understood because being in that state of fight or flight had become her standard.

"You want to say your goodbyes. You love Haeylo and you love your people. How can I take that away from you knowing we'll never see each other again?"

Casper's bony fingers tightened around hers. Her bottom lip quivered but she held it together long enough to ask, "How does it happen?"

His head bowed. "A ceremonial sword. It's... fast."

"And painless?"

He didn't reply. Arriette dropped to her knees and clung to the railing until her knuckles turned white. How could she murder her tutor, her *friend*, and the Recruit's leader? What were they going to do without his wisdom and experience; without his love and compassion?

"I won't do it. There has to be some other way."

Casper lifted her chin with a delicate finger. "Yes, you will."

Neither of them spoke for several minutes, unable to look one another in the eye. He left Arriette in the stairwell to think, and made his way down towards the exit. Alone, she sat on the top step and shared a comfortable half hour with the distant echoes of the infirmary's working. Life continuing regardless of her pain relaxed her nerves, lowering the adrenaline levels in her bloodstream. There wasn't much she could do until they located the wormhole Jet thought he could lead them to. Casper wasn't willing to hand over leadership yet, and she wasn't about to force him. So she set off walking to the Indalo store instead to keep herself busy with the archives in the basement.

When the shopkeeper welcomed her, she asked, "Got anything in here about Pandora?"

She raised a hand to Tabitha at the back, browsing ancient weaponry. Intrigued by Arriette's arrival, Tabitha laid the maul she was buying on the counter and hopped up. Her legs swung back and forth, drumming as they hit the wooden board beneath.

"Don't you mean her box?" he asked.

"No, her. My gut tells me she's important."

The shopkeeper nodded and lifted the wooden hatch beneath his feet to access the archives.

Tabitha laughed. "The *famous* gut feeling. All the great leaders get it."

"Laugh all you like. If I'm right, you're going to wish you'd stayed with Baby A," Arriette grumbled.

"She sent me here to buy weapons. She's afraid the orcs will breach our protection spells."

"She's smart. You should go back to the infirmary and use that thing to guard her room." She gestured at the maul and shuddered, hoping she'd never have to us such a brutal, destructive tool.

"I will, but first I want to hear what the archive knows that we don't already, even though our retainers have already devoured everything it contains."

"So you already know everything about her?"

"Pandora is an ancient Greek myth from Earth. She has nothing to do with Haeyloian history. Her *box* might have made it to our planet, but *she's* dead and buried if she ever existed at all. The shopkeeper will return empty handed."

Arriette raised an eyebrow. "We descended from humans on Earth and they have everything to do with us. If her box is here, Tabitha, then a part of her, if only a memory, is here too. Myths and legends are based on *some* truths, right?"

After an in-depth search of the Indalo store, the shopkeeper returned with nothing. He snapped his fingers and popped open the lock on a storage cupboard instead. Then, he sat a beautiful vase beside Tabitha.

"This is the best I can do. Be careful. It's delicate."

Arriette and Tabitha stared at one another.

"That's *not* Pandora," said Tabitha.

"Indeed. But Pandora's box is rumoured to have been Pandora's vase." He handed it to Arriette for examination. "A vessel that held all the evils of the world. Pandora herself was a gift from the God Zeus to Epimetheus. He sent her to the world with the box to marry Epimetheus as a form of revenge. That box was designed in anger and hatred, and so when Pandora opened it out of harmless curiosity, it unleashed awful things—all but hope remained inside."

"I know her story," said Arriette. "I read. Are you saying we need to get hope out of the box to fight the evil on Haeylo?"

The shopkeeper clarified, "Our conversation and your actions today prove hope is already a part of our world. It's what makes life bearable. Evil cannot be simply *coaxed* back in. It is born with us, not received into us or bestowed upon us. If we take anything from Pandora's story, it should be the morals."

Tabitha grunted, "I don't know what this means for us."

"It is said the box held sickness, strife, death, jealousy, turmoil, hatred, famine and passion. Gateway evils, meaning evil exists as a *result* of those things, and will therefore always exist. How we cope with it and control it is what matters. By returning the gateway evils to the box you can save future souls, but it would not save those already tortured. The damage has been done. You can rid us of incurable diseases, but not cure those already dying of them. Use Pandora's story as inspiration for your actions, Arriette. Go about this with curiosity and passion, goodness, sincerity; find and re-open that box for the purpose of saving and curing, and you will be blessed with positive things for your efforts. If we can indeed return those gateway evils in doing so, that's a bonus."

Arriette nodded. "I think I understand. There's a chance that what's done is done, and there's no going back." She turned to the shopkeeper then, who had begun to get back to work and asked, "Will you stay and fight? Do you believe that hope is enough?"

"Pandora's box held a fuel that burns deep within us all now. It is a powerful thing."

Arriette smiled, then replied, "That doesn't answer my question."

FOUR

The morgue didn't have the impact Arriette had expected. It sat beneath the infirmary, down that long metal staircase she and Casper bared their soul on, and then through two wooden doors. There were no half-autopsied bodies on tables. No bloodied tools on metal trays. The air was clear. The room was cool. The walls weren't deathly white, either, and the floors were clean and smooth. In places, carpeted. To Arriette, the morgue was just another boring office.

"Can I help you, Miss?"

She was greeted by a retainer. His long blonde hair was tied up in a high bun and his light blue eyes studied her through thick-rimmed glasses.

"I'm looking for this woman."

Arriette handed him Scarlett Evermay's identification. The retainer led her to a metal storage compartment. She sighed at her reluctant reflection in the door. This was about to be a painful reminder of her failure.

She yanked it open.

The retainer had inserted Scarlett feet first, so Arriette was met by a pale face. Peaceful, at least, and still pretty.

"Can we help you with anything in particular?"

Arriette jumped. Glaring at Scarlett's lifeless body, she'd forgotten anyone else living occupied the room.

Another assistant had joined them, and the two men awaited her instructions patiently.

"A friend said Scarlett was mutilated by wolves."

"Werewolves," said the first retainer. "I cleaned the lacerations. Most of them were to her stomach and legs."

"You covered her up."

He smiled. "Miss, why are you really here? We were not expecting anyone from our leadership—"

"She's here for the blood results," said a familiar voice. "Arriette will be damned if she can't find out what happened to her precious back-stabbing best friend, Susan. If Scarlett can provide the answers, then it saves her some trouble and might just help her to save another innocent supe."

Arriette almost spat at Tobias, seething with rage, as he came to stand beside her. He placed a gentle hand on Scarlett's head.

"I'm sorry you lost your life because of us," he said, then turned to the retainers. "I hope you don't mind us asking about the traces of magic in this woman's blood. We're looking for a hex."

The retainer nodded but replied to Arriette, sensing her authority over the dreamer.

"You're Arriette Monroe."

His words were more of a statement than a question, but still she blushed. At least word had begun to spread about the Recruit's new leader. They already respected her.

"Magic doesn't always leave a trace. I will let you both wait here for a moment while I find the paperwork, and you can say your goodbyes."

Arriette thanked him, fighting the urge to scream through her grief and guilt.

The second retainer said, "I'll bring you a drink while

you wait."

Quietly, they left the room.

Arriette and Tobias were now alone together again. He hadn't showered or shaved, nor had he bothered to present well at all. He looked tired and rough, and she could have slapped him for being so disrespectful.

Moments later the second retainer brought them a drink, then disappeared again. They sipped in silence until it became unbearable.

"Want me to leave you to it, Arriette? Is that why you slid in here on your lonesome? You look upset."

Arriette put her empty cup down and turned on her heel. "You should be thankful the others aren't here to judge me. Casper would disapprove."

He laughed. "Oh, you're going to kill me too, then? I'd like to see you try; dreamers can't harm other dreamers with their gifts. Supe biology basics."

Kill him too?

So many innocent lives had been lost in Arriette's name. Her heart quickened and she drowned her useless senses to focus only on her telekinesis, fuelled by her vivid imagination. She could picture Tobias writhing in pain on the floor of the morgue, begging for her forgiveness. But it wasn't fair to argue in front of Scarlett, so she slid her body back into the container and closed the door.

She cleared her throat. "Take it back."

"What?"

"Saying I will 'kill you too'. Take. It. Back."

"I wish you could make me," he said.

Arriette outstretched her arms and using her telekinesis, she lifted Tobias until his head knocked on the ceiling and kept him there. Having heard the clang of his skull, the retainers rushed back to the morgue and gripped Arriette, tackling her by her shoulders to the floor. Something stung her upper arm. She hissed, landing uncomfortably, but the palms of her hands were still free to control Tobias. The combined strength of the retainers was still no match for Arriette's intense fury, and she flung them off her.

Dreamers were supposed to be exempt from the powers of other dreamers, or so she'd been made to believe by Dion. Tobias was under the same impression.

But here she was.

Causing him pain.

"How are you doing this? Let *go* of me!"

From the roof, Tobias was able to offer a retaliation. He thrust out his palms, sending Arriette in a sliding motion across the other side of the room. The small patch of carpet burned her arms and her elbows.

Unable to deal with both the pain and the control of her power, she released her hold. Tobias fell, landing on his knees.

"Get Casper!" Arriette yelled at the retainers as she pulled herself up and dived under a metal stool. "Something isn't right!"

They were on their feet and running before she'd finished the sentence.

As if preparing to throw a ball, he opened his hand to reveal a blue flame, which he pitched at her head. Arriette launched her body toward the fireball and swung the stool like a bat. She deflected it. He rolled over an empty metal table to evade his own attack, which Arriette slid beneath and released her wings. They became her balance beam, allowing her to carry Tobias and the table on her back into the air.

"Stop this, stop this now!" said a new voice, the morgue's human assistant.

"Get out of the way," Tobias told him, using his power to throw the innocent technician out and bolt the doors.

"And get Casper!" Arriette screamed after him.

But he didn't. Instead, he shattered the glass window pane with his elbow and fumbled to unlock it. He yelped as a shard of glass stuck in his thumb.

"This is not the place to fight!" he said, sticking it in his mouth and mumbling about how disrespectful they were acting.

"What are you *doing*, Arriette?" Tobias spluttered, spitting from his bleeding gums onto the teetering table beneath him. "You're acting crazy!"

Arriette pulled her wings in tight and dodged to the left so the slab crashed to the ground.

Tobias groaned. "Point proven."

"Apologise for what you said!"

At full speed, she flew at him until she crushed his aching body against the doors, face-to-face with the assistant who hopped away in a panic.

"You're hurting me," Tobias moaned.

"Good!"

"Alright. I'm. Sorry."

Arriette released him.

Instantly, she felt exhausted. Her arm throbbed and had swollen but she had enough strength left in it to flick her wrist and unlock the bolted doors, allowing all three of the assistants back into the room. Before she blacked out, she felt arms take hold of her, then she collapsed in a heap.

FIVE

Arriette sat up in bed. Her bare feet hit cold stone paving and her eyes locked on a single box window above a filthy toilet in the corner. A large bruise covered her cheek and was beginning to turn an off shade of purple, and a pin-sized puncture was now visible on her upper arm where she'd likely been injected. There was a black eye forming, and several scratches and sore spots across her torso.

"Wait, they drugged me?" Arriette groaned and rubbed her eyes. "Ugh, hello? Can anyone hear me?"

Her voice echoed through the bars of her cell and down a long, empty corridor. There were rooms lining both sides and only a few held sleeping inmates, none of whom she recognised as they paced the bars.

One of them seemed to recognise her. "Arriette?"

"Jet? Oh thank Zìnnyi!"

Jet was the only invisible supe Arriette had ever met. He tapped the bars of the cell beside her and as he waved through them, she caught a brief glimpse of his fingertips which were bleeding, like he'd tried to claw or scratch his way free. Despite being able to turn his senses invisible, his power didn't allow him to move through solid objects, which Arriette thought would have been extremely handy.

"What *happened* to you?"

"I'm a bit roughed up but I'll live," Jet said. "Until I heard your voice my plan was to disappear until they opened the door to find me, but it's freezing in here. I can't hold my power long, it hates the cold."

Arriette kicked the bars, careful not to break a toe. "My cell is locked; the bars won't budge. Why are you here and where's Tobias? Where am I?"

"When you left for the morgue, Joy said she thought there was another underwater passage from the map I found. We got separated and next thing I knew, I was in here."

"You didn't think to go with her?" she asked.

"This is *our* lair. Who the hell would harm their own people? We should have stayed together, I'm sorry."

Arriette groaned and rested her forehead against the bars, trying to formulate a plan that wouldn't lead to their deaths.

"Has Tobias been in here?"

"I haven't seen him. We're in the castle you can see from the entrance where we came in. Perhaps one of the watchtowers, or the dungeon. It hasn't been used for centuries so I can't say for sure which parts are still in use, if any. I thought Tobias was with *you*?"

"He *was*," she snapped, now thrashing her body against various places on the three other walls in hope of finding a loose brick. "I passed out. We had a bit of a fight."

"Couples argue," he said.

"I mean a physical fight," she corrected. "It's crazy, but our powers worked against one another."

Jet hummed in thought, unsure how two dreamers

could physically attack one another given the boundaries of their biology. "There's got to be an explanation, and you should ask Casper if we get out of here."

"*When,*" she spat.

From her thrashing, Arriette had ripped a hole in her clothing. Only now did she realise her captor had changed her into striped nightwear material; an ugly grey with black stripes. The clothes Sebastian bought for her were nowhere around. Her top button was missing and her hair was matted with blood and dirt. She hadn't realised the blood had been seeping from a wound to the back of her head, but that had been hours ago when she'd collapsed at the morgue.

Above everything, she was most concerned that someone had possibly seen her naked, and had the audacity to kidnap the next leader of the Recruit.

"I hit my head, Jet," she told him. "I'm not dying, but I might need stitches."

"You sound angry."

Arriette hissed and examined the corners of her cell. "Oh, *I am.*"

He or she who dared to betray their own would pay for their preposterous actions.

"Are any of the others here?"

"No," Jet said, and Arriette was quietly thrilled, so her sense of isolation solidified. "I heard a woman scream about half an hour ago. They dragged her down the hall and into the interrogation room, but I never saw her face. Nobody else here has said a word. They're too afraid."

"Did anyone say her name?"

"No. She was blonde though, and slim. That's all I can tell you."

"Human?"

Jet rubbed his head as he replied, "No idea. She growled and clawed at the guard like an animal."

"Werewolf then, maybe."

Arriette spared no more time asking questions. She began to hunt for an escape route. There had to be secret compartments or switches in a Recruit castle. The top of the toilet had been sealed and the sink was ancient and stone with only cold running water. There was no shower and no privacy, and nothing she could use to pick the lock or signal for help. Shouting from this height would alert only birds.

"I'm *not* going to die like this. There has to be a way out of here. What use are my powers if they can't get me out of an old rickety cell?"

Arriette's telekinesis was useless if there weren't any keys or items nearby to steal and manipulate. Picking the lock was out of the question without something pointy. Still inexperienced, she hadn't yet learned to create her own items from imagination and memory and trying too much would only drain her energy, like it had filling Ma's kitchen sink with money. Even that had been with the help of Tobias. If she could start a fire or attract attention, the guard might open the door to investigate, but she'd seen nothing flammable besides her clothing and when she tried to form the incantation of *Monibah* as she'd seen Casper do that evening at the waterfall, nothing happened.

"Jet, I need your help."

"Do you have an idea?"

"I'm going to try and shift shape but I think there's something wrong with my powers. The Haeyloian language is dead in my mouth, and there's nothing here I can see that would pick a lock. You need to be my lookout; cough if you see anyone as you have a better view of the exit than I do."

Before Jet had agreed, Arriette focused her mind on the creature she needed to take the shape of. She stripped naked and shoved her clothes against the bars so she could easily reach them and redress later. She hadn't been anything but a tiger before and this power wasn't the easiest to control or the most comfortable to use. But in the infirmary, she'd summoned two types of claws from her knuckles and her fingernails.

Still, last time she'd been angry. *Really* angry.

She needed to get angry again. It didn't take much once she recalled Tobias's accusations, and soon she began to shrink. Her view from the window disappeared. Her back hunched. Her sight became defined, like looking through a magnifying glass. Fur, black and sleek, grew in a flurry along her arms which soon rounded to paws.

From somewhere in the castle there was a scream and a clang, like metal upon metal, but none of the other inmates reacted.

Arriette skulked through the bars and checked left and right for the exits. Catching sight of her, Jet gave the thumbs up.

The cell across was empty, but a child in shorts and a scruffy navy shirt sat in the next cell along, cross-legged on a bench. Once safely in her room, Arriette rubbed her feline face against the child's leg until she giggled. Then, she transformed back.

"I'm here to save you," she whispered.

The girl seemed normal, human, and powerless. If she's had any supe abilities, Arriette thought she'd have tried to use them against her already.

"What's your name? I'm Arriette." She ran her fingers through the child's auburn waves.

"I'm Angelica," she said.

"Where are your parents?" Angelica shrugged and lowered her head. "I need you to be brave for me."

Arriette squeezed her hand and examined the lock on the door. A three-pronged key should do the trick. She let go of Angelica and pressed a finger tight against her lips, telling the child to be silent. Then Arriette pointed to the lock.

"If I can transform my entire body, one digit shouldn't be too difficult, right?" She turned to Angelica. "I'm going to get us out of here. Don't be frightened."

Arriette shifted shape once again, this time concentrating on only her left index finger. She moulded her skin to the shape of the lock and turned her arm until the bars clicked open.

Arriette's palm began to sting as the outline of an X-shaped Gabo rune seethed into her skin. Although pleased with her progress, dealing with the responsibilities of a qualified shape-shifter now only increased the pressure for her to get this right, and Casper's rune was a painful one to bare.

She pulled Angelica into a tight hold, shaking off the itchiness, and jogged across to re-dress. Then, she unlocked Jet's cell. She repeated the action for his door and all the others, though none of them were eager to escape. Did they all know something she didn't?

"You're free, what's the matter with you?"

They didn't thank her. They barely moved.

Jet reached for Angelica's hand. The child stared into his dark saucer eyes, searching for some reassurance. The corners of his mouth stretched from ear to ear when he smiled but it was clear from his stiff posture that he felt uneasy and unsure. He didn't have children of his own, and spent very little time around those in the lair.

Angelica quickly realised Arriette was her best chance, so she switched to nestling against her instead,

"Are you coming?" she urged the others.

Blank faces. Silence.

"Do you think you can get us the hell out of here now?" Jet asked.

Arriette made haste for the nearest exit. "Working on it."

SIX

Jet, Angelica and Arriette ran for the cell block's exit, deeper into the heart of the Recruit's castle. However unused it was now, they could see evidence of past battles in the imperfections, of nicks in the stone where an axe or an arrow had chipped away at the structure, and in the missing doors, beams and other interior comforts like furniture. It has been stripped bare, and as though they ran alongside her, Arriette sensed the presence of the ghosts of its past.

The structure was a bland labyrinth now, and Arriette wanted nothing more than to escape her captors and get back to Casper. Without her, there would be no future for the Recruit. Dying anticlimactically in here without reason couldn't help their cause.

She studied Jet's faulty power as his invisibility began to flicker on and off. Angelica avoided him, stunned by his warped and foggy presence at her side like one of the ghosts Arriette had been imagining. Neither she nor Arriette could keep track of where he was.

They couldn't stop their teeth chattering or shoulders shuddering either. With only the thin inmate clothing they'd inherited to protect them from the castle's chill, they'd be more likely to freeze to death before finding a safe way out.

"Is that man OK?" Angelica asked Arriette.

"My power doesn't like the cold," he explained. "It's sporadic when I'm emotional, or my body temperature lowers."

"An unpredictable power won't help if we run into a guard, Jet," Arriette reminded him.

"You're right, so I think you should take the lead. Shift your senses. It might help us escape this place."

Arriette checked the next corner then gestured for her friends to wait while she shifted her senses from human to feline, surprised at how easy the partial transition was; like melting butter, or a light bouncing of a tumbleweed.

Behind them in the direction of the cells, Arriette heard intermittent screams and the clang of metal hitting stone. More damage. More deaths.

"Anything?" Jet asked.

Arriette flinched. There was a final clang immediately followed by a gargle and the chopping and hacking of meat.

Those poor people. Why didn't they come with us?

She must have looked terrified because Jet grabbed her shoulder. "*That* bad?"

"Not now. We *need* to keep going."

They continued down the corridor. Arriette had only moved another hundred yards before her sense of smell picked up on a familiar natural musk. She was so distracted she almost ran head-first into a wall, but Angelica cried for her to watch out.

Arriette shivered. "That's Susan."

He ushered her to the end but they were halted by a padlocked door.

"You said Susan was dead," Jet said.

"You should go on. Take the stairs, there." Arriette

directed them to an open spiral staircase beneath a stone archway. They had been walked thousands of times before, and the stone steps sank in the centre where boots had stomped and trodden and climbed.

"We're *not* leaving you here to chase a ghost."

"I need to follow her scent, it might mean something. And you can't stay here. You'll get caught."

"This is a bad idea."

"I can take care of myself."

"But I can't protect her," Jet pleaded. "Whatever you're planning, do it with us in tow, and do it quickly. We're running out of time."

Arriette scouted the corridor. A way back, there had been an opening in the wall where it had crumbled and fallen away over time. Arriette gestured for Jet to hide in the nook with Angelica and stay as quiet as possible. If anyone opened the door, they'd be out of sight unless the guard ventured far enough down.

"If Susan's not here, then it's not long since she was," Arriette told them. "This could be important."

Suddenly, that padlocked door rattled and swung open. A man and woman dressed in white masks and matching overalls started in their direction. They were unarmed, but without a weapon of her own Arriette couldn't fight them both off and protect her friends at the same time.

"Jet, time to test your power." Arriette grabbed his hand, then ushered Angelica back out of the nook.

"This is a *really* bad idea," he hastily whispered.

"I trust you. You can do this."

Arriette squeezed her eyes closed. Jet took them both in his hold, and prayed his power held. The white suits passed them by, so Jet carefully pulled Arriette and the child behind him and into another room. They peered through a murky window to see two patients laid on their backs. They were stripped of all clothing and strapped to metal slabs at the wrists and ankles. Tobias was one of them, barely covered at his hips by a wide leather strap.

Across the room, thrashing and writhing, was Susan. Seeing her again made Arriette's runes itch and her spine ache. The memories they shared must have been more painful than Arriette allowed herself to remember.

Susan's blonde hair hung over the edge of the table and she growled at every white suit she saw. Her lips were swollen and covered in blood. Her wide eyes were an electric blue and were alight with rage.

"That's the woman they dragged from the cells."

"She really *is* a vampyr," Arriette gasped.

A young brunette approached Susan's slab and jabbed her with a needle below the thigh. Arriette's arm twitched at the sight. Rage broiled inside her.

The vampyr struggled and spat, watching as red liquid was sucked from her bloodstream into a clear bag. The woman sealed it, slung it on a tray, and wheeled it through a different door, leaving the patients alone.

"What are they doing to her?"

"I don't know," Jet said, "but at least we know Tobias isn't in on it."

"Yeah, but *now* I'm thinking the mortuary assistants were. Perhaps moles in our organisation. They gave Tobias and me drinks and somebody injected me with something."

"Do you think they spiked your water?"

Arriette nodded. "Then knocked me out with whatever that was." She rubbed her upper arm.

"I don't think they're involved now," Jet said.

"How do you know that?"

He lowered his voice and leaned in to whisper, out of Angelica's earshot. "They're dead."

"*What?*" She let go of Jet's hand, re-appearing in the small space they occupied between the guard-riddled corridor and the lab.

"They were in the cell opposite."

"Why didn't you tell me?"

"I didn't know you knew who they were, did I? Whatever their purpose here, they were deemed useless and disposed of before you woke," he said, then ran a finger across his throat as not to upset Angelica with the gory details. "Two of them. Retainers, I think."

So the human assistant had been innocent.

Arriette sighed. "Do you think we can sneak in and free them before those suits come back? If we don't, they might meet the same fate as those we left behind."

She'd been timing their rounds. They had at least four minutes before someone else would re-enter to check on the patients. The room was big enough not to be spotted but they'd need to be fast and organised before anyone noticed they had escaped.

"We'll have to free them at the same time," Jet said. "Then make a run for it. I'd rather be caught by that young brunette than her partner. He's huge, and I'm not strong enough to defend us."

Arriette agreed. "Me neither with my powers acting up."

The suit's partner was at least six foot tall with wide shoulders and bulging arms. Even after releasing Tobias, they'd have their hands full. That's if she could get him out. From where they stood, Tobias appeared to be unconscious and the leather strap was so tight against his skin his thighs were white at its edges.

"Why can't he dream his way out?" Jet asked.

"He's unconscious. If he's weak when he wakes, his dreams won't last long or work at all. Like mine. We need to free Susan. She can help us. She's already awake and she seems fine, and she's deadlier than any of us."

Jet shook his head. "Wait, you want to *purposefully* untie a vicious vampyr?"

"If we help her, she won't bite us."

"Arriette, she's *not* going to recognize you. You know what happens to a vampyr's memories when they turn."

"Believe me, I'm aware," she said, huffing. "Well, I can't just leave her. I have to give her a chance."

Jet bit his lip. He peered through the window to assess the ideal route to both slabs. "Send me in and let me try to get Tobias out first. My power is the most reliable right now. If the guard comes back, I'll stay invisible and wait until she leaves."

"And if it fails?"

"I'll run like hell."

This was a stupid, irrational idea. The room's temperature was lower than the corridor's. She could see from the puffs of white breath around Tobias's mouth and the raised hairs on his limbs. Jet's lack of control over his invisibility wouldn't withstand that sort of emotional pressure. He'd compromise their mission.

"It's too risky."

Arriette shuddered again, this time from her head right down to her toes. Her hair flapped wildly in a breeze they hadn't noticed before. She span to check for an open door, which would likely mean guards approaching, and instead came face-to-face with the silhouette of Susan.

Arriette tried to scream. Jet wrapped his palm around

her mouth.

"Don't speak." Susan stated, "You'll get yourself killed."

"How are you doing this?" Jet uttered.

She ignored him and spoke directly to Arriette, her eyes unblinking. "Turn back."

Jet released her and checked through the window to see Susan's body now laid unconscious on the slab.

Arriette said, "I don't understand. What *are* you?"

"A projection. A spiritual duplicate. Get down!"

They dived to the ground as Susan's examiner patrolled past the door toward her body. Arriette's concentration shifted from the guard to Susan's fangs. Real, blood-sucking white fangs.

"One of our own is in there. I can't leave him."

"I'm not going to help you kill yourself."

Arriette scowled. "You clearly have no idea who—"

"I know who you are, Arry," Susan said, "but ego isn't going to save you."

Jet shoved Arriette aside. "What are they doing to you in there, Susan? Why do they have supe prisoners all over the castle? What did they do to Arriette's powers?"

"Supernatural experimentation," she whispered. "I overheard the guards talking about their orders. They're harnessing the vampyric and demonic power and transferring it to the physical form of a living being."

"*Why?*"

"Your friend is due to receive a dose of my blood any time now, Arry," she said. "You can try to save him but you'd be a fool. I'm already dead. They can't hurt me anymore."

"But supes can power-save," she argued. "How have they bypassed it?"

Jet interjected. "Power-saving is a choice you make at the time. You have to switch it on for it to work."

"And these supes have no idea what's happening to them because they're drugged and knocked unconscious before they can switch it on," she said. "Oh, this is a nightmare! I don't want to leave you alone, Susan, and that man in there is *really* important to me."

Susan shook her head. "Leave your lover. You've been warned."

Her spirit faded. Instantly, body sprang back to life just in time to launch at the throat of her examiner who had leaned a little too close. She missed, but only just. The woman scuttled out of the room, leaving Jet to sneak inside.

"Angelica, we're getting out of here."

They peered through the window. Jet's invisible hands untied Tobias's restraints, unbuckling each one including the tight leather strap from beneath, and hauled him up by the shoulders. He grumbled and opened his eyes, still fatigued by whatever drugs they'd been feeding him.

"Angelica, you need to keep hold of my hand. We might have to run soon."

"Your fingers are cold," she complained.

How could they keep a child so innocent and harmless captive in a place like this? They were inhumane.

Jet and Tobias disappeared and seconds later reappeared at the other side of the door. Jet pointed at Angelica and then at Tobias.

"Angelica, close your eyes."

She kicked herself for not grabbing an extra white coat or some more inmate overalls before sending Jet in after her friends. Panicked, she took three deep breaths and unbuttoned her shirt.

"What are you doing?" Jet mouthed.

Arriette pointed to Angelica and then at Tobias's naked body. Rather she is seen in her underwear than Tobias be seen running naked from the castle's gate.

Jet opened the door and took her shirt to tie around Tobias's waist. He groaned and rubbed his head.

"T-thank y-you," he said, his flesh covered in goose pimples. "They w-will notice we've g-gone."

Arriette closed the door, directing Jet to free Susan.

"No, t-they're coming b-back."

"Did you know that was Susan?" she asked him.

Tobias frantically shook his head. "No, b-but I knew she c-could astro-project."

"Astro *what*?"

She and Jet glared at one another, surprised their escape plan was working so far.

"I'll get you all out and come back for her," Jet said.

They set off running for the staircase. Arriette thought they looked like escaped convicts, though as far as she knew they were all innocent. She slid to a halt when she realized Tobias wasn't behind her, but he re-emerged carrying some inmate overalls, then handed back Arriette's shirt.

She tugged it on, blushing.

"F-found them on a b-bench back there," he said. "How are you going to save the b-blonde if she doesn't want to b-be saved?" Tobias asked, slowly warming up in his new stripy pyjamas. "She's crazy."

Susan had only ever followed her own instincts—her heart. If she wouldn't follow Arriette then she'd follow Kalvin. That's how she lost them both. Susan had followed Kalvin to the city where they both met their fate. The same fate as Scarlett.

"We need Kalvin to lure her anywhere. She'd do anything for him."

"The guy was a nut job and he tried to kill you. He's dead, so our idea dies with him," Tobias grumbled.

They ducked as another medically-dressed guard passed along the corridor ahead and threw their bodies against the stone wall.

Knowing Susan was alive and remembered her past meant Arriette could interview her at the town hall. If she could give them any more information about her death, it would certainly answer a lot of their questions.

Tobias inhaled sharply. "There are men and women in that room interfering with supe biology. If *any* of them get hold of *you*, we're all screwed."

"They had me, but I don't think they'd taken anything from me. I'm just weaker, perhaps from the drugs?"

"Then they were saving the best until last," Jet said.

"I've had three transfusions from Susan. You're powerful enough to stop this. Protect yourself *at all costs*. That means no Susan. You can't toy with a creature that's dangerous and out of our control."

She scowled, prepared to have yet another public argument with him at the wrong time and in the most inconvenient place.

"I'm supposed to save Haeylo from evil and if that means I need to lie to Susan to get some answers, then I'll tell her Kalvin is alive and waiting for her and I'll do with a clear conscience. We don't know what was in that water at the morgue. It messed with our powers, Tobias."

Susan would never trust Arriette without the mention of Kalvin, so she had no other option.

"It's not up for debate."

Suddenly the doors to the hall flung open.

Jet vaulted and Arriette and Angelica, and threw his arms around them both. They lay in an uncomfortable heap on the floor, but were invisible for the time being. Tobias, however, had already thrown a punch.

Still clung to Jet's arms, they scrambled to their feet and the three of them ran in the opposite direction. She had to get Angelica out of there, but the door they faced wouldn't budge and was locked from the other side.

"Move back," she told them both, then let go of Jet's hand.

She rattled the handle and kicked with her bare feet until the wood began to crack. She swore and cursed, throwing all her weight at the handle þut with no luck. She even tried to Shape-Shift to pick the lock as she had done back at the cell, but nothing happened.

"It's not working, Jet! Casper's power saved us before!" Confused, she grabbed a hold of Angelica's hand for comfort. "There has to be another way out of here. We'll go back the way we came."

"The bad people are that way," said Angelica, now in tears. "They're coming!"

The guards were heading straight for them. Tobias had defended them for as long as he could, but was being pushed further toward the door, unable to fend off the rush of laboratory coats with nothing but his hands.

"Arriette, dream the door open!" he bellowed.

"I can't, it's not working! Nothing's working!"

Arriette focused with all her might. Just one fireball like the one Tobias created in the mortuary would buy them some time.

Just one.

She glared down at empty hands. "Angelica, get

behind me."

"What are we going to do, Arriette?"

"I won't let them hurt you."

They'd have to kill her first.

They came galloping toward them. Arriette raised her fists.

SEVEN

Somewhere In Time And Space...

Today the canteen seems busier because she's earlier, catching the red and black uniforms in the joys of Town Hall's breakfast shift. Heels clack against shining marble floor and women chatter at the adjacent table about their supernatural families. Most share tales of successful grandchildren who've grown and joined the Recruit or the city's Guard.

She wonders if she'll ever be one of those women.

There's a sense of seclusion. She studies her speech for the upcoming ceremony. The unsteady rock of her table is distracting so she takes a moment to watch the individual routines of those around her as she folds a sheet of paper and stuffs it under the shortest leg.

If they can be normal, so can I.

Here at Town Hall, supes of all HPS ranks work long hours to ensure the safety of the Recruit and that the hunt for Pandora's box continues. Judges sift through case files, pleading for caffeine at the counter, while others stare helplessly into their cooling cups.

If anything like her, they'll be grasping hold of their remaining sanity to face the day ahead.

A librarian pre-orders her sandwiches in preparation for a predictable lunch, basking in the glory of this calm job and thanking Zïnnyi for the army that's about to protect their mass of knowledge, and the archives in the Indalo store.

She sits with her notes.

She sits and thinks about her fellow Recruit members and how they're coping, drawing her attention back to the ceremonial preparations.

***

Only the mild humming of magically powered refrigerators fills the canteen from where he stands. The red and black uniforms are scurrying to clear tables, barging past him and occasionally excusing themselves.

He strokes a long beard, wearing a trench coat despite the warmth of the building. His corner of the canteen is quiet as most of the employees linger toward the exit now, though a janitor mops around his unmoving feet.

He's been monitoring the movements of the young woman in the central table for a few hours now and she's barely noticed his existence.

He begins to pace toward her. The lighting dims all around them, causing the woman to look up briefly from her paperwork and glance over her shoulder.

The canteen staff scatter as he approaches the table.

The stranger lunges at her with a force she knows will either end in her hospitalization or her death. She barely noticed him advance.

She decides to run, missing his strangling fingers. The exit is open behind her and she charges for it, leaving the paperwork scattered across her table and fluttering to the ground.

He follows, gaining speed.

She dives into an open room and slams the door closed, falling to the ground and scrambling on all fours beneath a desk.

Turning the knob of the door, he enters stealthily. There's panic in the canteen now and alarm bells sound all around him.

He senses movement, but before he can turn to grab her swinging arm, he's knocked out.

His master will not be happy to hear he's failed.

EIGHT

9280 AD

The laboratory guards had been following the orders of a low, grizzly female voice. Its owner wore green camouflage cargo-style trousers beneath her lab coat, and had dyed each tip of her spiked hair an off shade of blonde. Her ears, nose and eyebrows were stamped with various piercings, and tattoos crept up her neck.

"Where did you go, little mice?" she growled, smirking as she scanned the corridor. She rubbed her cheekbone where Arriette's fist collided with it, before Jet leapt between them and turned her invisible. He'd intercepted Tobias's fight too, confusing his opponent when he swung but grazed nothing but stone.

Jet hushed Angelica with a finger to his lips as she began to stir in fear. Arriette glanced down their line of four, holding hands, invisible to the enemy's eye but not to one another. Shuddering, Arriette tried to pull herself together. She was so anxious and angry that screaming seemed the only logical outlet. But slowly, they were heading back toward where Tobias had been rescued and she couldn't risk getting them caught.

Susan's body still lay flat on the metal slab. Her fangs had retracted, leaving fresh blood on her lips and chin. Beneath the table lay the carcass of a chicken.

"They're *feeding* her," Jet whispered once they were away from the corridor, leaving the woman and her minions to conclude their pointless search.

"*What* do you think you're doing?"

Arriette startled as Susan's spiritual presence reformed behind them. Jet moved Angelica to stand behind him.

"You needn't be scared of me," she told him. "I can't bite in this form. You were foolish to come back here."

"How can you see us?" Jet gasped, still clinging to his friends.

Susan licked the blood from her lips and grinned, revealing the shimmering white fangs behind them. Arriette raised her brow; these meagre techniques to scare her off the rescue mission weren't going to work.

"Let me save you," Arriette said. "You can show those things off all day. I *know* you won't hurt me. I'm your friend and you sent Scarlett Evermay to give me that message. If you remember my name and my face, I'm hoping you remember that, too."

"Some of your story is... familiar," Susan hummed, "but my memories are cloudy."

"How did you become a—"

"Doesn't matter now," she said. "You are *so* sure I need saving, Arry?"

Arriette stood her ground. Unblinking, she said, "I'm not leaving you here either way."

"Those guards are by no means innocents, but they're sheep. I can take care of myself."

"Is the spiky-haired chick is their leader?" Tobias asked. "She looks like a piece of work."

"She's a werewolf of the Shou pack. Nasty and effective in her line of work. Against a vampyr, though?"

Susan licked her lips.

"What difference does her pack make?" Arriette asked. "She still has to die."

Werewolves were all the same to her. Brutal, savage, murderous and too smart for their own good. They'd mauled Scarlett in the forest for trying to deliver a warning. She bled to death in Arriette's arms, an experience she would never, ever forget.

Tobias checked the corridor for guards, then quickly explained, "There are three packs our group know of, all born werewolves, who are conscious in their wolf form. Only those bitten or turned by blood suffer memory loss. Born weres are proud killers and they live together in packs. Moon worshippers. *She's* one of them."

"So we need to avoid her and get out of here now," Jet interjected, "is basically Susan's point."

"I'd hate for my next meal to be your lifeless bodies. Cold blood is *much* less satisfying," she hissed.

Arriette glared at her. "Nice try, but I'm still not afraid of you, Susan. And vampyrs can't drink dead blood, it's poison."

"How do *you* know?"

"I've earned the right to be asking the questions."

Susan chortled, then gestured for her to proceed.

"Why are my powers messed up? Tobias and I could attack one another using telekinesis which is impossible."

"Arriette's right. Just before, when we were trying to escape, our powers failed. If not for Jet, we'd be dead."

"I cannot tell you any more here. If they suspect I can astro-project, they'll kill me. For real this time. You should just go," Susan said.

Susan knew why they had been taken prisoner. Arriette could tell by the way she held back, avoiding the question. She wasn't going to leave Susan alone to die in that laboratory, and she wasn't walking away without answers.

"If we had more time, I would," she clarified.

"We're getting you out of here. I'm not moving until I know what's happening. It's my job now."

Susan paused, glanced through the glass at her lifeless body, then nodded.

"Hurry up and release me. Then, we'll talk." She disappeared.

Tobias held Arriette back as she moved to free her friend. "You're *not* going in there. She's a vampyr now and we can't trust evil as far as we can throw a stake. We'll ask her the questions on the slab."

"We don't have time," Jet said, "and it's going to look strange if she starts talking to herself. We'll be invisible to the guards but Susan, for some reason, can see us. It'll draw too much attention and suspicion."

"Jet, she's hungry. If we free her we're all dead. Friends or not," Tobias said. "If she can astro-project, that's probably why she can see us in her spirit form. I mean, isn't that technically what we are right now?"

Arriette appreciated their fear of being bitten after all they'd been through, but she was still confident that Susan would never hurt her, despite her hunger. Susan had given her life to tell Arriette about her place in the Recruit. She wouldn't ruin their chance of success now.

"Tobias, get Angelica out of here. I want her safe and you're the strongest of us. If anyone can fight their way out of here using only hand-to-hand combat, it's you." Arriette turned to Jet. "You and I will free Susan. We'll follow Tobias's path of destruction and rendezvous back at Town Hall."

"What about the orc army, Arriette? There are still preparations ongoing. If I turn up with a kid in these prison sweats, there are going to be questions and panic. We don't know how long we've been missing."

"Tobias is right," Jet said. "The wormhole won't open itself. I had all the information and if I was kidnapped, so was everyone with me."

"Let's worry about getting out of here first," she said. "Susan said she'll tell us everything and I believe her. When we're safe, then we can move forward with the evacuation and save Pouki."

"Just don't forget about our primary goal here," Jet sighed. "The Recruit are depending on you, and their lives are more valuable than some selfish vampyr."

Arriette said goodbye to Tobias and Angelica and wished them luck on their escape. They broke from the group and ran back toward the cell block, leaving them visible and vulnerable. They'd established a possible escape route via their current position to be impossible, so the only way to find daylight now was to head back the way they came.

Arriette worried about how Susan might react to the sunlight and couldn't understand how she'd been smuggled in without their knowledge. Without the wormhole, the only entrance was via the cave and vampyrs were sleeping during its opening hours. Inside the Recruit lair, dreamers had built the night and day artificially, so Arriette hoped her skin wouldn't burn.

It took only a few minutes to free Susan's limbs and then they were up and out in half the time they'd allowed for the mission. Still, they weren't going to hang about too long, not when Tobias and Angelica were already on their way to safety. If they got captured, they'd need help.

"This way," Jet said, following Tobias's trail of open doors and dead bodies.

"Susan, why aren't my powers working?" she asked through jagged breaths as they sprinted.

She laughed. "This is not the time nor place."

"Tell me what they did to us. How did I not know about it sooner?"

"I do not miss my human life at all! Everything is always so *urgent*."

"This *is* urgent, Susan!"

They turned a sharp corner which led to yet another boring stone corridor. Arriette tried to regulate her breathing and keep pace with the others, but she had to pause to nurse a pain in her side.

"You are always worrying and searching for obvious answers. Supernatural experimentation needs no further explanation," Susan said. "They took my blood and inserted it into your boyfriend to research the effects. You too, Jet, though you were unconscious at the time."

"They took my blood or, gave me yours?" Jet asked.

Susan sniggered. "Does it matter?"

"YES IT MATTERS!"

Startled by the outburst, Arriette urged them all forward. Jet's power had begun to flicker with the pressure of the escape and the fear of what a vampyr's blood might do to him. And he had to have drawn the attention of a guard at that volume.

"Tobias will have heightened senses," Susan continued. "I do not feel my blood coursing through *your* veins, though. Ingesting vampyric blood rather than receiving it in replacement of your own merely acts like a drug."

"It's good that he's taking care of Angelica, then?"

Susan nodded. "They'll probably be fine."

"Wait, no. Tobias and I were struggling *before* we were captured," Arriette said. "Before they injected me."

"Let me guess, they gave you food?"

"Water," said Arriette, mentally kicking herself. "Whatever they wanted to test on us was in the water, and the injection was to knock me out and kidnap me."

Susan shrugged. She hadn't been there to witness Arriette's fight, but it sounded likely.

"The experimentation goes beyond blood. They're making potions and serums, too."

Arriette paused and hunched over to catch her breath for a moment.

Susan grinned. "Are you two a thing then? Two powerful dreamers in love and both in the Recruit? Seems you couldn't get farther away from normality if you tried, Arry."

"Oh shut up, Susan."

Ahead of them was a locked door. Arriette kicked the rusted padlock a few times to free them. Once through, they were met with a gust of fresh air. Tobias hadn't been here, though, because he'd have already removed the lock.

"So we're here for an experiment. What about you? The lair is protected from your kind. How did those guards get you past our defences?"

Susan's eyes flashed blue and her hair lifted, standing on end and shimmering in the corridor's candlelight. It was a familiar sight; Arriette remembered how Dion reacted in Manaia forest when threatened.

"Someone is coming," she hissed,.

Tobias emerged from a passage to their left, startling all three tense supes.

"It's us. Come on, this way," he hurried.

They followed the dreamer down six floors of winding stone steps, careening occasionally when they landed on an uneven one.

"How did they get you here?"

"They chained my wrists in silver. We lifted a wooden hatch and beneath sand—a beach, maybe—ran a long, thin tunnel. That's all I can remember."

"So there's a second entrance?" Tobias asked.

"We're at the heart of a war here. Our own are kidnapping innocent supes and experimenting on them, presumably to see if they can turn us all hybrid to withstand evil's attacks," Jet told her. "What other explanation *is* there?"

"To find our weaknesses?" asked Arriette. "Or turn everyone supernatural to avoid inequality?"

Susan stopped to peer from an open window on the ground floor. "I haven't seen the sun in a long time. The darkness and the limitations bring back... memories."

"Keep moving," said Jet, nudging her forward, and Susan's flash of humanity was gone before Arriette could register its presence.

"You needn't manhandle me. In case you haven't noticed, I'm unlike the other vampyrs this world breeds. That's probably why your wards didn't work on me. Be careful how you treat me. You have no idea what I'm capable of."

Jet grumbled to Tobias, "She'll kill us all, that one."

"You accepted Dion!"

"Arriette, Dion isn't some astro-projecting mutant murderer with a grudge."

They followed behind Susan, doing their best to keep pace. There were several guards on the ground floor. All were fast approaching, shouting to others for their help.

"Why are there werewolves in here? I was always under the impression they are incapable of anything but hunting after being forcefully changed beneath the full moon?"

Susan shook her head. "The moon packs are conscious throughout." She paused. "I'm... *hungry*."

Tobias grabbed hold of Angelica and pulled her from the vampyr's line of sight.

"Tell your bloodsucking best friend to keep her retched dead hands away from us," he said.

Arriette rubbed her aching head. "Susan, I don't approve of this but I see no other way. Do you think you can get rid of those guards?"

"How humane does this need to be?" She narrowed her eyes, counting her opponents.

Arriette shuddered. "As humane as possible. Try not to kill them."

"You know that's impossible."

Arriette brushed back her hair to show Susan her scars. "Just do it, and don't make a mess!"

Susan rolled her eyes and skulked off down the corridor to dispose of the werewolves. "You're no fun."

"I can't believe you let her do that," said Tobias.

Arriette groaned. "What choice did I have?"

"Vampyrs aren't great at controlling their instincts, Arriette. It's going to be a bloodbath," Jet said, his eyes fixed on the stalking vampyr as she pounced on her first victim.

"For once, I think those instincts will be beneficial."

NINE

The canteen seemed busier because Arriette was so pre-occupied, and Town Hall's activity reflected her skittish mind. Her brain was frantic—things to do, people to speak with, a speech to write, and all the people she was failing to protect. Although she'd only escaped yesterday (and she was thrilled to be back in a comfortable bed again) a strange sense of deja vu overwhelmed her.

She'd dumped her documents at the closest table, wanting nothing more than to blend in. Hours passed. She couldn't seem to finish any task in particular, flitting between the sheets of paper and tearing out her hair. When she did manage to relax, flashes of the laboratory, her cell, and the screams her feline senses picked up on were haunting.

Supes scuttled by, their shoes clacking on the shining marble floors. Many had attended for court whereby high ranking supes on the HPS passed judgement on petty crime amongst their own within the lair. It happened, though they were supposed to be friends... everyone on the same side. Others were office workers chatting over breakfast about their families and the rumours of a war. Arriette felt a sense of seclusion despite the people surrounding her. She studied her speech for the upcoming ceremony, trying to clear her foggy head of all other issues and think clearly. Casper had already admitted he wasn't ready to hand over leadership yet, but Arriette was terrified the time would come and she'd have nothing to say for herself.

Although every face in the canteen knew of Arriette and what lay ahead, none dared approach as she sat staring at her notes, thinking of her fellow Recruit members and how they were holding up.

Tobias. He'd recently learned a harsh truth about how he came to know Casper. Shot with an arrow by the man he now considered a father, grandfather, mentor, and leader.

Reiko. He still had no idea Casper steered him to the Cabin, and had been training him to learn potions with every cooking lesson.

Baby A. Resting in the infirmary after losing her unborn child—the imagined offspring of the man Arriette was falling in love with, but wasn't yet ready to admit aloud.

Unable to concentrate, she looked up to watch the canteen staff hurry back and forth to prepare for the lunch hour. As the judicial employees filtered out, only the mild humming of magically powered refrigerators filled the tense silence.

Arriette frowned when her eyes spotted a tall, broad man lingering by the door, with scraggly hair and a beard. His trench coat reached below the knee. *Why is he dressed for snow storms?* was her first thought. Her fingers began to tingle, the lights overhead flickered, and the refrigerators cut out suddenly. Then the canteen staff dispersed.

Oh, he's here to kill me. She already knew what his

next move would be somehow, but she froze, allowing his fist to slam into her chest, flinging her body like a rag doll against the nearest table. Still not confident in her telekinesis, Arriette abandoned her paperwork and set off running for the exit, her feet thundering and her heart pounding.

She lunged through the open library door and kicked it shut behind her as she threw her body to the ground. There was little to use as a barricade so she crawled beneath the desk and hoped the darkness would hide her if she could only control her laboured breathing.

The man turned the doorknob and entered, unafraid. He paused in the doorway, distracted as chaos erupted in the canteen and a security alarm sounded throughout Town Hall. Arriette seized the opportunity. She crept from beneath the desk and lingered in the shadows, then slid a hardback book off the nearest shelf. As the man searched, she struck the side of his head, then struck him again, until he collapsed.

"Security! In here!"

It only took a few seconds for two retainers to relieve her of the weapon. Arriette's entire body ached from the man's strike; an injury she didn't need right now. She staggered back to her table and cursed.

A small voice welcomed her back to temporary sanity. "Arriette, are you hurt?"

"Angelica, *what* are you doing here? Were you caught in that commotion?"

Her eyes widened. She pulled a chair out.

"Jet says the vampyr lady wants to see you."

"Oh, yes, *Susan*." Arriette had almost forgotten they'd rescued her. Or had *she* rescued *them*?

"I heard the alarm. I thought there was a fire!"

"No, we just had an unwanted visitor. I got rid of him, don't worry. Until the guards have him locked up, you should go back to your new room and wait for one of us to come get you."

When Angelica had gone, Arriette made off for Susan's room.

This ought to be good.

TEN

Arriette hadn't been in Susan's room more than a few seconds when the vampyr leapt out and pinned her to the wall by the neck. Her nails were scratchy and jagged and her breath the stench of rotting chicken.

Arriette swallowed hard but held Susan's gaze. She was not going to be so easily intimidated in her own territory.

"The sunlight didn't burn your skin then. Pity."

"Where have *you* been?" Susan grinned. "Hiding?"

"Hardly. Trying to free my mind with a bit of ceremonial prep but I was rudely interrupted. I thought if I could get ahead of this upcoming *exchange* of leadership, these innocent people wouldn't be so tired of me screwing things up." Arriette squirmed when one of Susan's nails nicked her skin and drew blood. "Is this necessary, Susan?"

The vampyr loosened her grip but didn't fully let go. She swiped a fingertip across the wound to savour the fresh drips and stuck it playfully in her mouth.

"The kid says you got yourself in some trouble. A regular occurrence, I predict."

Arriette sighed. "I told Angelica to go to her room."

"She did, but she wanted to reassure me she'd given you my message first. She smells like a sweet girl. *You* smell like a wet dog."

Arriette freed the crick in her neck as Susan backed away. "I got attacked in the canteen by a werewolf. Funny thing is I remembered it happening before it did, like deja vu or something."

"Time-travel," the vampyr stated.

"Maybe. So, what's your deal, Susan? You're circling me like I'm lunch. Are you going to kill me? Please, don't keep me in suspense."

"You're not afraid?"

"I could use the time off."

Susan searched Arriette's clothing for a weapon and once satisfied she wasn't there to harm her, let down her guard a little. "You're unarmed."

"I'm beginning to consider carrying Kalvin's scimitar everywhere these days."

"So *you* have his blade. Interesting."

"After he stuck the damn thing in my side, I thought I'd rather earned it." Arriette sighed before she added, "Look, I'm in no position to kill you. So, why am I here?"

"You couldn't kill me. You're too distracted."

"I have reason to be."

Arriette rubbed at her aching temples and walked toward the stove. Every living area came standard with water boiling facilities and a small kitchenette for cooking, but Susan wouldn't be using it. Vampyrs had no need for such amenities.

"*Why* are you distracted?"

"Apart from being attacked by *another* vampyr?" Arriette chewed her lower lip to keep her temper. "I'm due to become leader of the Recruit soon, but you already know about that somehow. I can't lead my people when I can't find most of them or when werewolves are taking us prisoner for illegal experimentation. To do as I'm destined, I'll have to kill someone I love, but there's enough blood on my hands and I'll miss him so much, my heart aches at the very thought of this planet without him. So get on with it, Susan, seen as though you summoned me. How are you alive, if that's what this is?" She gestured to Susan's vampyric form and folded her arms.

"Could life treat you any worse, I wonder?"

"*Sure.*" Arriette retaliated, "I could be a vampyr."

Susan sucked her teeth and sneered. "At least you know who is behind the experimentation. Who tried to turn you all into something you were never supposed to be."

"Yeah, because these werewolves are obviously going to admit such a crime. I feel so violated and unreliable. Why didn't you just tell me everything back at the castle, Susan? How did the weres get in here? How did you?"

Susan gestured for Arriette to take a seat. "Your powers are only weakened. They were saving you for last. Jet's powers seemed relatively unaffected too, but turning invisible is something I have not seen before."

"He could already do that." Arriette rolled her eyes.

"We vampyrs have amazing senses," Susan said.

"Oh, I know. What's your point?"

"I overheard a lot in the castle without trying. They steal supe blood. They mix it up and re-insert it to test the effects. They couldn't find a demon so they grabbed the nearest vampyr they could find. At the time I was weak and vulnerable. They said you would be their boss's most valuable prize if they could harness your power and hand them out to every supe."

Arriette shook her head. "Wait, you said '*prize*'?

Coyote called me his prize back in Drakonta. He claimed to have been sent by someone, too."

Susan shrugged. "Means nothing to me."

"Means lots to us, though."

When Susan stared at her blankly, Arriette elaborated, telling her everything about the shape-shifting orc that attacked her mother, how he had been hexed and sent after Arriette on behalf of his master.

"So why are weres openly wandering our lair and how did they get in here without my knowledge? They're technically evil, right? The wards aren't supposed to let them in. Do you know if Falkon had you turned?"

"I could not tell you who my parent is. They likely entered the same way I did, though." Susan paused and waited for Arriette to cease fumbling in the chair. She'd always been fidgety and impatient, even when reading. "They're here to work."

"Who authorised *that*?"

"Harriet Foley. At least, that's what I—"

"Overheard, I got it."

"You should speak to her about this."

Arriette closed her eyes. "She's dead."

"Unfortunate."

"I *knew* there was something else off about her." She bashed a fist on Susan's bedside table, spilling a drink of water Susan had no interest in consuming. "Casper said I had weird senses and I didn't believe him. Too stubborn for my own good."

Susan narrowed her eyes and retracted her fangs, which had prepared to defend her at Arriette's outburst.

"Nobody is interested in a job unless there is payment involved, Arriette. Most of the weres in here came for protection, weaponry, and a chance to survive. The city are experiencing unusual side-effects of Pandora's box being re-opened."

"Hundreds of years ago!" Arriette groaned. "But I understand, and you're not the only one to say the box is the cause of everything weird on Haeylo right now."

"Not all wolves wish to side with your enemies."

"Then why provoke me by kidnapping my friends and attacking me?"

Susan brushed back her blonde hair. "They are using the genuine wolves as camouflage to sneak through your wards."

Arriette clapped her hands. "You're onto something here, Susan," she said, excitedly. "Do you think Falkon has them working in the castle?"

"Plausible."

"Then we'll tell Casper. Come on." On their way out the door, Arriette paused and scowled to herself. How could she have forgotten? "The orc army on the river bank. Did you see them when you were kidnapped? They took my friend, Pouki. He's short, with a long white beard and he wears robes like Casper."

"My memory is sketchy."

Why does the Tōgædere bond between a new Vamp and their parent have to wipe everything useful?

Slamming Susan's bedroom door behind them, they made their way to the Town Hall's main meeting room to speak with Casper and anyone else present who'd listen.

Upon entry, Casper and Jet sat discussing how he, Tobias and Arriette had been imprisoned, and found Angelica on the way out. The air was thick and stuffy with an acrid stench of wet dog. There were two security officers on the inside of the doorway. At the far side of the room sat the werewolf attacker, chained to a wooden chair.

"Oh great, another deja vu." The last time she'd strapped an enemy to a chair, she'd been in her mother's living room with Coyote in his orc form. "You get anything out of him?"

"Nothing more than you already know. He's working for Falkon Lou."

"Shocker," Arriette said. "I've *got* to meet this guy. He's haunting my entire existence."

"You should wait until you are at full strength before you take on this everlast, Arriette." Susan suggested, her brow raised.

At the use of her full name under these serious circumstances, Arriette blanched. She was used to hearing sweet human Susan call her Arry. Now, it seemed, vampyr Susan had an... edge—one where her old habits came and went with her attitude.

"Why do you care?" Arriette growled, unconvinced the vampyr's concern for her safety was nothing other than self-preserving deception. "My powers are fine. *You* obviously didn't get the memo about me, then?"

Susan folded her arms, blending with the guards and leaning back against the door frame. "I sent that memo."

"Oh, so you *do* remember."

"Ladies, there'll be plenty of time for you to catch up when this is over but I think we need to find this wormhole sooner rather than later," Casper interjected. "If people are being kidnapped and taken to that castle, we need to send out some kind of warning."

"Luckily they didn't keep us for long. Imagine if we hadn't have come back when we did." Jet said.

"They didn't *keep* us, they *kidnapped* us. I wouldn't have been thrown against a refrigerator and chased through the library, that's a certainty," she said, glaring at the unmoving werewolf. "If we try to warn anybody now, Falkon will know we're on to him. He'll disappear, taking any evidence with him."

"Alright, then we go back to your plan. We stay here and fight whatever breaks through," Jet said.

"There is no need for that wormhole you were all searching for," Susan added. "I can show you an alternate exit, most likely where the wolves were welcomed in by Harriet."

Casper sighed. "*She's* behind this?"

"I think Harriet did this with good intentions and I'm still confident most of the working weres in this lair are camouflaged, but mean us no harm." Arriette hated to admit Harriet may have been trying to do the right thing. "Susan only knows what she overheard. You can take us there?"

"I can try."

"Hang on," said Jet, "I thought you wanted to save Pouki? How can we make a move on Falkon Lou or do anything about his experimentations when half of us are gallivanting across Haeylo? Dion and Reiko have no idea any of this has happened. Pouki is missing. And if the Wolves got in through this mystery exit, they'll be waiting on the other side."

Casper gave Jet's shoulder a firm pat. "Dion relies on Arriette's leadership and believes in her capabilities. They're sitting tight until we arrive, I can guarantee it," he said. "There is always the chance the wormhole will fail, or send our people to the centre of their swarm. We cannot be so sure of any exit's safety."

"Can the Four Saviours help us prior to an evacuation, Casper? They possess a crystal ball."

He mulled this over, then asked Susan, "How do you

know about the Four Saviours?"

Susan raised her brow. "I left a note from beyond the grave. Somewhere deep in my subconscious, I know more than any of you, or at least... I did. I was turned vampyr, but I can astro-project. I remember some of my human life —enough of it—which is unusual. I am no ordinary vampyr."

"Could you astro-project before the experimentation?"

Susan said, "I never tried. I wasn't a vampyr long before they took me, and I've been held here since."

Arriette grabbed Susan by the arm. "How much *do* you remember?"

"Some, but you are not the only one who reads, Arriette Monroe, and I can fill in the gaps with research. I remember enough to help you find Falkon Lou, maybe, but not enough to explain why I hate that man more than my hunger."

"Why didn't you tell us all this in the castle?"

"Between escaping it, fighting off guards, disposing of werewolves for *you*, and being instructed to wait in my room until you came for me, I suppose I forgot to reel off my endless knowledge," Susan hissed.

Arriette grimaced. She hadn't mentioned to anyone else yet about allowing Susan to feed off those werewolves.

"Yes alright." Casper motioned for her to calm down. "Emotions are running high; we have all done things we are not proud of." That had been directed at Arriette. He didn't look her way, though, and gestured for Susan to explain as much as she could.

"My memory begins when I moved to the city with Kalvin. I don't remember why I left or how we arrived, but

I remember being given my job. It's patchy. Bits and pieces of a life lived. The job resulted in my death, but I learned a lot about supe politics before that, and people talked freely around me like I was invisible."

"What did the job entail?" Arriette asked.

"I was the Chaos Bearer. A glorified babysitter."

Casper interrupted and clarified, "It was Susan's job to care for the Chaos Wheel. It's a pendant based on the symbol holding a similar name. The wheel represents infinite possibilities and once belonged to an everlast who gave her powers up a long, long time ago to marry a retainer. The pendant was passed to her staff's successors who just so happened to be led by Falkon Lou's rulecast. It is by no means powerful, but valuable."

"So a lawyer hired you?" Jet asked.

Susan continued. "On behalf of the rulecast. The pendant was due to change hands. They wanted to sell it and the lawyer hired me as an unknown, unrelated face to protect it until the interested party could pay."

"Give a nobody a something to hide. Fair enough."

"Exactly."

"And why is it so special?" Arriette asked.

"It's no more powerful than any other everlast pendant but it's extremely expensive because of the materials it contains, and its symbolic shape. The everlast who originally owned it decided not to wait for her true pendant and instead, created one. Nobody else has ever managed to do this, and her combination doesn't work if replicated, so it's unique."

Susan sighed as she thought about the upcoming tragedy in the story—*her* story.

"Unfortunately, before the sale went through, I fell ill. The lawyer didn't trust me with it and so he fired me and found somebody else to take my place. I believe my job got me murdered. Somebody hoped by hexing me, I'd be weak enough to steal from."

Casper explained that the Recruit thought the hex had killed Susan, cast to toy with Arriette's emotions and delay the onset of her powers. Susan denied the theory, saying others in the city were also falling ill with similar symptoms. Arriette remembered her time in the city well and had already figured out they must have suffered the same way she and Tobias have, via a potion or serum of some kind. Falkon was trialling the process.

People were dying.

Arriette said flatly, "So they used the people they wanted rid of as guinea pigs for experimentation. That included you."

"It seems like a lot of trouble to steal an everlast pendant; one with no more power than any other," Jet voiced.

"Susan, do you remember why you wrote me that letter and had Scarlett deliver it?"

"I remember copying lines from a book." Susan nodded. "I was sorry to hear about Scarlett's death. She was a kind friend. Before that, the lawyer and the buyer were talking in front of me about a saviour that would lead the Recruit, and they were going to bribe you with it in exchange for some information."

"He knew my name?"

"No." Susan paused and entwined her fingers. "He just knew of your role. I can't remember how I found out *you* were the leader they meant, Arriette, or whether that knowledge got me killed instead of my job. I know they wanted to ask you some questions, and potentially gain your protection against Falkon Lou."

"He wasn't the buyer?" Casper asked.

"No. They were both so terrified that he'd be furious once he found out another supe held more power than the HPS."

Arriette thought about the bribe. Would she have taken it? Everlasting life through that pendant in exchange for... what? Information on the box's whereabouts? The names of the other Recruit leaders? Perhaps so, because at that time Arriette knew little of evil and less of Falkon Lou. Given their fear, she'd have likely taken them in and fallen for their trickery.

"How much is the wheel worth?"

"Millions."

"To an everlast, that amount of money is not life-changing," Jet told them.

Arriette sighed. "Well I have *my* theory. I think Falkon Lou is behind all this because he is on the hunt for Pandora's box. He's threatened by humans. Baby A told me supes would become extinct if the human population increased."

"That's true," said Casper.

She turned to Susan. "Your job did put you at risk, but your knowledge of me prior to overhearing that conversation with the buyer, *that's* what got you killed."

"Falkon probably wants to remain in power; have everyone be made supernatural against their will," Casper further explained. "These potions and experimentations could be to ensure he can control them or limit their gifts. That's the only reason *I* can think that he'd want Pandora's box. If he holds ultimate power, and the divide between good and evil, then all will bow to him."

"If the box is empty, what use is it to him?" Jet asked.

Casper replied, "He or she who wields the box can

control the contents. They would become the next Pandora.”

Arriette knew what to do. They would gather as many of the Recruit's leaders as possible and head to the city. Staying to fight in the lair was unwise now. She wasn't looking forward to travelling and given a choice, staying put seemed an easier way out, meaning she could defend the beautiful homes of innocents within the sanctuary. Plus, her powers needed strengthening again and she could feel them returning to her tingling limbs, but without practice, she'd be dangerous. Arriette missed being able to conjure her wings or use her telekinesis reliably.

“I can't understand how you knew about me, though. Are you *sure* you don't remember anything else, Susan? Seems odd for Falkon to hex you just for jewellery, especially after you wrote me that note. Something had to have connected the dots between the mention of a new leader and... well, me!”

“I can't tell you any more because I don't remember,” said Susan, “but there was a time-traveller who lived next door to us. Perhaps I paid her to take me forward. Curiosity kills.”

Jet nodded. “It has been done before. That might be how Falkon Lou found out too.”

Casper turned to Jet. “Is Sebastian still on good terms with the Four Saviours? Susan's suggestion may be the way forward.”

“One in particular. She used to work for an everlast. Sebastian isn't going to appreciate her involvement.”

“Why not?” Susan asked.

“They have history.”

“I see,” Casper said, realising something intimate had likely gone on between the sorcerer and Jade, one of the quadruplets. "They have crystal balls to keep track of those undergoing training, drawing their power from the elements. If anyone in this lair can help us to determine where everyone is and if the threat to all exits is real, they can."

"OK, so we can ask Sebastian to introduce me to them," said Arriette. "Jade would talk to *me*, right? But, how do *you* know of them, Susan?"

"I don't personally. They're legends. The city library is filled with records of their abilities."

"Are they here?" Arriette asked Jet.

He nodded. "Sebastian's uhm, contact, is close by. Jade's office is in the village centre, just around the corner. If she's with somebody else, we might have to wait. People pay her good money to hone their gifts."

Arriette scoffed. "And *we're* paying with the lives of thousands of innocent people. She'll see me."

Jet had no comeback.

"There's a chant they can perform to find people," Casper said. "We can start with that. A location spell will open a projection of Haeylo. We supply the names and the Four Saviours provide their location. It's not live; if they move, it won't follow them."

Susan smiled. "Good enough."

"Be wise, Arriette, when you approach Jade. The last time they were asked to help the temporary leader, there was a *falling-out*." Jet stifled a laugh. "Something else you can thank Harriet for!"

Casper straightened his robes, doing his utmost to keep a straight face. It seemed Harriet was the cause of most problems in the lair, behind Arriette at least.

"What shall we do with the werewolf?" he asked. "He's at your disposal, Arriette."

"Well we can't let him go. He'll run straight to Falkon and tell him everything. Besides, if the Four Saviours are kidnapped next, we're screwed," she reasoned.

Casper thought that made a lot of sense. Ultimately, it was up to him. "We are not going to release him."

Susan moved to sit beside Angelica, who'd been listening to their chuntering, most likely overwhelmed with the politics. They began to swing their legs back and forth in unison, enjoying this small, childish act together.

Arriette found herself smiling.

Susan saw Arriette's reaction. Her legs ceased to swing and her ocean blue eyes met Arriette's khaki. "Arry, can I ask, did I *really* die... because of *you*?"

Susan didn't seem angry or upset. She wasn't hostile at all.

Arriette lowered her head. "I'm so sorry."

Susan's eyes widened and Arriette caught sight of her pearly fangs, horrified by the defensive stance she'd taken. Jet and Casper gasped when Susan started to charge.

"Not as sorry as you're about to be," she hissed.

ELEVEN

Arriette held up both hands. She swallowed her fear and took a tentative step away from the vampyr's narrowed gaze, careful not to fall over anything.

"Susan, please, just think this through."

She lunged and grabbed Arriette by the wrist. Her fixated sapphire glare never moved, as if she was looking through her friend and seeing something within her nobody else was. She flung Arriette at the others and, crying out in pain, Arriette cradled where a fresh bruise would be tomorrow. The vampyr hopped effortlessly over the meeting table and dodged between two chairs to where the werewolf had been sitting. With one hand and her vampyric strength, she lifted him by the throat until his legs dangled helplessly.

Arriette's breath caught. "He's... *free*?"

With her other hand, Susan threw the ropes at her, which had been sliced clean. *Foolish*, she thought, *to pay so little attention to such a large beast*. The wolf lashed out at Susan with shifted fingers, displaying brutal curved claws and fur-covered hands. She evaded the attempt, then slammed him to the ground and rolled the wolf over, pinning those claws to the floor.

He scratched and growled but to no avail when Jet and Casper scurried to help her better restrain him.

"Get chains instead," she said, "and a gag."

"No, leave the gag," Arriette told her, stunned by her friend's new instincts. "We might need to question him. How did you know he was free?"

As she shrugged, she said, "I don't trust anyone, and he fumbled," then hissed at the wolf beneath her strength. "Who are you? What's your name?" She crunched his head harder against the floor.

He groaned but managed to say, "My name's Nazar."

"Is it true then?" Arriette asked him, still in shock. "Is Falkon Lou behind this? Are you here to experiment?"

"Obviously," Susan sniped.

The wolf spat at Arriette's feet, so Susan pulled him up by the fur on the back of his neck, then crashed him against the nearest wall. The paintwork cracked as the wall fought back against Susan's anger, standing its ground. Gawping, Arriette had never seen such physical dominance, even from the likes of Dean Constable and the vampyrs Angelo and Roberts back in Manaia Forest.

"There will be no second warning," she said, releasing her fangs and dragging them across the back of the wolf's neck. "Answer. The. Question!"

Jet escorted Angelica out, just in time for the wolf to admit he had been assigned to their cell block, and instructed to hunt them down after their lucky escape. Retracting a claw without risking disarming himself completely, he pointed a single finger at Arriette.

"They sent me to find *her*."

"You're working for Falkon Lou?" Casper asked.

The wolf nodded as best he could beneath Susan's thrusting palm. His face was squashed, restricting the movement of his lips.

"Did he pay you?"

Another murmur sounded out the word, "Pro-tec-tion."

"I assume Falkon wants these experimentations done so he can either boost our chances of winning the war against evil or to infect everyone with a supe power to eliminate humans," Arriette said, shuddering at the thought that Nazar could have taken her back to that acrid cell had she not somehow managed to predict the future.

Nazar struggled to lift his mouth. "None of us... even like him... umph... watch it! But... what other choice... do we have?"

"Then *why* take his side?" Susan asked.

"He said he had... Pandora's box! He said *she* could manipulate it."

"He's lying," said Arriette, assuming he meant her.

"I know that *now*."

Arriette suddenly felt immensely sick. Without another word, she ran for the door, barging between Casper and Jet like skittles and he re-entered. She needed a minute, but Jet was hot on her tail. Once in her room, she sat bewildered on her bed, concentrating on dulling the butterflied in her churning stomach.

It can't be, she thought, rubbing her face vigorously, attempting to knock the thoughts loose. *It contradicts everything Baby A saw on her journey to the future.*

There was a gentle rap on the door and Jet Carter's concerned face appeared around the frame. Scowling, he crept toward her and offered his hand, which she took and squeezed.

"Are you alright? What happened in there, Arriette?"

She sniffled. "I—I think I had *another* vision or something. Maybe my powers are returning, I don't know. I feel sick. I feel *so* sick!"

"Like deja vu? Because that's common for angels and time-travellers. You have the blood of both. What did you see?"

Arriette cringed but admitted, "I... saw my death." She leaned her head against his shoulder and began to cry.

"When? How? You can tell me," he whispered. "It could just have been a vision from Zïnnyi."

"I didn't know I could use my power without actually travelling. Is it possible to experience something without being there? Is that possible?"

He rubbed her shoulder. "Some can, but it's uncommon. Your *mind* travels. That's what deja vu is—a glimpse into the past usually. Do you need me to ask Baby A if she's well enough to explain this fully?"

"No, she needs her rest."

"So what happened in this vision?"

Arriette sniffled and wiped her eyes. "There's a cliff and the sensation of water hitting my face."

Jet scratched his chin. "The only cliffs near enough that I know of are above Enzo Beach. The village is quiet and its inhabitants are all deeply religious, but they're human. Few would wish harm on anyone so I can't imagine they'd want to hurt *you*."

Enzo Beach. Arriette had seen paintings of its golden sands, beautiful turquoise seas and tranquillity in all its glory. A holy place. A peaceful place. A tiny fishing village effectively, run by harmless human women in robes, overlooked by a gorgeous temple up in the mountainside.

"Baby A said I'm alive in the future, and this vision is contradictory. Do you think this really could be a warning to save an innocent rather than a premonition, then?"

"You received your blessing, right, where your senses heightened?"

"Just before we arrived here, and Baby A did say I'm alive in the future she visited."

"How far in the future?" Jet hated to ask, but he reassured her anyway. "It's highly likely if your powers are strengthening that this was a vision. When Baby A's feeling better, perhaps you should ask her. Until then, don't worry. Either way we're far from Enzo." He slicked back his dark hair with a sweaty palm. "I don't see you as the suicide type, despite everything, and someone will be with you at all times, so you'll not be pushed either. I promise." He paused and waited for Arriette to return a smile. "Feel better?"

Arriette released his hand and inhaled deeply. She did feel better, but if this *was* an innocent to save, Zïnnyi had chosen a busy, dangerous time to assign Arriette her first angelic duty. Baby A told her to give each case deep thought; is this person worth risking their current mission to save? Could she do both with help from the Recruit? Was their creator testing her ability to focus on what was most important?

"Thanks, Jet," she said, hugging him and grateful for the bond they now shared, even if it was born from trauma. "It could be worse."

Jet's brow furrowed. "Worse than your death?"

"We could be back in that castle!" They laughed, then she added, "Let's keep this between us for now, alright?"

He agreed and excused himself. Arriette splashed cool water on her face and neck, dried her eyes and psyched herself to get back out there. If anyone asked, she'd tell them the rush was due to anxiety-related sickness. *That* they would believe.

When she returned to the meeting room, Jet had already covered for her, explaining she'd felt poorly and had to run to the bathroom. She winked at him from across the room, thankful for his kindness. Whatever had been in that experimentation drug was backfiring, or so he'd had them all believe. For effect, she rubbed her stomach on the way in.

Casper asked if she was feeling better, then suggested they split into groups. The first would go in search of the hatch Susan used to enter their lair. Group two could go to the wormhole to survey the area. Was it a suitable, safe exit? Then they could summon the quadruplets for their help in locating everyone else and evacuate as planned before the orc army gained entry.

"Hey," Susan said, nudging her. "Your friends aren't going to try to stake me, are they? I mean, I'm hungry and I attacked that wolf, but I would never harm anyone unless they came at me first. My outburst was in self-defence. Can you protect me?"

"*Me* protect *you*? I think you'll be fine," she said. "Casper, I think Susan should lead me to the hatch. She remembers sand so I have an idea where it lets out. The rest of you head for the wormhole. It may be completely useless but it'll be handy to have on record either way."

Jet raised his hand. "Don't we need a traveller for this to work, though?"

Arriette pondered. "I think Baby A will want to help any way she can with her doctor's approval but if she does as she's told for once and wants to rest, just ask someone else in the town. It's important I follow this hatch with Susan."

Jet shook his head, worried about Arriette chasing a vision she may not be able to change and risking both hers and Susan's lives in the process.

They glared at one another for several seconds,

confusing the other supes in the room, but he broke eye contact when she said, "You know I can't ignore this."

TWELVE

Out in the corridor, Arriette decided she wanted to say a quick goodbye to Baby A before heading to the hatch with Susan. If the angel felt able, she would ask her to activate the wormhole. Susan agreed to wait in the visitor's room until Arriette had finished because the two hadn't officially yet met.

"I need your help," Arriette told Baby A as she closed the door behind her. "It's important."

Baby A sat up and swung both legs off the edge of her bed. She gestured with a tilt of her head at the handsome face sat on a chair in the corner.

"Oh, you're busy. I'll just go."

"Arriette, wait. We owe you an explanation."

"*You* don't owe me anything," she told the angel.

"An apology at least," she said. "*Please* sit down."

"This isn't why I came here," said Arriette.

Baby A pointed to the spare seat beside Tobias. Arriette sighed and obeyed, wishing this was just another of her time-travel visions she could later avoid like a nasty plague.

"You both mean the world to me. Tobias has been a huge part of my life and I trust him. He'd *never* intentionally hurt me," Baby A said, turning to the dreamer in question, "but what you did *was* dangerous and irresponsible, Tobias."

Baby A moved to stand but soon realised her strength wasn't up to the task and sat back down, cringing through her aches and pains.

"I can't forgive you," Arriette told him. "It's too weird. Tobias, you and I were close to something special, or so I thought. But to think of you two—"

"It wasn't my fault," Tobias said, "and nothing happened, I promise. We were never intimate like that. Baby A is promised to our creator."

Arriette sighed. "You got her pregnant, Tobias. It's as much *your* fault as it could possibly be. Women don't get pregnant without, well, obviously now isn't the time for a biology lesson!"

Baby A shook her head. "Tobias and I were together briefly several years ago, but our relationship was never physical. I can't. I'm bound by Zïnnyi to remain pure. What happened to me was an accident, not a miracle."

Tobias shuffled uncomfortably. "I'm not proud of it, Arriette, but the baby was the product of my imagination."

Arriette stifled laughter. "*What?*"

Tobias folded his arms and sat back in the chair. "You're *real* supportive."

"Sorry but this *is* ridiculous. You dreamt Baby A would get pregnant and she did? How is that possible?"

"I was lonely. Even with my friends around, I longed for a family; my own flesh and blood. My emotions were unsteady and so my powers were too. We both know now how inconvenient that can be. Baby A was the only female to project this dream upon for miles near the cabin. I didn't even know I was doing it."

Arriette stood and went to the door.

"He didn't mean to. Tobias and I aren't in love, Arriette, nor have we ever been. We're just friends."

"He attacked and threatened me in the corridor. He told me I'd caused the deaths of my friends. He yelled at me for thinking the worst, despite refusing to tell me the truth. He's an imbecile. How can I trust someone like that? I can't place my body or my life in the hands of a supe so reckless."

Tobias stood abruptly. "Hey!"

Baby A wagged a stern finger; Arriette was within her rights.

"If you hadn't behaved the way you did then I might have a surmountable level of sympathy for you," Arriette continued. "If not for Casper intervening, well, we'd *both* be in the infirmary."

Tobias lowered his head. "I panicked. You *have* to believe me. I'm ashamed of myself. That's the truth."

"Then why keep this a secret? Why not tell me sooner and avoided all this? I'd have understood and helped!"

"He didn't want Casper to find out and think poorly of him. He just wants *your* forgiveness."

"I can't deal with this right now. I need loyal friends to fight alongside me. We can't keep secrets from one another, particularly life or death ones. This isn't about me, Baby A, it's about *you*."

"Me? What did I do?"

Arriette sighed. "You did nothing. It's what he almost did *to you*. You could have been killed. Aren't you angry?"

Baby A shrugged. "What else is new?"

"I'll be more careful." Tobias held out his hand for Arriette to shake but she hesitated.

"What do you say, Arriette?" Baby A said, smiling.

"He'll never push his luck again."

Tobias chewed his lower lip. "I'd do anything."

"Can you leave Baby A and I alone?"

Tobias entwined his fingers, paused, then left silently. Arriette shook his hand on the way out and opened the door for him, but when he leaned in to kiss her cheek she turned away.

Not yet, she thought.

When they were alone, Baby A patted the blanket beside her and Arriette collapsed against her shoulder.

"Thanks for that, I guess," she said. "He's been on my mind. I think I'm falling in love with him, Baby A, and it's scaring me. I'm sorry about the baby," she said.

"It's nobody's fault. I know how you feel and it's mutual. You're scared he'll do to you what Kalvin did, or that I'll do what Susan did. You're wrong about us both, but you didn't come here for that. Now, what's *really* the matter, Arriette?"

She broke down sobbing and told Baby A everything about the upcoming ceremony and her visions of the future. She spilled her worries and her fears across the bed for Baby A to gather and dispose of.

The angel agreed her visions were likely messages from Zïnnyi because she also received confusing sights and sounds. The job of an angel was to decipher them and make the decision to act. Sometimes they felt real. Sometimes they were vague, like daydreams.

"I have to go now," Arriette said, sniffling. "Susan and I are going to find where the wolves brought her inside the lair. The others are going to help you with the wormhole activation, if you're up to it."

Baby A scowled. "With help, but why do we need both? Surely we can all use the same exit if it's safe?"

"It'll be handy to have a working wormhole here again too, particularly if it only works one way."

"Yes, I suppose you're right. Why go now, though? I thought you wanted help from the quadruplets? They were hopefully going to explain how Falkon Lou found out about you."

Arriette nodded. "I think I know how, but we weren't sure if it was even possible."

"Oh, it's possible," Baby A said. "Only an everlast would be so bold as to use magic for personal gain. It'll be useful to have their insight still."

Arriette grinned. "*We* used magic for personal gain at Ma's house, remember?"

"Well *we* aren't trying to destroy life as we know it," she said. "I think we can be forgiven that minor sin." Baby A winked and nudged Arriette. "They can at least show us where our friends are. It's all going to be fine you know."

"I have to go," Arriette said, smiling.

"Hey, speak with the quadruplets first. Let's get everyone together, as many as we can, anyway. I'd round them up for you but walking unaided is... a struggle."

Arriette hugged her friend and headed out into the corridor. She explained the change of plans to both Susan and Tobias and sent them off in separate directions to find as many of their friends as they could. Arriette crossed her fingers for Joy and Paulei who'd gone missing at the same time Jet was taken prisoner. They hadn't been seen by anyone since the meeting prior. Hopefully, the Four Saviours would be able to find them.

She headed out into the street. Surrounded by a sea of unknown faces, she moved swiftly through the crowds, scowling. She searched every face for familiarities until she grabbed a lookalike by mistake, prematurely giddy that she'd bumped into one of her missing friends.

Arriette apologised to the black-haired young female and paused, stunned by her beautiful brown eyes.

"No bother," said the woman. Arriette was anxious to keep moving. She tried to excuse herself but the woman shouted, "Aren't you Arriette Monroe?"

"I thought you were someone else. Sorry."

The woman took Arriette by the arm before she could escape into the crowd. She pulled her into an embrace. "You mistook me for Joy Johnas."

Arriette backed away. "How did you—"

"My sisters and I have been watching you. It's quite alright. Do you need my help?"

"Do I know you?"

The woman laughed and shook Arriette's hand. "Forgive me. My name is Jade. I'm a Recruit Trainer here in the lair. My sisters and I are better known as the Elite Four. Or, the Four Saviours. We're quadruplets."

Arriette squeezed Jade's hand. "A gift sent from Heaven at the perfect time." Her luck was beginning to turn.

She led her back toward the town hall, explaining who they were looking for on the way, although Jade already knew of their troubles. Arriette hoped the Elite Four would be able to locate her friends: the telepath Paulei Leigh, their old boss Pouki Hallidae, and the young everlast, Joy Johnas.

THIRTEEN

Once Jade had contacted her sisters, Arriette asked all four women and the rest of her friends to join her in the lair's archive. Inside the Indalo Store, after everyone was comfortably seated, Jade began to explain how their powers worked in line with the elements: earth, air, fire, water. They discussed whether collectively, the Elite Four were capable of locating Sebastian and Joy, Pouki and Paulei.

Arriette had been admiring their tattoos, identifying which of the quadruplets controlled which element on Haeylo. In the Haeyloian language, their tattoos were one of a kind supe birthmarks as per their title: Urt, Ayre, Fori and Walta. These were variations of a basic triangle with a wide base and a sharp point and were small, but noticeable —domineering.

Jade, the controller of Earth, had an upside-down black triangle tattooed at the top of her spine. Each of the women's markings were in the same location and Arriette noticed this only when they tied back their long brown hair in preparation for whatever would come next. The tip of Jade's triangle was cut off with a green horizontal line from the base, suggesting what she represented was beneath the ground or upon its surface.

Saph, short for Sapphire, was the controller of water,

and she had a basic black upside down triangle minus the unusual line. Arriette recognised this mark as a representative of the vast oceans across Haeylo's surface, its rivers, lakes and streams.

Dianne's triangle (though her sisters called her Di), signifying her control of air, was the opposite of her sister Jade's, with a light blue horizontal strip and black outline. Her influence was above ground level.

Naturally, Arriette then predicted Ruby's to be similar to Saph's, completing two pairs. For fire, hers was a regular black triangle with no special markings or lines (as far as Arriette could see).

Despite their control of the elements, each sister had inherited their own responsibilities and skills, closely linked to that element though not complete manipulation of it. Alone they were professional, intelligent women. Together they were more powerful and influential than any first-class everlast, so technically the girls could not be placed on the HPS. Arriette thought them a scale three. They were all Sorceresses with the same abilities as Sebastian Sky, the sorcerer, only modified to fit their roles as trainers of new or struggling Recruit followers.

Jade's profession lead her down the route of biological warfare, human biology and environmental studies. Saph's took her beneath the oceans, to river banks, ponds and lakes. She was also studying marine life and oceanic currents, which Arriette found fascinating because Mousique had been close to fishing grounds. They fed her neighbours when a failing harvest couldn't. Di specialised in unusual weather patterns, freak storms and related natural disasters. She also knew quite a bit about pollution and Haeylo's delicate atmosphere. Ruby's knowledge, however, was dissimilar. She thrived on learning everything about chemical, volcanic eruptions and the forging of weaponry.

Anyone could approach the sisters alone, hiring them as mentors or private tutors in a chosen field. Because of this, priceless skills were being passed through every generation of Recruit followers. Arriette remembered the children in the street sharpening stakes and forging weaponry. Had *they* been students, perhaps of Ruby's, putting their hours of study to some practical use?

After the chatter had settled, Arriette began by thanking the Elite Four for participating. She'd been afraid of asking them for help in case it highlighted weakness within her leadership, but after Jade's kind greeting in the street, she'd found them all to be more than agreeable and so far, pleasant company. Of course, she'd likely offend them in future if she couldn't remember which name matched which woman, but it was clear they respected authority and knew their place in the Recruit food chain. Their tattoos would help.

"We'd need a list of the missing persons' names," said Jade.

Arriette gestured at Jet who passed Jade a small piece of parchment with the four names written neatly in list format.

"This should do it," she said.

Jade pulled a long brown rope from behind the counter and the women each took hold with both hands, twisting their corner to create the shape of a shield knot.

"Arriette, we need you to keep your people back from the knot, which symbolises protection. We should, using a chant, be able to summon the location and status of a vulnerable person in the centre," Jade said.

"*Status?*" Sebastian asked.

Jade sighed and turned to confirm, "Alive or dead."

She glanced around the store at those present: Baby A and Tabitha, Jet, Tobias, Sebastian, Susan and Casper. The creases across her forehead and doubt in those bottomless blue eyes told Arriette they others were likely dead despite her efforts.

"Wait for us to complete the chant once, then you can join in. When we're in unison, I'll throw in the parchment. Ready?"

In a calm, quiet voice, Saph began with the first line of the projection chant, saying, "We call upon the elements of four."

Her sisters spoke the next line without her. "On the solid Earth, as the soaring wind, in the ocean depths, by the heat of the flame."

Arriette backed away and gestured at her friends to participate. Together they repeated the chant three more times then watched as Jade released the parchment. There was a mighty clap and an eruption of force which threw back those not part of the knot, pinning them to the walls of the Indalo store. Arriette fought to keep her eyes open.

In the centre of the knot flashed the faint faces of her friends. A transparent screen surrounded the Elite Four and the stronger it became, the more the others were able to move around.

Joy Johnas's familiar face formed first. Her eyes were wide and panicked and she was rushing through a field of long, sand-coloured grass. Her clothing was dirty and ripped as though she'd been hiding. Arriette glanced at Sebastian who nodded to confirm he knew her whereabouts, then directed Jet toward the door to retrieve her. He struggled and closed the shop door behind him. If Falkon's wolves had chased her, she'd been brave to run so far from the lair's population and to attempt to make it back by herself.

Paulei's face was upon a floral background of what appeared to be bedding or carpet. He was awake and mumbling, though Arriette couldn't make out what about. He appeared shaken and upset with puffy red eyes and a dripping nose. Again, Arriette looked to Sebastian for answers. He shrugged, then pointed as the projection zoomed out to a small shack, somewhere on the outskirts of the lair. Wherever Paulei was, he was unharmed and safe... for now.

The image changed suddenly and panned along the riverbank to a small, frail body floating unconscious in the reeds. Arriette squinted and gasped as she saw blood seeping from a head wound and disappearing with the flowing river, like leaking red ink.

The Elite Four moved toward the projection, slackening the ropes, which in turn caused the images to fade. Arriette yelled 'stop!' just in time for Reiko's gritty voice to fill the air. He was standing outside the diner in Haeylo's city, looking handsome in a white shirt and black lace-up shoes. Beside him was Dion. She'd combed back her luscious red hair and put on some lipstick.

"How are we seeing this?"

"I wrote their names on the back," said Sebastian. "I thought you might like see they're safe and waiting."

Arriette wrapped her arms around the sorcerer. She squeezed until he giggled. "Thanks, Sky. That means a lot."

Jade gathered the rope in from her sisters. The projection faded and the air cleared, leaving those remaining stunned but ultimately happier.

"Let's go find our friends!" said Arriette.

Casper stopped her. "Wait, what about Falkon? Is it possible, Jade, that Falkon sent a time-traveller to find out about Arriette's position with the Recruit?"

"Yes it's possible," she said, "but that's not how he found out." Jade walked toward Susan and took hold of her pale fingers. "I'm sorry, Susan, but only *you* can unravel your memory. I leave you all with our best wishes and our prayers."

Silently the Elite Four packed up their things and left.

FOURTEEN

Joy Johnas, now home, sat cross-legged at the edge of her bed. Paulei and Jet sat with an arm around either side of her shaking body and Arriette knelt at her feet, trying to meet the everlast's gaze.

"Can you tell me what happened?"

"The orcs, are they here yet?"

Arriette smiled and took Joy's hands in hers. "No they haven't broken our wards yet." Arriette held up a palm before Joy could argue. "I would have evacuated sooner if I thought they would."

Joy wrung her hands together, then shook them as if to chase away negative vibes and memories. "We were out in the field like you said, searching for the wormhole. I thought we'd cover more ground if we were to split up."

Paulei shuddered. "Never imagined she'd be ambushed in our own sanctuary."

"Nobody could have predicted this," Arriette assured.

Joy continued. "So we each went off in a different direction. Paulei decided to head for the hunting shacks at the edge of the lair. Jet said he'd search in the old territory, around where the castle is. There are a lot of ruins there. Before our dreamers became so technologically advanced and creative, this whole lair looked a lot like the castle. It was medieval and stone built. I thought I'd search the fields where you entered via our tunnel.

"They came out of nowhere like an ambush out of the grass from all directions. I set off sprinting and just ran for as long as my legs would carry me. I twisted my ankle and fell. I woke feeling groggy with a bump on the head; I must've hit a tree or a rock."

"And the wolves?"

"Nowhere around," she said, "so I thought I'd try for Town Hall to warn you. Jet intercepted me, and we walked home together. Now, I'm here."

Arriette gave Joy's shoulder a firm pat and handed her a cup of Reiko's tea, this time brewed by Casper in his absence. Joy swilled it, sniffed it, then gulped the whole cup down in only three swallows.

"Paulei, same problem?"

He nodded, wrapping his jacket around Joy's shuddering shoulders. "There were only two on my trail. I didn't lose them."

"Then how are you alive?" asked Jet.

"After a while they just stopped chasing me and veered off. On purpose, I think. I ran until I reached the shack and bolted myself inside. I couldn't figure out what they wanted with an old telepath like me but I was going to make them work for their dinner! I dare not step outside so I waited until Jet and Joy found me, and we walked home together. That's how I found out others were attacked."

"Did you figure out *why* they veered off?" Jet asked him. "Picked up someone else's trail, perhaps?"

"Food, maybe," Paulei replied. "I didn't stick around to ask where they were leaving. I didn't realise just how long I'd been sheltering there. You escaped the castle!"

Jet shrugged. "Fear does things to us."

Arriette and Jet explained everything they could about the kidnapping and the wolves' involvement, including the capture of Nazar and their suspicion that Falkon Lou was behind this whole thing.

Arriette excused herself, leaving Jet to fill in the missing pieces. She couldn't wait much longer.

Pouki needed her.

***

Baby A hobbled nearer to the closed wormhole, folding the map with one hand and clinging to Tabitha's arm with the other. The area was barren and unlike anything else Baby A had seen so far, and couldn't have been more than a half-hour walk from the castle. Surrounding them were overgrown ruins of what looked like homes or outhouses, and a crumbling well that had long since dried.

"Are you sure you can do this?"

Baby A nodded. "Looks like something terrible happened here."

"It malfunctioned and exploded; began sending people all over Haeylo without warning. It spiralled out of control, taking most of this area with it and leaving us with tree stumps and animal carcasses. The time-travellers decided to close it forever and allow the land to regrow." She paused. "Arriette has a way out, Baby A. This is optional. If you're not up to it, she and Susan have an alternative."

Baby A released Tabitha's arm and stood straight. "You won't know my history, but I'm stronger than I look. Casper found me orphaned and alone by the river with nothing but a single picture, and I've been searching for my purpose since. I'm a survivor, but I needed a place to belong. I needed a reason to exist. *Why* had Zìnnyi spared me? Your lair has given me a home, a job, friends and family, a sense of belonging and a *future*. If you think I'm going to crawl away from anything beneficial to our operation here, you're mistaken."

Tabitha Hope cleared the area, asking the helpers and Baby A's Retaining doctor to allow her enough room. She spread her fingers evenly and began to push out toward the wormhole, now just a deep, intricate spiral carved into the bark of a lone tree. She extended her palms from her elbows and moved them aside as if to stretch the spiral wider. Soon it began to turn hypnotically.

The ground quaked as though a building had collapsed close by, sending gusts of thick air their way.

"Here we go," Baby A said, smiling. "Another memorable moment in Recruit history."

FIFTEEN

"Arriette, *where* are you going?" Casper was on his way to the library when he intercepted Arriette sprinting from Town Hall with an outstretched arm. "Slow down!"

She came skidding to a halt and almost crashed into a passer-by. "I'm going to save Pouki," she said, then apologised to the startled pedestrian.

"I'm taking care of it. You and Susan are to go in search of the wolves' hatch. Our people are getting anxious." He paused, then leaned in toward her. "I, too, am worried about that orc army. I'll have Pouki rescued once Baby A returns with confirmation of the wormhole's activation. It'll be safer that way."

"But I can try to save him *now*," she protested.

"Alone, what are your chances of success?"

Arriette exhaled and folded her arms, defeated. Casper was right. She needed to trust his wisdom and judgement, though it was difficult for her to agree and leave Pouki's rescue in another person's hands. As originally planned, Arriette would make haste for the hatch with Susan. Then they could begin evacuating their people before the wards protecting their sanctuary were finally demolished.

"What about everyone else? They'll be waiting."

"Let *me* worry about them. Those wards should hold long enough."

"If they don't?"

Casper hurried her. "Better get a move on."

When Casper had gone, Arriette sat on a nearby wall until Susan emerged from Town Hall with her gear. As they set off walking, Susan turned to Arriette, walking backwards down the cobbled main street.

"The last journey we took together was from Mousique to Harvest Fields for a picnic and we forgot half of our supplies. Kalvin was painting the fences. He wanted us out of the way, remember?"

"Yes, but we're more prepared this time," she said, gesturing at the heavy backpack strapped to her shoulders.

"I'm relying on you," Susan told her.

"That's reassuring." Arriette rolled her eyes. "It could be midday out there. I don't need you exploding on me."

Susan smiled awkwardly, appreciating the hidden sentiment. Both women needed one another equally.

"I don't think I will react the same way, but do you mean that?"

Arriette raised a brow. "Jade said only *you* could recall those memories and if you explode into a giant ash cloud, who's going to tell me how Falkon found out I was next in line for Casper's job?"

"Oh." Susan lowered her head and turned back around, fiddling with the straps on her backpack. "You need me for information."

Without Susan, Arriette would never know the truth. Had Falkon convinced a time-traveller to find her or was she missing something?

"You haven't missed me... at all?"

"At first I didn't."

Susan nodded. "Well, you must have been pleased to be rid of me after what I did."

"Losing Kalvin was a shock," she admitted. Arriette wasn't sure how else to react. She opted for honesty. "I blamed myself for your death, though I hated you for leaving. I thought better of you. I loved him and you were my best friend. Both of you took a knife to my back."

"I had my reasons, I'm sure. I knew you'd be a great leader, Arry. That's why I left you that parchment."

Arriette frowned. "Can you tell me *how*?"

"No," Susan said softly, her fangs protruding from her rosy lips, vibrant atop her pale skin. "I don't remember. I've always had faith in you, though. That's etched deep, in a heart which no longer beats. I feel little now I'm a vampyr, but my confidence in *you* dominates the emotions I do have. There is no love remaining in my chest for even Kalvin, though I don't remember feeling much for him anyway." Susan scowled, more to herself than Arriette. "I'm not sure I ever truly loved Kalvin, Arry."

"Then why did you leave Mousique?"

"For another reason. I just don't know what that is yet." Susan huffed. "I let you down. I'm not like the other vampyrs so there's got to be a way to revive my memory. Dion's different too, right?"

Arriette shook her head. "Not like you. Human blood makes her sick. Her physical form is vampyr. Her spiritual form is human. She can't remember much of her life before death. Pouki can usually read vampyrs, too, up until their last breath anyway. Not her, though. She's quite unique."

"Could he read *my* mind?."

Arriette hummed, deep in thought. "We'll have to try when he's home and rested. It *would* answer an awful lot."

They walked for an hour in silence. Susan turned to Arriette, stopping her in her tracks. She lowered her bag to the ground and indicated Arriette should do the same.

"Kalvin's dead," she said.

Arriette's heart skipped a beat. "I'm so sorry, Susan."

"He fell, didn't he?"

"You died within hours of one another. He and a retainer called Dean Constable came after me. It's a long story but he stabbed me and we fell a long way to the city centre. Baby A caught me but Kalvin didn't make it." Arriette lifted her shirt to reveal the scar which had almost healed with the aid of her angelic blood. "I *am* sorry. It was self-defence."

"I'm sorry, too," said Susan.

"You had nothing to do with it."

"Actually I think I did," Susan said, slumping to sit on a fallen tree. "It's odd. I remember him but as if through a storm. There are images and sounds but none of it fits. Like a jigsaw with missing puzzle pieces. I think Jade was right, Arry."

Arriette sat beside Susan. "What about?"

"I think only *I* can tell you how Falkon found out you were next in line for Casper's job. Why else would I leave you the note? Why else would I have these memories? Maybe I *wasn't* killed for the Chaos Wheel but so Falkon could silence me before I reached you? Or, for some other nasty reason."

Arriette placed a hand on Susan's knee. "It'll come back to you. Jade would've told us in the store if not. *She* believes it and I trust her. Give it time, alright?"

Susan grabbed her things and slung her bag hard over one shoulder. Although their losses meant different things, they were both suffering. Arriette knew from befriending

Dion that sometimes even vampyrs need a trusting companion.

"He was a good man," Arriette said.

"No, he wasn't. He was selfish and stubborn," Susan replied, grinning, "but I appreciate the sentiment even if you're lying."

They walked together for another hour before Susan dropped to her knees in a clearing and rummaged through the fallen leaves.

"Can I help you?"

She snapped her fingers as her left hand found a metal ring attached to a large wooden trap door.

"No need. Got it."

She yanked the ring as hard as her vampyric strength could muster and after several tugs, the door popped open, releasing a rancid stench of mould and decay. Arriette turned away and sat beside the hole with her legs crossed.

"Why do you think you're different?"

"Everything supernatural happens for a reason. You're religious, so you tell me."

Arriette shrugged. She had always believed in a god, although until meeting the Recruit hadn't really named him or prayed to him. She'd been open-minded, curious but cautious.

"I can't. Not yet, anyway."

Susan laughed and dropped down onto the first rung of a creaky wooden ladder. It descended into the darkness. Arriette cringed at the thought of following her.

"I never thanked you properly for saving my life."

Arriette scowled. "I didn't. A vampyr turned you. I just rescued you from that awful laboratory. You weren't for it though, remember?"

Susan reached out for Arriette's hand, preparing to

lead her into the unknown tunnel, no doubt plagued with rats and insects.

"That vampyr saved me physically, but emotionally, Arry, I'm all yours."

***

As the wormhole opened, Baby A turned to address those accompanying her. Some were there to support the Recruit, others to support Baby A's medical requirements but most attended out of curiosity.

The magical doorway to the outside world began its steady clockwise rotation, sucking stray leaves and bugs through the portal. Baby A waited to be sure it wasn't going to malfunction again, then turned to her friends.

"We're leaving the wormhole active. For now it moves one way, and that's to the outside world but I can't tell you where until somebody uses it."

"Why not?" Tabitha asked.

"I didn't create it, I'm just re-activating somebody else's portal. So, travel at your own peril, because unless you're a time-traveller you won't be coming home unaided."

"But you did it!" Tabitha said, hugging Baby A. "Arriette is going to be so proud of you. Now, let's get you back to the infirmary."

SIXTEEN

There were no lights in the tunnel. Arriette used her practised *Monibah* to summon a small candle in the palm of her hand. She slid past Susan to light their way, desperate to reach the other side. She had never been claustrophobic, but the stench of death and decomposing foliage was enough to churn Arriette's stomach and make her feel consumed by the narrow hall.

"So the old guy, he's like your teacher?"

Arriette swung her hand round to light Susan's ocean eyes. She stopped, seemingly not phased by the intense heat or her proximity to fire either.

Unusual, Arriette thought, as fire had killed Angelo.

"Yes but he and I are friends too." She lowered her head and with it, the flame. "Not for much longer."

"Because he's old?"

Arriette shook her head and turned slowly to continue her fight through the sludge and slime. The grime made a sloshing noise when she picked up her feet.

"Because I'm going to kill him."

There was silence behind her as Susan processed this. Arriette continued walking because nobody was ever going to understand how knowing that made her feel. The human in her said murder was wrong, but the Recruit leader in her argued it was necessary. Casper would agree.

"Arry, why do you want to do that?"

"I don't. He says I have to," she replied, "by decapitation using a ceremonial sword. Only then can I take his job and put him to rest. End his suffering."

"Your conscience is pure at the moment," Susan said.

Arriette stopped once more. "I wouldn't say that." She lit a second candle and handed one to the vampyr. Susan's brow was creased with confusion, but she didn't balk at the potential danger.

"What are you getting at?"

"It's just... the leader of the Recruit should be pure and if you're a murderer you're not pure, are you?"

"If *anything* it's assisted suicide," she reasoned.

"Again, a sin," Susan argued, raising her hands. "Just saying. I can't see you going ahead with the ceremony. I think you're better suited to another role."

Arriette narrowed her eyes. Susan hadn't been back long enough to have an opinion about her destiny or the planet's, and *certainly* not Casper's. He'd told her that his death would end his reign and begin hers, just the way Zïnnyi intended it.

Sin or not, she'd do her job and do it well.

"This isn't optional, Susan. I don't think you've been here long enough to know about this organisation's long-term goals, *certainly* not in depth. Killing Casper will end his suffering. He's lived life over and over since the beginning of this planet, challenged by our creator to find *one* person. Only then can he be free.

"That task is over now. If I have to chop off his head to give him the peace he deserves then so be it. I'd sacrifice my purity for that man in a heartbeat after all he's done for me and it is no place of yours to tell me otherwise!"

Stunned, Susan lowered her hands and gestured for Arriette to continue down the narrow way. Perhaps she'd been wrong about her after all.

SEVENTEEN

Baby A stumbled back through the overgrown brown grass, clinging to Tabitha hope's arm for balance.

"Do you think he's doing the right thing?"

Baby A turned to Tabitha, puzzled.

"What do you mean?"

"Well," said Tabitha, "do you think Arriette is ready to take over from Casper. Our circumstances suggest otherwise."

"I believe in her," she said, honestly.

And she did.

Baby A believed in Arriette more than she believed in herself sometimes. She'd seen how powerful and influential her friend was and the extent of her capabilities. Arriette was a born leader; educated, loving, kind but firm and most of all, she cared about the future of the human race. A trait none of the supes held or ever would hold.

"How can you be so sure?"

"We don't have a choice sometimes. Our hearts believe and our heads follow suit. Don't *you*?"

"These are dark times. Arriette is a bright light, yes, but is she *the* bright light?"

"You're not questioning her potential, you're unsure of Casper's integrity, aren't you?"

Tabitha, embarrassed by her guilt, paused at the base

of an oak tree to allow Baby A a moment's rest. The others had already left, leaving them alone to discuss the elderly shape-shifter's motives.

"She won't give in until she meets the expected standard, but how can Casper be so sure? How do we know he hasn't selected the next best thing so he can finally receive his peace?"

Baby A sighed and sat beside Tabitha Hope on a large rock. "Because I know him better than you."

Tabitha entwined her fingers. "I'm sorry."

"Look," Baby A began, "Casper is honest. Zïnnyi watches his every move and has rebirthed him each time he's failed. If he tried to cheat the creator, he'd never find peace. Casper's smart and after all these years, he's confident he can fix this planet and give the human race the second chance they deserve. I'm not saying Casper or Arriette are perfect, but they're as close as I've ever seen." Baby A paused to take a drink from her canteen. "Casper and Arriette have already met. In Casper's past and Arriette's future. He *knows* she's the next leader and in her heart, she feels their connection too. I sense it; it's my job."

Tabitha nodded and helped Baby A to her feet. "I'm sorry I questioned it, I'm just anxious."

Baby A squeezed her hand. "Me too. Casper did awful things to keep Tobias and Reiko with him all these years, but they were necessary. Once you see that, you'll understand."

There was a snap of twigs ahead in the bushes and Baby A's eyes narrowed at the sight of a young nurse emerging from the shade. She brushed down her uniform and tidied her pretty red hair, then smiled and made her way toward them.

"*There* you are. The infirmary sent me. You're too sick to be out of bed. Your doctor hasn't cleared it."

Tabitha scowled and looked to Baby A who shook her head gently and feigned a wobble. The nurse rushed to her side and grabbed hold of one arm, gesturing at Tabitha to let go of the other. Baby A smiled and signalled it was fine, so Tabitha hung back and pulled her maul from its floor-length pack strapped across both shoulders. She held it out with both hands. The metal felt heavy but powerful between her fingers.

"Let's get you back so we can find you the best care."

Baby A paused. "I don't need your care."

"Of course you do!"

"No, I just needed you to think I did."

The nurse's eyes widened when her peripheral vision saw the maul. She yanked Baby A into a choke hold.

"I knew straight away who you were," Baby A said, struggling to remain upright, "because my real doctor came with us!"

Baby A's wings catapulted free, flinging the nurse off her feet. She grabbed hold of Tabitha and together they sprinted away from the ruins across the lair's open fields, pausing only briefly for air despite Baby A's aching limbs. She cradled her stomach as they approached the Indalo store and threw open the doors, slamming them shut behind and racing for any ammunition already in sight.

But it wasn't long before the nurse was on them. She leapt at Baby A, throwing her delicate body through the glass cabinets behind. Weaponry tumbled down covering both their faces. Glass cut into her pale skin.

"Monroe was a fool to leave you unprotected."

"She's going to kill you," Tabitha spat, nursing a wound to her forehead and searching the debris for her weapon. "Whoever you are."

Baby A gasped beneath the nurse's weight and fumbled for anything sharp or heavy. Her clawing fingers found and tipped a box of unused silver arrowheads. Baby A struggled to throw the nurse off her body, then flipped and pinned her down.

"She's a wolf, and soon to be a dead one!"

The wolf laughed and shifted her teeth and her fingers, preparing to rip and shred the angel's beautiful white wings.

"Silver won't mutilate a wolf."

"You mean like you mutilated my friend, Scarlett?"

"It was only a matter of time, Baby A, until we managed to kill *one* of you and look how easy it was."

Baby A plunged the arrowhead deep into the wolf's carotid artery. Blood sprayed across her face, covering both the floor and the walls behind. She screamed and flailed, but Baby A's firm grip and stern glare never faltered.

"You killed her," said Tabitha, crawling on her hands and knees to check Baby A's wings.

"I'm fine," she promised.

"We could have questioned her, you know!"

Baby A batted her away. "Stop fussing. She'd only reel off the basics; Falkon harnessing all supe powers to rid Haeylo of humanity forever, gain control of Pandora's box, rule the world and cause chaos and misery."

"You forgot destroy the Recruit. I'm assuming he'd want to be rid of all who challenge him."

Baby A grinned. "We can't be destroyed. We're a religion, a belief, a heart, a soul. You can't take that from people."

Tabitha aided her to her feet. "The shopkeeper is

going to be *so* angry when he sees the state of his store."

"Oh please, Tobias and Arriette can have this cleaned up in the blink of an eye."

EIGHTEEN

"Susan, slow down. I can barely keep up with you," Arriette yelled, her voice echoing down the empty tunnel ahead.

Susan tapped Arriette on the shoulder and she span, lighting a few feet behind until she saw the vampyr's concerned face.

"I'm right here." She passed Arriette her candle. "You sound like you could use both of these."

"*You* sounded as though you were running away," she said. "*Sprinting*, even!"

Arriette glanced down at the rippling sea water a short way ahead of them and pointed. She thought she'd seen a shadow.

"Rats, maybe?" Sue suggested, passing her.

Arriette jumped and screamed when a fat brown creature dashed between her legs and disappeared behind her.

She shuddered. "You were right. Disgusting creatures."

Arriette looked up just as Susan's fangs found another rat's flesh. She grinned between the dripping blood. "They taste good to me."

"I'll rephrase—*you're* disgusting. For as long as you're eating them though I suppose they're not eating me.

So how much further to go?"

Susan dropped the rat's corpse and wiped her mouth. "Not far."

Her footsteps began to splash again and Arriette panicked. She blew gently on her candle and whispered '*Monibah*' to increase the effect, then held it at her arm's length.

A cold palm grabbed Arriette by the neck and hauled her off her feet. Her backside landed firmly in a puddle of sand and seaweed and she cried out as more disease-riddled rats came scurrying toward her. Thrashing with both arms, Arriette decided she'd had enough of whatever game the vampyr was playing.

"Get me the hell out of here!"

The presence behind her disappeared and Arriette found herself worrying she was either losing her mind or being followed by a mischievous ghost. Then a huge splash of water covered her as the shadow charged past, knocking her onto her side.

Arriette cringed and wiped her eyes. As she hobbled to her feet, a throaty gurgling sound could be heard from up ahead. "What's going on? This isn't funny anymore, Susan! Where *are* you?"

A bright light shone as she rounded the corner, temporarily blinding her before a silhouette stepped in the centre, shielding her from the rays of sunlight. It was Susan, clutching the limp body of a half-shifted werewolf in her hands, his throat chewed up between her fangs.

When their eyes met, Arriette backed away. Those blue saucers, once so innocent and harmless, were now electrified and bright. Arriette set off running back along the tunnel but she didn't get far.

"He was trying to kill you," Susan said, blocking her

path.

Arriette held the vampyr at bay. Like a sharpened stake, being set on fire was *supposed* to kill vampyrs just as easily, so Arriette thrust the candles at her just in case.

"Back off! Take another step and you're toast." Arriette shook her head and staggered away. "*Literally!*"

Susan crept around Arriette slowly, then threw the wolf's body into the sunlight. She held up both bloody palms.

"Put those out, Arry. I'm telling you the truth. He tried to strangle you back there, then he came at me. I don't think he knew I was a vampyr."

The passage, now growing brighter as Arriette's eyes adjusted, was a widening, half-stone and half-wooden structure which ran beneath the beach and through to the Recruit's lair. Long wooden planks held some of the walls in place and leaking seawater dribbled through in various places. Rocks and sand were scattered about and Arriette had to watch her footing as they emerged into the daylight.

She put out the flame and nodded once to Susan, then gestured she lead their way out of the tunnel.

"Where did he come from?"

"Followed us, I suppose. Won't have wanted us telling the others about this passage," Susan said.

They sat out of breath beside the wolf's corpse, looking across a golden beach toward the turquoise, crashing ocean.

After a few minutes, Susan began to laugh. "I'm not burning. I knew I was special."

Arriette had completely forgotten, but before she could say anything the vampyr was on her feet and running to the water's edge to clean her face and limbs. The water around her turned crimson as she washed a fist full of matted blonde hair, thick with sludge and sand. Chunks of the wolf's flesh fell from her clothing and she swilled her mouth as the salty tide moved in.

"Sorry about before," said Arriette, kneeling in the water beside her. "You really scared me there."

"Don't worry about it, Arry. Wash your face, you're covered in blood and dirt," she said, helping to splash the back of her neck. "I don't remember why I left you that parchment," she said suddenly. Arriette looked over at her, curious. "I wish I did, but flashes of memory keep hitting me in segments—out of sequence—but they're returning slowly. I told you about the Chaos Wheel. I took that job because I thought, *if this thing is so special then someone honest should be in charge*. That, and I had to make up for something terrible I did."

Arriette's brow furrowed. "What?"

"It's still a mystery, but the guilt is clear and painful even now. Whatever I did it was criminal, *evil!* When I found out I was dying I think I asked Kalvin to tell you because there was so much I needed to say. I was running out of time. Apologies, revealing secrets, and no doubt to tell you how I valued your friendship, however brief and one-sided."

"Why send *Kalvin* back to get me, though? After what he did, you can't have thought I'd trust him again."

"I never saw his monstrous side." Susan dug her fingers into the sand, watching as they sank deeper and deeper. "He loved you. Love is a tether. It drew him to you. He did what he thought necessary to find you, despite his ulterior motives in the end. Kalvin learned there was an everlast girl missing, the daughter of someone he owed money to. The girl's fiancée was on his way to find her, travelling toward Mousique. That's when Kalvin decided to go too."

"So he didn't actually *want* to see me?"

Susan shook her head. "Not at first. The everlast said he'd clear Kalvin's debts in exchange for his daughter," she scowled, trying to recall further information, "or someone who might be able to resolve problems like mine in the city. They were his top priorities, I guess. I remember the everlasts panicking, though between Kalvin leaving and my death, my memory still hasn't returned."

Arriette continued to wash, considering diving in to clean her clothing and her hair too. The water was clear and sparkling, filled with shoaling colourful fish. Further down the beach it crashed against a rocky cliff face.

"Do you remember how you met Scarlett Evermay? She was your retainer friend in the city."

"Scarlett found *me*. I don't think we were friends at first. She told me she knew people who could protect us."

"But *why* did you want me protecting, Susan? What did you and Scarlett know? If you didn't love Kalvin then *why* leave Mousique to live with him in Haeylo's city? It's a huge step to take without reason."

Susan sighed and shook her head. "Why? Why? Why? I don't know! I'm sorry but my head—" she paused, smacking it repeatedly with her sandy palm, "—it hurts."

Arriette slumped back onto her bottom. She was a fraction closer to knowing the truth and that had to count for something.

"Do *you* think I can do this, Susan?"

"Do what?"

"Be the leader of the Recruit and replace Casper."

Susan took hold of Arriette's hand and smiled. "There are thoughts inside my mind I can't control and can't recall, but I *feel* this in my heart, even though it no longer beats."

***

At Town Hall, Baby A and Tabitha Hope told Casper about their encounter with the wolf.

After examining her corpse closely, they found she wore a wig masking her short spiky hair and contact lenses. Tobias rushed in to check on Baby A and informed her the wolf she'd killed was, in fact, the leader of those in the laboratory. He recalled their experimentations. He remembered vividly seeing her in the castle's hallways, giving everyone orders.

All the while Casper seemed distant, though concerned for them all, still worried about the ceremony.

Baby A paused mid-conversation with Tobias and took hold of his hand. "Casper?"

"You can tell us what's on your mind," said Tobias. "We won't judge you."

Casper inhaled then released Baby A's hand. She and Tobias looked at one another anxiously.

"I told Arriette that she must kill me in order to replace me and I am not sure she has the strength."

Tobias sat beside him. "You're wrong."

"She *must* kill me," he said. "I told her I needed time because I'm delaying the inevitable. I needed to say goodbye to you all."

"I'm not saying that she doesn't have to kill you. I'm saying she's more than capable," he said.

Baby A scowled. "You can't believe she's going to back out of her duties, not after all we've been through together."

"She's more than ready but she's grown to love us all as family. It is cruel of me to expect so much."

"I'm a little worried about the ceremony, too. We all are," said Baby A honestly. "Arriette is inexperienced in making those difficult leader decisions. This is likely to be her hardest so far, but I'm confident she won't let you down. Arriette knows this means *everything* to you and to our planet. I've seen the future," she reminded him, "and the sights I witnessed indicate we're right to trust her."

Casper's tear-filled eyes met Baby A's. "You didn't see me there, did you?"

Baby A shook her head. "If you're afraid she's going to resent or hate you, then before the ceremony you have to ensure she understands *why* this is necessary and what she can accomplish by swinging that sword. Don't leave any of her questions unanswered, Casper. I think then, once fully informed, the decision will *finally* be her own."

NINETEEN

They headed toward the steep ascent of the mountain, sharing its base with Enzo in the east and Drakonta in the west. Susan and Arriette wanted to stay in the water to cool off; Susan more so due to her fascination with being unaffected by the sunlight. Her pale skin was already beginning to gently tan, giving her a more human appearance. Her blue eyes glistened with delight. Arriette had asked her not to reveal her fangs to the people of Enzo. If it became public knowledge that vampyrs were beginning to conquer the daytime, there would be widespread panic.

"Where do we go now?"

"There's something I have to do before we turn back." Arriette pointed to the village, cosy at the base of the mountain and surrounded by trees. "There are humans there, and I think one might need my help," she said. "In a vision I saw a cliff. My instincts say we walk uphill until we find it."

"We're going to look suspicious whichever route we take."

"Why?"

Susan rolled her eyes and pointed to some steep stone stairs, secured with a wooden rail. "There's only one way on and off this beach. Nobody saw us come down, so when we go up, there'll be questions."

They began their ascent, pausing only briefly half way for Arriette to catch her breath. She was cautious, keeping a careful watch on her footing and gripping the rail until her knuckles turned white, despite it being wobbly. Susan stayed close behind but when Arriette finally made it to the top, the view was worth her effort. She exhaled thoughtfully and brushed back her mane of hair, pleased to have made it in one piece.

Susan ushered Arriette along a winding path, sheltered by overhanging trees and into the village. It was a single dirt track, lined with sweet-smelling pink flowers and grass banks.

"They're staring at us. It must be our clothes."

The local women wore sandy-coloured dresses with their hair tied up in either a bun or if short, loose by their shoulders. Floral embroidery decorated their hems, necklines and sleeves. They faces were pale and bland except for the circular symbol of Enzo painted in black on their foreheads—a perfect circle drawn in one brush stroke.

Arriette hadn't changed clothes since returning from the castle and now felt groggy and unclean. Although they looked normal in their own cultures, in Enzo they stood out as tourists.

"What do we do now?" Susan asked.

"You look lost," said a passer-by.

Arriette was startled by the elderly woman and her proximity, but asked her how to reach the highest point of the mountain. She shuffled towards the vampyr, something she thought she would never do, for comfort and reassurance.

"Whatever for?" asked the woman, her wrinkled

hands trembling as she pointed up a steep hill. "It's dangerous."

Arriette cleared her throat. "We're artists looking for some inspiration."

The woman's eyes narrowed. An obvious lie.

"Nobody goes up there. Turn back. This is no place for weak city folk."

Susan balked, "*Weak?*"

And Arriette added, "*City* folk?"

"There *is* a path, though?"

"Mythology warns us away. It is forbidden to venture."

Arriette discreetly elbowed Susan in the ribs. She let out a yelp and turned away, pretending to look at the scenery.

"We were hoping to paint some portraits of men, but we haven't seen any yet."

The elderly woman lowered her hood and a long, grey plait fell loose, dangling below her stomach. Her wisdom-filled slate eyes were beginning to darken with age and the symbol above her nose wrinkling. Arriette thought she had a look of someone she once knew; a memory or a vision brushed her subconscious. Had she known a relative of this human woman in Mousique, perhaps?

"The men live in the temple. Along this cobbled street and up the hill. You will reach a freshwater well and beyond that, the path will fork. Take a right. You'll find a narrow tunnel with the Enzoian symbol painted above the door."

The woman bowed her head slightly and with the tips of both index fingers, touched the symbol as a sign of respect. Arriette knew the symbol well from her books. It had been drawn in a single, smooth motion to symbolise simplicity. These women lived basic lives, with little need for material possessions or riches.

"Thank you," Arriette said, dragging Susan behind her. "And goodbye."

"Beware!" she shouted after them. "Do not roam the left path, or curiosity may take your soul."

Arriette span on her heel to ask what she meant, but the woman had already disappeared. She jogged to catch up with Susan who had mumbled something about the woman being insane, and continued up the cobbles.

"What was *that* about?"

"She's crazy. Don't let her scare you."

"I'm glad you saw her too. For a minute there I thought *I* was going crazy." Arriette chortled. "It's easier for you to live fearlessly. You're already dead."

Arriette followed Susan to the end of the road and up the hill, just as the woman had said. She allowed the vampyr to check behind boulders and trees and scout the hillside before Arriette went any further.

She thought about her friends awaiting their return in the lair and hoped their magical wards had continued to hold. They were all brave, strong survivors and she knew if the entrance gave way, they'd fight for their sanctuary with or without her.

When they finally reached the well, Susan skipped down the path to investigate. Arriette paused to rest her aching limbs and leant against the well for support. Her eyes found the fork in the road and the enticing right tunnel she'd been warned not to approach already beckoned her. She didn't trust the water from the well, so she swigged from her own canteen and wiped her brow with the back of her hand.

Soon she was rested enough to move on, following Susan up the right turn. She noticed the symbol carved into the stone above the tunnel so they were on track.

"I wonder what's down that left path," said Arriette, glancing over her shoulder.

"If she hadn't have warned you, would you be so curious?"

Arriette laughed. "Probably not, but if there's treasure in there I'm blaming you for my future poverty."

"Classic trap."

She scowled. "I'm sorry?"

"Planting a seed like that in the mind of a future saviour and then disappearing mysteriously. Of course you're going to go down the left path. You can't help yourself. It's a trap. She *wants* you to go that way."

"Why would she want me to break a bunch of their rules? She doesn't even know me."

Susan hushed Arriette. Up ahead there were deep voices chanting the words 'De'va mightie zìnnyi, de'va' over and over. They crept forward; their way was well lit with candles and both the walls and the path were decorated with intricate paintings. Some of them were beginning to fade with time.

Arriette's stomach nervously contracted when her eyes found the painting of a dragon surrounded by treasures just as they'd joked. It was devouring a woman that looked a lot like her with large emerald eyes and long, brown hair. In her left hand she held a sword and in the right, what looked like a box. Around the woman, butterflies had exploded from the lid, and they scattered in vibrant colours across the walls.

"I didn't think dragons were real," said Susan.

"They were," Arriette confirmed, "but nobody has

seen evidence of their existence in hundreds of years. Zïnnyi placed them on Haeylo as guardians of his treasures. Unless provoked and unlike most books depict them, they were supposed to be rather gentle and loyal creatures. Some scholars, in my books at Mousique, claim to have ridden them." Arriette traced the image with her fingers, appreciating the detail in each brush stroke. "Someone put their heart into this drawing."

"Green is a typical dragon colour then," Susan said and sucked her teeth. "Come on, this is all fantasy and we have work to do."

Susan led Arriette past the other drawings and deeper into the tunnel. All the while, Arriette thought of the box in the picture, wondering if the artist intended it to represent Pandora's box. Could the image be warning locals away from that tunnel as not to disturb a dragon guarding it? Zïnnyi wouldn't have left it unsupervised.

"I think we should go back," she said. "I think that picture was of Pandora's box."

They both came to a halt. Susan rubbed her eyes, frustrated by another distraction. Arriette explained everything she'd learned so far about Pandora's box and that it made sense for a dragon to guard Zïnnyi's most precious treasure.

"What did I *just* say about the trap?"

She raised an eyebrow. "I heard you. But Ma once told me Drakonta was named after a myth. A warrior is said to walk the streets of Drakonta warning people of a fire-breathing beast. The village shares this mountain's base and the dragon is painted here, clear as can be."

"And this has *nothing* to do with the bearer of that box being a brunette?" asked Susan, arms folded.

"It's a coincidence but now you mention it."

Susan grumbled. "Enzo and Drakonta are miles apart. We don't know where we are. We don't know if Casper managed to save your friend, Pouki. We don't know if the wards held. We can't confirm any of those things if we stay away from the lair any longer than planned. Please don't start a wild chase for a box that may not even exist. These mountains are full of tunnels that led only to labyrinths and underground streams. You'll get lost and I'm in no mood to fetch you."

Arriette shook her head. "It exists. You have to trust me."

They stared at one another blankly for a few seconds before Susan threw her arms in the air.

"Let's go this way first and save your innocent."

Arriette grinned. "You won't regret this."

Susan offered half a smile back.

"Oh, and we should be quick. I'm hungry and you're the only food I've seen in over an hour."

Arriette chewed her nails. "What happens if you don't feed? Can you survive as long on animal blood?"

"I'll tire and become aggressive. I'll go paler, weaker, and my fangs will be hard to hide. People will know I'm a vampyr."

If Arriette didn't find Susan something to eat and fast, she would either be running from a murderous predator or they would both be running from an angry mob.

"Does it always hurt when you bite someone?"

Susan shrugged. "I don't bite myself. Probably when the skin breaks, if I don't kill them. You should know," she said, gesturing at Arriette's scarred neck.

"I was almost drained *twice*," she said, remembering both encounters. "They were terrifying experiences."

The first had been during a picnic with Rihaana and

the second after her escape from Kalvin and Dean—the *first* time!

"I'm sorry," said Susan. Her eyes met the ground. "I'd imagine if done properly with no intention to kill it would feel like a bee sting."

"Honestly, how hungry are you?"

"I have a little while to go before we should worry. I can make it there and back. I'll warn you in plenty of time."

Could she risk Enzo paying the price for her cowardice? If she was to lead her people, any sacrifices made would be hers.

"You can drink from me," she said, moving her hair aside to allow Susan access to her jugular veins.

Susan's eyes widened. "No, I can't. If I can't control myself I could kill you, Arry"

Arriette closed her eyes and tilted her head. She took three deep breaths, then gestured for the vampyr to get it over and done with.

"I've survived two already. I'm... different, designed to withstand attacks like these. And I trust you," she said. "Now bite me. Just... aim for my existing scars so nobody asks any questions later."

TWENTY

The temple was a magnificent building with golden archways, marble flooring, and smooth, shining walls. Arriette paced through their foyer on her toes as not to disturb those praying in the next room. A few of the Enzoian men passed her by, their heads lowered to the pages of religious writing.

Susan opened one of the sliding doors in the foyer and beckoned Arriette over. Behind the panels were rows of sandy-coloured robes, all with hoods and belts attached. They grabbed one to cover their more modern clothing and to blend in as they returned through the village on their way home.

"May I help you?" asked one of the men.

He was older and smaller than most of the others. His long greying beard almost touched the floor and his sandals looked to have been swallowed by his over-sized robe. Arriette's heart ached for Pouki.

Where is he?

"We're here to study your temple," Arriette lied. "We were told there's a lovely view of the beach from here. May we have directions?"

The old man placed his fingers together and bowed his head to touch his symbol. Then he turned to lead Arriette and Susan through the temple. They weaved between columns, ventured up and down various sets of stairs—none more than two or three high. When they stepped out onto patio-style decking, the man left them to their thoughts.

The view was stunning. Waves lapped against the cliffs below and at hip height, a wall ran the full length of the deck.

Susan hung her head over and whistled. "That's a *long* way down. Is this the place?"

"I'm sure of it."

Glancing around, Arriette saw a private pathway trialling off to a wooded area at the back of the temple. This place of worship was breathtaking, secluded and quiet, just as she'd expected.

"Who are you?" Susan and Arriette turned to see a young woman sitting on the wall at the far side of the deck. Almost in a whisper, she said, "They promised I'd be alone."

Susan scowled. "Who's *they*?"

The girl shuffled to the edge of the wall, dangling her legs loosely over the ocean beneath. Her sandy robes fluttered in the breeze, her long golden hair following suit. Her eyes were sad and swollen, red from crying.

"The monks," she said. "Who are you?"

"I'm Arriette and this is Susan."

They glanced at one another, puzzled. But when they turned back to ask the girl her name in return, she was gone. Arriette screamed and lunged forward, throwing her head over the edge of the cliff to see only a tiny splash.

"She jumped! She jumped!"

Susan pulled Arriette away by her shoulders and sat her down against the wall.

"There's nothing you can do now, Arry."

Arriette sobbed, tears flooding her flushed cheeks. "Suicide, right in front of me. I did nothing! Why aren't you more upset?"

Susan checked to see if the girl had re-surfaced, which she hadn't, then knelt to wipe Arriette's tears.

"I only looked away for a few seconds," she added.

"It's not your fault. If someone is set on ending their life then no-one can convince them otherwise. I think this is what Zïnnyi wanted you to learn. You can't save everyone despite your efforts and your kindness."

"Zïnnyi is going to reject her soul," Arriette said.

"He'll what?" Susan asked, scrunching her nose.

"Suicides don't go to Heaven."

"Nonsense. She did what she did for a reason, Arry. Zïnnyi forgives. *You* once taught me that."

"So my vision was just like Baby A said. It was a test and I failed."

Susan frowned and helped Arriette to her feet. "What do you mean?"

"Zïnnyi knew I'd try to save her but my curiosity about Pandora's box would delay me. Baby A told me back in Manaia Forest that angels judge if a life is worth saving against everything else. Zïnnyi wanted me to see I was wrong to chase a ghost this time."

"Or perhaps he was trying to show you something else," she replied. "Come on."

Susan gave Arriette a firm pat on the shoulder then led her away from the decking and back through the foyer. Throwing her body over the edge after an already dead girl wasn't going to save anyone, nor would it progress the resolution of their own problems.

They moved steadily through the temple and down the tunnel to the fork with their hoods up, hiding Arriette's tears. The Enzo symbol above the entrance mocked her.

Before she could curse her poor luck, Arriette's stomach contracted in realisation.

"Susan, these tunnels are *man-made*."

She shrugged, seemingly uninterested. "So?"

"Caves are natural and random. *These* walls are all smooth and direct. Both the tunnels are, see? Why didn't I notice before?" Arriette pointed up at the archways, narrowing the further you ventured.

"What are you thinking?"

Arriette's eyes brightened. "Nothing yet. I need to see for myself, though."

"Wait! This is a *bad* idea, Arry."

They crept down the left passage against the Enzoian woman's warning. Their road took sharp turns, dipped and smelt. It became even narrower after about an hour in the depths of the mountain, until they were funnelled into a single file line and in places, crouching. Arriette extinguished the *Monibah* flame she'd summoned in the palm of her hand when Susan announced there was a flickering light ahead.

"I think we should get the others before we go any further. If you're right about a dragon and Pandora's box, we'll need full power."

Arriette grinned when the path ended, opening out onto a steep ledge. Beneath them. Straight down and curled around various sizes of stalagmite in what appeared to be a bowl-shaped cavern, was a dragon. With every exhale it growled, snoring through a deep sleep.

She felt Susan stiffen beside her, then hands gently tugged Arriette away from the ledge.

Arriette's breath caught in her throat. *A dragon! A real, living and breathing scaled creature. Exactly as I have imagined them.*

She knew there were few weapons capable of piercing its natural armour. Just to see one with her own eyes was enough to satisfy the bookworm in her.

"They're not a myth," she whispered.

Susan slapped a hand across her mouth and gestured with her luminous eyes at the exit. Arriette nodded once and followed Susan back through the tunnel. It was unclear how long they'd spend beneath the mountain, and Arriette felt guilty for leaving her friends to cope in the lair alone for any longer than necessary. But this was worth the risk.

In shock, they sat at the base of the well, their mouths agape with nothing to say.

After a few minutes, Arriette began to laugh. "I know the Recruit will want briefing. I can't believe it. Pinch me, I'm dreaming." Susan nipped Arriette's neck. "Ow!"

"This is serious. *Don't* go back in there alone."

Arriette gave herself a few more minutes. Her racing heart pumped adrenaline ferociously through her veins.

"How are we going to defeat a dragon, Arry?"

Arriette snapped her fingers. "The ghost from the Drakontan story. Maybe he exists for a reason?"

"Or *maybe* he's a bedtime story told to stop children exploring and getting eaten alive?"

She soaked in her surroundings one final time before she and Susan set off back to the beach. The hillside trees were blooming, showering them with pale pink blossom. Insects thrived in the bushes and thick blades of grass swayed gently in the breeze. Arriette thought Enzo to be the most beautiful place she'd ever seen.

When they reached the beach, they removed their robes and hid them on the inside of the tunnel. Next time they visited, if needed, they wouldn't stand out so much.

Quickly but carefully, they headed back with Arriette's palm flame guiding the way until they came to the lair's entrance at the other end.

"I remember this hatch," Susan hissed. "They were... handsy."

She offered half a smile. "You're with us now."

Arriette was the first to poke her head up through the hatch. They were met by a handsome looking everlast wearing smart city clothing—trousers, a shirt and a tidy jacket. Clearly, Arriette thought, he had never known poverty, or hunger, or *war*. And he was *not* happy.

TWENTY—ONE

With gritted teeth and bound fists, Arriette hauled herself out of the hatch and stood face-to-face with a man she already hated. *Falkon Lou.*

"The famous Arriette Monroe, I assume?"

He was a stunning creature; tall and muscular with a square, firm jaw. Not at all as Arriette had expected. He had short dark hair and piercing eyes.

He offered her a handshake, which she ignored. Quickly, he retreated. "I'm glad I found you. Where have you been?"

Susan climbed out of the hole behind Arriette and stood alongside her friend, arms folded and fangs purposefully protruding.

"Not that it's any of your business, but we were in Enzo," she said, "to meet the inhabitants."

"Of course you were," Falkon said. He opted not to offer a handshake to Susan.

She hissed at him, flinching at a the sound of a snapping twig somewhere behind them.

"We have questions for you," said Arriette. "Can you follow us to the town hall?"

"Actually," he said, halting her with an outstretched arm. "*I'll* ask the questions, Deary."

Two armed guards emerged from the tree line and

grabbed both of Arriette's arms. She struggled and cursed, managing to break free from one of them. She used her telekinesis to remove his sharp weapon, separating it from the belt around his waist. Susan moved to bat the other away but he let go in time to avoid injury. Now angry and impatient, Arriette compelled both of Falkon's guards to their knees and held them there, then turned to glare at him.

"Looks like your guards bow to me now." She grinned and threw both guards backwards and into the tree line with a flick of her wrists. "So you were saying?"

"I do b-beg your pardon," Falkon replied, gesturing Arriette lead the way. "After y-you."

Arriette grinned at Susan as she fell back, sandwiching the everlast between their bodies. If he tried to run, either the vampyr's speed or Arriette's telekinesis would stop him.

They trudged in silence to Town Hall where the main meeting room filled behind them in anticipation of a fight between the city's leader and the Recruit's saviour. Casper had already placed his bet with confidence.

"Why are you here, Falkon?" she asked. "How did you get in here?"

Falkon ordered his men to stand aside, allowing him the room to speak to Arriette's people. Obediently they moved, blocking the exit to the corridor.

"Your lair wards off evil. I'm an everlast so it allowed my entry, and I need your help."

"Help you don't deserve," Arriette said, her eyes unblinking. "Nor do you deserve your life. Sadly, that's not up to me."

"Your threats don't frighten me, Deary."

Casper grumbled, "They probably should."

Arriette asked Falkon to take a seat. She leaned against the wall opposite.

He perched on the edge of a wooden chair as if ready to flee. "Charles Melovich sent you a message."

Arriette nodded but said nothing. She wasn't going to give him any ammunition. *He'd* approached *her*, not the other way around.

"The messenger, Scarlett Evermay, was a retainer. I heard she was killed. I'd like to offer my condolences."

Arriette chortled. "Spare me, Falkon. We don't accept your condolences. Scarlett's death was planned and executed by *your* wolves." She tutted. "You everlasts think me dumb. What you don't know is that I *am* one. I understand how you think, what you want, and the power these things provide."

Arriette retrieved the pendant from her cleavage and leaned closer so Falkon could identify it. His eyes widened and for several seconds he was lost for words.

"You're an intelligent woman, Deary," he said, "so let's not waste time with pleasantries. You should know my experiments are not intended to cause harm. My wolves have learned how to power interchange for any species, regardless of their biological limits. The basis is, I presume, how your people created their new leader. With blood."

Falkon paused for a reaction but there was none. The Recruit were already aware of how Casper, Tobias, Reiko and Baby A saved Arriette's life. It came as no surprise.

"I can take your friends' blood and give everyone equal power."

"You already tried that and it lasted merely hours," Arriette said. "I can demonstrate, if you'd like."

Falkon held up both hands. "No need, Deary, but you

cannot blame me for testing my discovery on the most powerful and influential organisation on the planet. You were human so you must see how weak a species they are. We *cannot* allow them to govern."

His eyes strayed back toward Susan, whose fangs were two dominant glints in the candlelit room.

"I see you've been reunited with my vampyr."

Susan hissed and lunged for him, only to be held back by Jet and Sebastian. "*Your* vampyr?"

"Yes, Deary. I hired your father to turn you."

"My *name* is Susan."

Her eyes narrowed and her fists balled.

"Don't do anything you'll regret." Arriette bit her lip.

Susan spat at Falkon's feet. "Oh, I wouldn't. I'd *delight* in exsanguinating him." She left the room, slamming the door behind her so hard it cracked the walls either side.

Arriette groaned and shook her head. "Thanks for that. Clearly, you've never had to deal with vampyrs before. I'm losing count of how many repairs we need to make."

Falkon waved a hand and immediately his guards left the room in silence. The chains on their black boots could be heard chinking as they retreated down the corridor and out into the street, where they also stuck out given their Guard uniforms.

"Might I have a moment with your leader *alone*?"

Arriette's friends paused until she gave them the nod of approval, then they filtered out one by one, leaving Tobias and Casper for last. Tobias squeezed her hand before closing the door behind him.

"The *new* leader," Falkon clarified.

Casper winked and followed Tobias into the hall.

"A leader you must be to hold such an influence."

He leaned forward to pour himself a cup of water, then folded his legs as he sat back, relaxed. Arriette pulled a chair out from the table and sank into it, suspicious of his demeanour.

"Where did you enter, Falkon?"

"The same place my armies will in a few more hours, I expect. Look, I like you, Deary, so I'll level with you. My wolves *did* kill your friend Scarlett. She was one of my most loyal retainers."

"Did you kill her to prevent Charles's message from reaching me?" she asked.

Falkon shrugged off the question. "I was sorry to learn of Scarlett's involvement with your vampyr, though at the time she was human—*almost*. She and Susan were my first batch of little experimentations. Unfortunately, the consequences were noticeable. Ageing! Who could have predicted such a strange side effect? Several others fell sick shortly after and I couldn't have them drawing more attention from Mr Melovich. I had them disposed of."

"So that's a yes, you wanted to stop her reaching me." Arriette cracked her knuckles. "You hired the wolves. You hired the orcs."

"Very clever, Deary," said Falkon. "Werewolves are loyal. They *are* pack animals after all. Orcs on the other hand, well, they're fearful and idiotic but disposable. I gave them a few humans and low-level HPS supes to eat or enslave and in return, they gave me loyalty and access to the Underworld. Easy, really."

Arriette sighed. "Falkon, Pandora's box *isn't* in the Underworld. You're wasting your time."

"I know that *now*," he said. "My armies are tearing

apart your pathetic barriers as we speak so it shouldn't be long until we're able to search our next location."

Arriette stood abruptly, sending her chair across the room behind her. She slammed both fists on the desk, knocking over Falkon's water.

"You think we have it here?"

"You may not have it, but I believe it's down here somewhere, Deary."

Arriette dug her nails into her fists to keep from punching him in the face. "One of my friends is missing. We haven't been able to find him even though we know where he was. Did *you* take him?"

"Ah, the telepath! Yes, yes he's fine. I had my men transport him to the city. Pouki, I believe his name is?"

"Is he alive?"

"Perhaps—"

"IS HE ALIVE?" Using her mind, Arriette twisted the chain of Falkon's pendant around his neck, tightening it against his windpipe until he nodded, frantic and panicked. He gasped when she released her hold and retrieved the chair.

"You know I am immortal," he said.

Arriette feigned disinterest, flippantly reminding him, "Unless murdered."

He swallowed hard and shoved his shaking hands into his pockets.

"I promise, Deary, he's alive. It's my job to know everything that happens in my city. Now you have that out of your system, let's talk business."

"I'm not going to help you."

"Clearly," Falkon said, rubbing the red line across his throat. "Though this is a proposition you can't deny. The wolves in your lair—those working to aid your people—

are here of their own free will. Only the Shou, Tri and Choku clans, still worshipping their individual moons, are under my control. Currently, they're working in your castle."

"Yes, I found out the hard way," said Arriette.

Arriette thought she saw the flash of a wry grin. "These clans are eager to gain status and power on Haeylo, above the humans who will, if our creator gets his way, become the overlords. I'm asking you to approve *their* power exchanges for some... information."

"What kind of information?" Arriette asked.

"Valuable information. Life or death information. Do with it what you will or nothing at all. I care not. Do we have a deal?"

"No," said Arriette. "Why ask my permission to carry out your experimentations on the wolves? It never stopped you before."

"At the moment I can only do this temporarily. I plan to turn them against my orc armies. Vampyr venom is deadly to an orc. When I have no further use for them."

"You'll dispose of them, too," she finished.

Falkon smiled. "Now you're getting it. If I can give the clans temporary fangs, I can dispose of the orcs once and for all. I now have Underworld access. We can sweep through their lair and execute the demons' slaves. No orcs, no surface influence. And that means a limited food supply and perhaps their eventual extinction."

Arriette exhaled. A world without orcs might be beneficial in the long run, but she'd have to allow this power-happy everlast to play God. And what would he do with the werewolves once he'd finished with them?

"My request is merely out of respect for you, Deary."

"The effects wear off?"

Falkon nodded. "You're living proof. Temporary fangs to serve a purpose and then back to their wolfy selves."

"I'm... not sure. What if you create something... else?"

"Which reminds me! *What* of the young astro girl?"

Arriette scowled. "Who?"

"The little girl your boyfriend escaped our castle with."

"Why do you want her?"

"She's a unique little girl, but *someone* has to break the news to her that both her human parents are now vampyrs." Falkon held up his hands. "She was brought to me after an attack on her village. I had a telepath read her mind, and they told me what she was. Though, I don't think she has ever used the gift. I thought her powers of astro-projection were worth... trying."

"So she was born with them?"

"Looks that way, Deary. Why would the telepath lie?"

"Susan can do that too," said Arriette, more to herself than to Falkon.

"Yes, I know. An uncommon gift. And rather unlike the child's parents who were human. I'd like to examine her."

Arriette shook her head. "Absolutely not. You have your permission, Falkon, for now. But if you attempt to contact Angelica, I'll have you killed. Do we understand one another?"

Falkon stood and made haste for the door. "I think I can live with that."

TWENTY—TWO

Arriette used her telekinesis to stop Falkon as his arm reached for the doorknob. "Your end of the bargain. Now."

With a swivel of her wrist, she turned the everlast and snapped her fingers, then pointed at his empty chair. Falkon rolled his eyes and shuffled back, still under Arriette's control. He slumped down, displeased with being manhandled and manipulated into sitting on that uncomfortable wooden chair.

"You said you had some information for me."

"Some might say ignorance is bliss, Deary."

"An amendment to your deal. Stop calling me Deary."

Now impatient, Arriette narrowed her eyes, tightening her grip on his mind. Falkon cringed and squirmed uncomfortably, feeling her influence at the back of his skull.

"Fine. Withdraw, and I'll tell you," he said.

Arriette did as she was asked, then sat back down. She reached for a pen and a sheet of parchment.

"You won't be needing that," he said. "What I'm about to tell you will haunt your dreams, *Arriette*. The choice to hear this is yours. You may still back out."

She shook her head. "I'm confident I can handle

whatever you have to tell me, *Deary*."

Falkon snarled. "I gave you fair warning."

He paused and ran a sweaty palm through his dark hair. Arriette watched him with curiosity and intrigue. He really was a handsome supe.

Pity he's such an arrogant monster, she thought.

"It's about your vampyr friend, Susan Petter. Is she suffering memory loss at all? Oh, she must be. If you knew *this* you'd be *outraged*, I'm sure!"

Arriette slammed her fist down, harder this time. The entire room shook, knocking frames from the walls and items from the desks. Feeling the tremor, Tobias and Casper quickly barged in to check on her. Arriette held up a hand to pause them. Her dreaming ability was certainly growing stronger by the day, particularly in the presence of such an infuriating and pompous everlast.

"Susan wasn't born Susan Petter. Nor was she born human. She came to you as a troubled soul, cowering beneath Zinny's wrath and answering to another name."

"What name?" Arriette held her breath.

"*Pandora,*" he sang.

"You lie!" Casper said, storming toward Falkon and towering above his seat. "How do you know this?"

"Susan worked for me as the Chaos Bearer. Part of the application was to have a mandatory background check by a telepath."

"Susan would have known not to allow this if she had such a history. She'd have withdrawn her application. You're a liar!" said Arriette.

"It's the truth," he said, scowling. "Susan signed her contract without reading any of the requirements. She was desperate for a job, rather stressed at the time. Why else would I have selected her for my first batch of experimentations? To exploit a power like *that*? I couldn't wait."

Arriette sat back and bit her nails. Was this true? Could Susan, now a merciless vampyr—an evil predator of the Underworld by nature—*really* be the source of the planet's evils?

Pandora the curious.

Pandora the hunted.

Pandora the... vampyr?

"She doesn't believe any of this," said Tobias. He crouched beside Arriette's chair with his warm hand resting on her knee. "Do you?"

"Oh, she believes me, Deary," said Falkon, interlocking his hands and leaning forward across the desk. "There's more, but how deep down the rabbit hole do you wish to fall?"

Arriette stood abruptly, knocking Tobias off balance and onto his bottom. "*All the way,*" she said. "This isn't a fairytale, Falkon, this is serious. If Susan really is Pandora, she can lead the Recruit to her box; it can rest in safe hands."

"As Susan intended," he said, "which is the next chapter to our story. You have longed to know how Susan found out about your leadership? You have ached to understand why she wrote you such a baffling message?"

"How do you know—"

"I know everything about Susan Petter. Until she died, her mind was an open book. Once made vampyr under my orders, she disappeared against my wishes. I've been searching for *her* as much as her box since."

Tobias took hold of Arriette's hand. "You should know where the box is if you read her mind," he said.

"I wish," he replied. "Sadly, the image we had of the

box was merely somewhere dark and dank. Hence my assumption she must have hidden it in the Underworld. The last place any human filth would dare look!"

"What do you mean *in Arriette's hands as intended*?" Tobias asked.

Falkon raised his brow. "Oh, I think that's rather obvious, Deary, don't you?"

His eyes narrowed. He squeezed Arriette's hand a little harder. "Pandora wanted the box to land in *our* hands?"

"In Arriette's hands," Casper said. "The message she gave was not to encourage her to take *my* role as a leader." He shook his head. How could he have been so blind? Casper recited: "One chose to use their power for personal gain, enforcing evil and greed throughout mankind. Angered, Zïnnyi struck her down, stripping her of all power and banishing her to eternal suffering."

Arriette covered her mouth with her palm and lowered herself to her seat. "Zïnnyi help me."

Tobias put his arm around her waist. "It's alright, Arriette, we'll figure all this out. We always do."

She burst into tears. "She *was* trying to tell me about a job. She *was*! We just had the wrong job. *'To see a world in a grain of sand, and a heaven in a wild flower'.*"

"The poem from the crowning ceremony?" Tobias asked. "What does that have to do with Pandora?"

"She was trying to tell me I was to inherit Pandora's box, to be its protector. There is no power greater in this universe than that of Pandora's. She knew that poem would lead me here to this moment. This... realisation."

Tobias helped Arriette to her feet and dried her eyes on his sleeve. He walked her out the office, asking Casper to find Susan and bring her to Arriette's room for a quiet, private discussion.

When they left, Casper and Falkon stood alone in the meeting room. "You're not off the hook *yet*, Falkon."

"I have no doubt," he said.

"And if I find you are lying about any of this—"

"I'm not," he said, straight-faced, "and you already know it, Deary. Why else would I be here to search your little sanctuary? She is next in line to receive Pandora's box. She's the guardian now Susan's somewhat pathetic excuse for a human life is over. The box *is* here somewhere. My armies are already inside your hidden world, Casper. It's too late to evacuate now."

"But the wards... how did you—"

Falkon laughed. "You silly old fool, there *are* no wards, merely traces, like a distant memory. Those wards died with the wiccan who cast them."

"*Harriet?*" Casper slumped down in Arriette's seat and placed his head in his hands. "I, I didn't realise—"

"Oh, Deary, from that look on your face I'd say she's... dead? And by your hand! Perhaps it is time you left leadership to another."

"What will you do with the box when you have it?" asked Casper. "Give it to Arriette and give up *everything* you have been working toward? You're not going to, are you? You're going to steal it."

Falkon grinned and started toward the corridor. "Try not to worry, old man, because you won't be here to stop me when I do."

Falkon closed the door quietly behind him, leaving Casper shaking, terrified, and alone with his thoughts.

TWENTY—THREE

Whether she deserved the recognition or not, Arriette's next rune was the P-shaped Thurisaz she'd been hoping for, and against Baby A's promises, her time-travel power bonded excruciatingly to her body. The tattoo appeared at the base of Arriette's spine like a blistering brand, plunging her consciousness deep into a tricoloured whirlpool. Her lungs drowned in an acidic fog and a ruthless migraine hammered in her skull, delivering fatigue and nausea that she couldn't shake.

After what felt like hours of torture the fog lifted and it left behind beautiful imagery of Mousique and Drakonta but mostly of Enzo's golden sands and crashing turquoise waves. In Arriette's opinion, Enzo was the prettiest, most tranquil village on Haeylo and the ultimate destination for a religious pilgrimage. She remembered the sweet pink flowers during her ascent to the temple, mentally revisiting the smooth marble floors, intricate cave paintings, and breathing in the fresh mountain air.

Her friends, the handsome dreamer, Tobias Shallow and his human hunting companion, Reiko Port had offered to build Arriette's new home there when she sat everyone down and told them of the dragon they'd seen. It would be the Recruit's future public headquarters; a place of safety, reassurance and reliability for all. However, selecting any human location posed a significant risk to the Recruit, particularly if Falkon Lou found Pandora's box before they did.

She took comfort in her knowledge that deep in the Drakontan mountainside beyond a fresh water well and paintings of a feisty young brunette girl, that fire-breathing dragon guarded what Arriette believed to be Pandora's box. During her time with the Recruit, however, she'd assumed the species was extinct or fictitious with little evidence to support past sightings. Falkon Lou would be unwilling to bet his life or slay the creature alone, which meant Arriette had more time to retrieve it herself.

Despite the risks, nothing could reverse Arriette's love for Enzo or the good fortune it promised. She wished she could feel Enzo's cool, warm breeze in her hair as the swirling vortex returned, this time meshed with a panoramic rainbow that triggered a disorientating, hypnotic and almost paralysing episode.

A male called out to her from afar. Arriette opened her mouth to ask for help but found she was mute. After several desperate attempts to scream, she managed merely a whisper.

"Who are you?"

The voice was sweet and harmonic. It said, *"You know who I am. This is the paradigm between time and space. Many travellers use it to pause between destinations."*

Her vision span faster the more she fought to find her way. Feeling queasy, Arriette pinned her eyes shut.

"Make it stop. I feel sick to my stomach!"

"How can you when you have no stomach?"

Arriette regained her balance. She watched her body disintegrate, uncontrollably, into silver flecks of dust. Her consciousness was time-travelling but her body still felt present somehow; a ghostly sensation like a phantom limb.

The sickness lingered in her knotted gut because where Arriette's body was physically planted in her bedroom at Town Hall, she was in danger.

As if reading her mind, the voice said, *"You're here for a reason. A revelation. Open your eyes!"*

Arriette followed the instructions. She was a cloud lingering beneath her mother's ceiling, watching her body fidget at the kitchen table as Ma was washing pots at the sink. They were talking, but she couldn't recall the conversation. In her peripheral vision, Arriette also recognised her shape-shifting mentor, Casper, drinking tea.

She sank to his eye-level and gasped. *"I must have travelled forward in time and space."*

"This is one of many possible futures."

"Casper is alive and well here," she said. *"There's a chance I choose not to kill him."*

Ma's kitchen was clean and had been repaired from the Recruit's encounter with Coyote. His orc form had obliterated any chance of their group enjoying a peaceful vacation in Drakonta, but Arriette missed his shape-shifter form.

"I'm still not sure why I'm here now," she admitted.

"You want to return to visit your mother," the voice said. *"You have questions about your father."*

"Yes I do," she said. *"I need to ask her how he died, but I've been thinking about Casper, too. I don't want to lose him. Now after what I've just learnt about Susan!"*

"Your actions and reactions influence Fate," said the voice. *"The people of Earth—your ancestors—believed Fate was permanent. What do you believe?"*

"I read that in a book once," Arriette said, *"but I don't have an opinion yet."*

The voice replied, *"Free will helps Fate decide our path. It gives us directions to a satisfactory outcome. The choice to kill Casper is yours alone but act foolishly and you should expect to bring injury, pain or death upon yourself and others. Act wisely and you may still meet that Fate, but others can be saved."*

Her whole existence sighed in this place. *"How can I choose between what I see here and Casper's freedom? It's not fair!"*

"Life isn't always fair. You should trust your instinct."

"My instinct says to free him," she said. *"My heart says I love him too much, and I'm afraid."*

The image of Arriette's mother faded. The colourful streams returned, softer this time. She wanted to talk more but sensed her body's pulse quickening. Her skin was hot. Her non-existent stomach was churning.

"Something isn't right," she said.

"Go with my blessing." The voice slowly faded into the distance.

"I don't know how to leave this place!" Arriette reached out, hoping her telekinesis would pull the voice back. It was no use. *"Wait!"*

Palpitations jolted her awake.

She was on the floor of her bedroom and concerned faces, including Casper's, hovered over her. Falkon Lou's head of dark hair and piercing green eyes leered into her line of sight.

"Can you stand?" he asked.

Arriette stood, using Casper's arm to regain her balance. She straightened her hair and dress, embarrassed that she must have fainted.

"We heard a crash," Casper said. He picked up a fallen chair. "Did you hit your head?"

Arriette apologised for frightening him and smiled when Susan appeared in the doorway, arms folded. Fangs protruded from her upper lip. Without them, her beautiful blonde hair and clear blue eyes made her look human, particularly in Tabitha Hope's blue dress.

"We should let Arriette rest," she said.

"No, I need to talk to you," Arriette insisted. "It's—"

"You went somewhere," Falkon insisted, interrupting them. He turned his back to Susan who hissed and moved to pull him away.

Arriette raised a hand. "I'm OK, honest."

"So where did you go?" he repeated.

Susan growled. "Don't make me manhandle you, everlast."

Falkon grabbed the hem of Arriette's dress and yanked it up. He pointed to Thurisaz at the base of her spine. "How to you explain this?"

Arriette blushed. "*Excuse me!*"

"I'd recognise the stench of burning flesh anywhere, Deary. I've branded enough people in my time," he said, rolling up his sleeve to reveal the figure eight of infinity burned to his bicep. "You time-travelled, didn't you?"

Arriette batted away his hand and yanked down her dress, disgusted with his lack of manners and the violation of her privacy.

"Don't be foolish. Are you trying to back out of our deal?" Falkon started to remind Arriette of their arrangement but a knock at the door halted him.

She exhaled with relief. Susan would have been humiliated and in no position to defend herself.

Their visitor was the werewolf, Nazar. Now his bright eyes were wide. His hands and face had partially shifted from either fear or excitement and his ears were long and pointy, coated in grey fur. Nazar's body had also bulked up and out. He looked muscular and intense.

Susan slid between Falkon and Arriette before Nazar had entered the room. Without knowing his intentions, she thought it best a strong and capable vampyr was in the line of fire, not her recovering friend.

"The wolves are fleeing," he told them. "There are rumours, Falkon. I tried to stop them."

Falkon grumbled. "*What* rumours?"

"That you'll turn on the clans after the orcs."

Startled by the accusation, Falkon shook his head. "Where did you hear these lies?"

Casper and Susan each took one of Arriette's arms. They led her toward the door while Falkon and Nazar were pre-occupied, but they didn't move fast enough. Falkon backhanded Nazar's cheek, causing him to stagger into Arriette on her way out. The werewolf immediately raised both hands and backed away from her to apologise.

Falkon raised his fist. "If you are to fear *anyone*, fear *me*."

Now obedient, Nazar lowered his head and pressed his body flat to the floor. Falkon was on him in an instant, shouting and accusing the wolf of betrayal. Arriette remembered how Nazar had claimed to hate Falkon Lou, siding with him only for protection. With teeth and claws he could easily overpower the everlast and flee. To Arriette's surprise, he chose to take the humiliation. He cowered at Falkon's feet.

Using Casper and Susan as a brace, Arriette kicked Falkon up and over her bed with both feet. She gestured for the wolf to run but he was stiff and stunned by her sudden retaliation. It was obvious to everyone now that the rumours about Falkon's true nature were justified but Nazar was still afraid of what Arriette might do to him. He was also disappointed with himself for being loyal to such a monster.

"You forget your place, Falkon Lou. You're no longer the most powerful or influential everlast on Haeylo. Followers should *follow*, not *fear* their leaders."

She looked down at Nazar and offered him a hand, despite struggling to stand herself. He accepted it and took a place by her side, nodding to indicate his gratitude.

"To treat one of your own like dirt I doubt there's an inch of decency or honesty left in you. In Nazar's position I'd be suspicious too." She rubbed the itching rune and groaned. "It took an unexpected journey to remind me that we write our own stories. I don't think I want to be the reason an *entire* species is made extinct no matter their crimes. I can't help you betray everyone else, either. *My final chapter will be a great one.*"

Casper gripped her arm a little tighter and smiled.

"It doesn't matter if I approve of your plan," she said, "because there is only one Zïnnyi and it's not our place to imitate Him. I don't trust you. I never did. I should have listened to my gut instinct that you're not here to help us."

The everlast mumbled as he pulled himself up, using the chair as a hoist. "So why *am* I here, Deary?" he asked, cradling his bruised ribs. "I offered to rid you of your orc problem, return the telepath, *and* supply you with enhanced warriors. What more can I do to gain the Recruit's trust?"

Susan cracked her knuckles. "You think we have Pandora's box. None of us know its true location, Falkon.

This is all for show; when you get the box, you'll betray us too."

"You're lying! Arriette already knows who you once were, *Pandora*. I told her everything."

"P-Pandora?"

Susan's head suddenly swam with flashes of memory. "I-I'd have told her myself a long time ago if not for you!" said Susan, distracted by flickers and reels of a past she'd been so eager to remember, and now so eager to forget. "You're not going to support Arriette's hopes of rebuilding the human population. You want eternal life at the top of the HPS. With Pandora's box you could control everyone and everything but that's not what Zïnnyi intended," she managed.

"How do *you* know what He wants?" Falkon asked.

Susan lowered her voice, saddened. "He told Pandora... many years ago."

Arriette pointed to the door. "I'm sorry but the deal is off. You need to leave now and you should take the clans with you. They're no longer welcome here, either."

Falkon dusted down his jacket and casually called for his guards. Three other werewolves marched down the corridor and Arriette could hear the chains on their boots chinking as they approached.

"Stay away from her," Susan warned. "I haven't eaten."

"You're not going to leave Arriette unprotected long enough to feed on me," Falkon said.

He remained still and silent. Any swift movements might provoke Susan to attack him anyway. No supe had ever survived a vampyr bite besides her, because Zïnnyi really did have a plan for her.

Falkon decided not to run. An everlast's speed was no

match for a vampyr's, nor was the collective strength of his werewolves.

"You have no authority here now, Arriette. When my clans have destroyed the orc species we'll return to finish off the Recruit. We're going to sweep your lair for Pandora's box. The clans still trust me enough."

"*The box isn't here!* Susan's memories were wiped when she turned vampyr," Casper argued, "and *you* told Arriette the rest only hours ago. Can't you see we're on the same side? We're not the enemy. Increasing the human population will not mean an imminent death for supes. That day may *never* come."

"He's right, Falkon," Susan reiterated. "How can you wish extinction upon such a harmless species? Humans have no powers. Why fear them?"

Falkon clicked his fingers. The guards moved in. "They killed Earth. I can't let them kill Haeylo."

"Pandora's box will destroy you, Falkon," Casper said. "The temptation to open it is too strong. That's why it must go to Arriette where it can be safe."

"He's not going to listen," said Arriette.

The werewolves moved without warning. Arriette pushed her friends aside and grabbed Falkon by his collar. Using her telekinesis, she pinned him between her bed and the wall. The werewolves tried to restrain her but were intercepted by Susan and Nazar. Casper fled to get help.

Arriette used her wings to build a barrier between them. She clenched her rune-marked hand around Falkon's neck, using her free hand to rummage in her long bedside draws for Kalvin's scimitar. When her fingers found the hilt her memory was transported to their campsite in Manaia Forest. She thought about Scarlett's mutilated body, Susan's deterioration, and Kalvin's betrayal of her trust. She thought of Dean and of Roberta. She thought of her now tarnished home in Mousique.

Her grip strengthened. She raised it high. The others stopped to watch in silence.

"Arriette, wait!"

Jolted free of her longing for revenge, she dropped the blade. Her hands were shaking and she gasped for breath.

Falkon ducked and crawled under the bed.

Prepared and dressed for battle, Jet Carter occupied the doorway. His dark hair was shaven, his face painted in cherry-red and grey tribal designs to cover his Eiwaz rune and he wore military trousers. His off-white shirt was open at the collar and he wore shiny black boots. On his belt hung a sheathed dagger.

Her eyes widened when the source of the voice, Reiko Port, pushed between Jet and Casper. He was bare-chested, revealing a scarred torso and he carried a full-length sword on a leather strap across his back. His face was painted like Jet's and he wore similar clothing. Arriette couldn't take her eyes off him. She'd almost forgotten how much she missed his company.

If Reiko had found his way safely to the Recruit's underground lair, Dion and Pouki were likely to be with him.

She reached out and touched his face. *"How are you here?"*

TWENTY—FOUR

Reiko stepped over an injured werewolf guard and picked up Kalvin's scimitar. He shook off droplets of blood from where it had landed in a pool on the carpet, then sheathed it.

Arriette's upper lip, nose and eyebrow were oozing.

"Come on, Arriette, let's get you out of here."

They walked hand-in-hand to the door. All the while their eyes were fixated on one another. Arriette barely noticed the damage to her bedroom or the injured werewolves awaiting their punishment. Broken picture frames lay at the foot of her bed and chunks of wood were missing from her bedside table.

Falkon had slithered out without a word. Arriette hadn't noticed his absence. She was too stunned to see Reiko.

"*How are you here?*" she asked.

"Casper sent a messenger to Haeylo City when you were in Enzo with Susan."

"I promised you I'd give everyone a job," Casper reminded her.

She wrapped her arms around Reiko's neck. "Did I hurt anyone with that—"

"No," he said, offering Kalvin's scimitar back to her. "He ran off, but he won't get far."

Arriette scanned the room and found nothing but a trail of red spots from Falkon's dripping wounds. She limped after him on a twisted ankle, using her friends as a crutch and winced whenever she put too much pressure on it.

Casper hung back. He asked Nazar to round up some willing volunteers to detain the injured werewolves. Nazar agreed to make sure they couldn't harm anyone else or assist with Falkon's search for Pandora's box.

"You *will* thank her for me, won't you?" Nazar asked, gesturing at Arriette's back. "If I thought they'd listen to me, I'd speak to our Alphas myself."

Casper gave his shoulder a firm pat. "Of course." Then he hurried after his friends.

They helped Arriette into the canteen and sat her on a chair beside Susan.

Reiko cleared his throat. "Everyone else is coming. Dion and Pouki are safe."

Arriette heaved a sigh of relief. She squeezed Reiko's hand to thank him for returning her friends safely.

"I have some bad news, though," he continued. "Falkon's orc army is already inside and they're heading toward the town. We raised the alarm and the townspeople are getting ready but we're going to be greatly outnumbered. Can you fight on that ankle?"

Deep in thought, Arriette tried to massage her foot to alleviate the throbbing. Soon she would be nursing broken bones, third-degree burns, and stab wounds if she even made it off the battlefield alive.

"I'll be fine. Baby A's blood will kick in. But I'll need a change of clothes. I can't fight in a dress." She smiled. "I'm so pleased you're back, even under these circumstances. How did the messenger find them?"

"They went to Charles Melovich's office. His daughter took them to a tavern in the everlast district and introduced us. Charles and Rihaana are on their way, too. I told him not to bother, but he insisted. We were laying low waiting to hear from you," Reiko said.

Arriette was overwhelmed. She wished they had more time to catch up and celebrate.

"We told Charles everything but he'd been suspicious of Falkon for a long time anyway. He'd even sent men out that day to find him but it was too late."

A light knock at the door drew Arriette's attention to her telepathic friend Pouki Hallidae and the red-headed vampyr, Dion Delavious. It took all her strength not to throw her arms around them both. Instead, she stood with Reiko's aid and with tears streaming down her cheeks, gave them both a tight, welcoming hug.

"I'm so pleased to see you! What happened to you, Pouki? We saw you were injured but we couldn't reach you in time. Falkon's orcs beat us to it."

The telepath's robes were torn, muddy and grass-stained from his struggle. There was blood in his beard and down his face from a broken nose but he insisted he wasn't in pain. Pouki told Arriette he'd been talking to the Harriet Foley for a while before she left to fulfil her Recruit duties.

"Take it easy on her," he said. "She didn't do this."

"Harriet didn't make it. She and I had a disagreement and Casper, well, it doesn't matter now," Arriette said.

Pouki lowered his head, though they had never been friends. Still, it was a loss to their cause.

"Orcs came out of nowhere and ambushed me," Pouki said. "I got knocked out and the next thing I knew I was in Haeylo City. Werewolf guards had me handcuffed in a basement in an everlast building. I don't how long I was there or why Falkon wanted me, but Charles let me go. Telepaths are valuable and he likely wanted me flustered. All that matters is you're safe. I'll thank Charles when I see him."

Dion drowned Arriette beneath her dishevelled red hair. She wore a long brown coat over baggy trousers and a pair of leather boots which Arriette thought suited her attitude.

"And how are *you* here?" Arriette asked, smiling.

"Used ya underground tunnel. Jet said daylight in the lair was artificial." She paused and shrugged off the risk she'd taken to see her. "Why didn't ya follow us to the city?"

"I'm sorry we worried you. We got sidetracked."

Arriette loved seeing their smiling faces; to know they were alive and well despite being separated for so long.

Behind Dion and Pouki, Tobias led Joy Johnas, Sebastian Sky and Paulei Leigh in to see her. She hugged them all. It wasn't long before Baby A and Tabitha Hope joined the group. They wore dark blue clothes and sturdy footwear. Some of her friends were armed with a dagger or a sword and had their faces painted. Others were yet to raid the armoury.

Tabitha was examining the maul she bought from the Indalo store with pride. Arriette was thrilled to see Baby A up and about after her miscarriage with Tabitha on her arm. Her blue eyes were gloomy with loss, though, and she stayed close to the retainer.

Charles and Rihaana Melovich were the last to join the meeting. They arrived late but well prepared and told her the orcs' numbers were growing and the clans were filtering out of the castle. Word had spread that Falkon Lou was missing after a struggle at Town Hall. The clans were beginning to panic. It wouldn't be long until they targeted the Recruit and accused them of kidnap.

It was still the happiest Arriette had felt in weeks.

Taking them by surprise, Nazar flung open the door. He threw Falkon Lou into their reunion, causing everyone to gasp and back up.

"Look who *I* found!"

Arriette wished Nazar hadn't gone in search of the everlast. Any violence from his werewolves would, in their eyes, be justified now.

"Lock him up. Keep him hidden," she said. "If they find out he's here, we're in trouble."

Falkon tensed when Nazar tried to restrain him. "Wait, please listen to me!"

"Unless you're calling off your orc army, I'm not interested in what you have to say. By the time you realise you're making a mistake, it'll be too late."

The crowded canteen was stuffy and claustrophobic. The group clanged their weapons and drummed their fists on the tables.

At first, Falkon cowered beneath the noise and covered his ears. All of a sudden, he dived forward and grabbed Arriette's throat to strangle her.

"Oh. No. You. Don't!"

Falkon was quickly apprehended by Tobias, who used his elbow to crack the everlast around the back of the head. Reiko punched him in the stomach and together they dragged Falkon out by his jacket.

They locked him in another room to calm down, and his makeshift cell was an office with no windows. Falkon had few friends in the building; nobody would come to his rescue.

Arriette waited for Tobias and Reiko to come back before she spoke again.

"Now *he's* out of the way, I can confirm Susan and I *do* know where Pandora's box is but we can't retrieve it without help. There are people who want to stand in our way. If Falkon or his army find it first, he'll wipe out any species he deems a threat, starting with the human race. A battle isn't what we need, but we want his forces distracted. If they're searching here, they're off the trail. I want to tell you everything we discovered in Enzo in more detail but there's no time now. Orcs and werewolves are already in our lair and they're threatening the innocent families living here."

Between concerned faces, Tabitha Hope raised her maul so Arriette could see she had a question. "Now that we have Falkon as our prisoner," Tabitha said. "we can use him to our advantage. Would they trade?"

"They will kill anyone on sight without giving them chance to negotiate," Casper said. "Orcs do not think logically."

"Then what do you propose we do? What if they're with their masters?" Tabitha asked.

"Do your best. Hope they're not. Remember, if we win we can re-build the barriers," Arriette said. "There are experienced sorcerers, wiccans and dreamers here who can replace the charms that died with Harriet Foley. It's too late now and no use unless we can clear the invaders first."

"What happens if we lose?" Tabitha lowered her maul.

Arriette exhaled, defeated.

The room fell silent.

TWENTY—FIVE

Arriette followed Jet Carter and Reiko to the armoury. Weapons ranging from bows and arrows, long swords and daggers to silver throwing stars and arrowheads were stored here, all specifically designed to take down the brawniest of horned demons. Anyone not already carrying a weapon took something from storage and the majority of them agreed to carry a shield despite the thickest ones being clunky and heavy.

If the orcs *were* accompanied by their masters—thick-skinned brutes or their ghostly cousins—the Recruit would need specialist tools to fight them. She handed out their supply of sharpened wooden stakes and silver-dipped arrowheads.

Arriette changed into a plain white dress, something she'd seen hanging in the closet of her bedroom but had avoided asking about. Perhaps because she knew its purpose and what it represented.

Susan took off Tabitha's borrowed dress, and she was given something more durable and similar to their friends. All the while, Arriette tried to explain as much about their visit to Enzo as she could, taking her own battle leathers with her to change before the fight. She wanted everyone to know the reality of their next battle, but anxious and busy, only a few were listening.

After gearing up, they joined the townspeople outside Town Hall. Arriette was stunned to see so many battle-ready supes, all dressed in navy-coloured clothing to make them easily identifiable on the battlefield. Their faces were hidden beneath helmets and paints or behind tall wooden boards. Arriette realised these were makeshift shields and barricades. Occasionally, her eyes settled upon a child weaving through the crowd. They were acting as runners, carrying messages and extra weapons. She never intended for anyone under the lawful age to go into battle and these children only looked about ten or eleven years old. The Recruit watched, horror-stricken, as they practised their aim on straw-filled dummies.

"Reiko, can't we do something?"

Reiko shook his head. He gave Arriette's shoulder a squeeze, cutting her off. "We need the numbers. Try not to think about it. Your people need you."

The Recruit lair's townspeople gathered around Arriette and her friends. Casper had been brief before Arriette left her quarters. The crowning ceremony would happen, but in its shortest form, and with Retaining elders present at the front to document the historical moment for their scrolls and books.

Prompted by him now as she faced these people, seemingly copies of the same wrinkled, greying scholar in white robes and glasses, she climbed to the highest step in the square and scanned the row upon row of loyal, inexperienced supe merchants and peasants behind them. Crammed into the main street in front of the Indalo store and the infirmary, they formed an ocean of dark blue and black waves. Behind her makeshift stage hung silky silver curtains, hung prematurely under the assumption she'd be crowned respectfully.

At any moment, orcs were going to storm their residences and businesses, setting fire to everything they touches, demolishing homes and killing innocent people. Interspersed among them would be the three werewolf clans, still under the impression that winning the battle would earn them Falkon Lou's mercy and protection; that he would favour them above the other species.

Little did they know he'd already planned his betrayal.

Arriette's fingers gripped the hilt of the ceremonial sword so tight that her hands shook. It wasn't much to look at and a plain, forgetful design. All except for the engraved lines along one side of the blade—the side to strike Casper's neck first.

It read:

'To see a world in a grain of sand, and a heaven in a wild flower.'

The poem she'd committed to memory.

The skin on her knuckles turned white. She glanced at Casper standing on a lower step, afraid and unable to think of anything but those poor, defenceless children, and what they would be witnessing.

"It is customary to announce the names of the current leaders before a battle," Casper told her, "to honour those leading and, perhaps, dying for us. We will have to be quick." He touched Arriette's arm. "May I?"

She nodded, closed her eyes, and took a deep breath. Trying to think of anything and anywhere else, she straightened her dress.

Try not to think about what this means. Your people need you. They're relying on you to be the fearless leader they've been expecting. Put on that front. Be brave. They trained you for this.

Instead of asking for help from these people, Arriette knew she should be apologising. Had she and Dion not taken Coyote to the orc mirror that day, the Underworld wouldn't have been alerted, and the lair would still be hidden. Had she and Susan not wasted time investigating the left path at the temple, this could have happened properly and with time to spare.

"You came here today for the greater good. You're here to fight for freedom. We're willing to die for, and in the company of, our families," Casper said. The town was silent. "When this ceremony is over, Arriette Monroe will claim her rightful place as your new leader. Until then, here are names of the Recruit's *current* leading powers."

A thick black line had formed in the meadow where Arriette first entered the lair. It moved steadily in their direction.

Orcs.

Demons.

Vampyrs.

Her palms began to sweat. Her knees wobbled.

Casper reached out and squeezed her hand as he read the names of his chosen Recruit members aloud. But Arriette wasn't listening. She shuddered when distant groans and the clang of metal were carried into the town centre on a breeze across the meadow. She kept a straight, courageous face as Casper announced the first eight names and abilities of the eleven they once valued most.

Sorcerer, Sebastian Sky
Retainer, Tabitha Hope
Telepath, Paulei Leigh
Everlast, Joy Johnas
Jet Carter, Invisibility

Potions Master, Reiko Port.
Dreamer, Tobias Shallow
Angel and Time-Traveller, Baby A

Casper paused, saddened that the next two names would not be joining them, especially when one of those deaths, he was wholly responsible for.

Wiccan, Harriet Foley.
Retainer, Scarlett Evermay

That was the first and the last time Arriette would hear the full names of Casper's chosen Recruit members during his reign. Once satisfied, he gestured for Arriette to take the lead. She was welcomed with a respectable applause. She chose to end with a prayer for friends they had already lost and those about to die on the battlefield, but mostly, she prayed for Zïnnyi to be with her.

She released her wings.
She raised her fist.
And she shouted, "For freedom!"
The town roared back, "For freedom!"

TWENTY—SIX

Arriette paced down the rows of townspeople, occasionally wincing through the pain of her swollen ankle. Unable to offer words of wisdom or comfort, she stared blankly back at anyone who bowed a courteous head her way. Some trembled with anxiety. Others sobbed with fear. Most, however, were straight-faced.

Jet Carter pushed through them, panting. "The ceremony is going to have to wait," he said, breathing heavily as he rested his hands on his knees. "The orcs are too close to our town. We've got to move... now!"

Arriette heard whimpers and cries of women and children who had overheard Jet's update The front line fighters were their husbands, brothers, sons, and fathers, and their blood was about to be on her hands. She nodded to Jet to acknowledge his message, then continued along the front row until she finally reached the end where, smiling, was a young woman of her height and build.

They clamped eyes immediately. Her face was still and calm; she seemed unmoved by the imminent conflict.

It's unnatural to feel indifferent to war, she thought, until she realised who that woman was. She was lost for words. The woman said hello and shook Arriette's hand as though they were old friends.

"You must be surprised to see me," the woman said.

Arriette hadn't recognized the brunette hair, though choppier than hers, the khaki eyes, or the unflattering way she stood, arms folded. Unlike others in the Recruit's infantry, the woman was unprepared for war and carried no weapons. Her dress revealed her bare shoulders, fastened like a corset up the front, flattering her curves.

"You're... *me*," Arriette said, dumbfounded. "But... you're also not me."

She waved her friends over from their places in the formation. If they too could see this woman, she wasn't insane. Tobias froze, stammered, but was lost for words. Arriette knew then she was not alone. This woman was real.

Casper began to ask how it was possible when the woman interrupted and grinned. "I thought you could use a friend and a good luck gift," she said. "You can't fight on foot with that injury."

"Are you here to help us?" Tobias finally asked.

This version of Arriette replied, "I'm not here to fight. My war has ended for now. It's good to see you all, though." This Arriette's eyes lingered on Casper, but she said nothing directly to him.

She was missing her mentor, confirming Arriette's greatest fear. This confident posture and overwhelming presence was unlike Arriette; something in her future must have changed, or in an alternate universe, she was stronger and braver and... *more*.

"Don't be afraid. I remember this moment well. You're wondering if you're going to wake up or if you've lost your mind. It's not a dream. You're just... overwhelmed." She leaned in closer and lowered her voice. "I know you dread the ceremony, and by now it is likely to have been delayed a little. But be reassured that Casper's death is quick. It's *easy*."

"So we win," Baby A said before Arriette could ask her future self for more detail. "I mean, if you're here then *our* Arriette doesn't die today."

"Try not to sound *so* surprised," Arriette said, scowling at her future self.

"I'm sorry but this is surreal. In all my time as a time-traveller I've *never* crossed my own path," Baby A said. "I'm not even sure it's safe. Why are you here now?"

The group turned in unison to face Arriette's future self with eyes wide. She brushed back her hair, revealing glowing skin and a healthy, pink complexion.

"I was given strength in this moment. I'm here to pass it on. Over the past few months I've been studying, trying desperately to clear my mind for a new... adventure. I've found some peace now. I know what I have to do."

"And what's that?" Arriette asked.

"All in good time. I wanted to help you find your way. You have too much on your mind and you need to clear it, or you'll get people killed."

"I've lost so many friends already," Arriette told herself, "and I'm about to lose more no matter what I think!"

"I can't tell you any more. Remember those you've lost. Only then can their memory be eternal. Death isn't the end,Arriette."

She gestured for the group to follow her toward the curtained stairs. The lines parted to allow them passage. On the horizon, the enemy were preparing to advance but the werewolves had already begun a search for Pandora's box. Despite the distant growls, howls, screeches and war cries, a gentle clacking broke through the terror and drew

Arriette's attention to the other side of the street.

"What *is* that?" Reiko asked, silencing the group.

Arriette watched as her future self disappeared around a corner.

"You're *different* in the future," Tobias said. "More confident. You've put on weight... it suits you."

Baby A elbowed him.

Arriette paid no attention to their squabbling. She was too worried about the front line and if her future self was coming back, or if those brief words of wisdom were the 'gift' she'd mentioned.

"You're a *real* gentleman," Baby A snapped at Tobias.

Arriette swallowed hard. "Is anyone else kind of worried about that clomping noise?"

Reiko took a few steps forward. He listened intently, trying to figure out what was making it. "I think it's a horse. Sounds like hooves."

Arriette hoped it was; she was pleased she'd be fighting above the heads of her opponents. Orcs were thin and frail. On horseback, she could plough through their front line and knock them aside like bowling pins, all the while taking the pressure of her aching ankle.

As her mind raced, a beautiful white stallion rounded the corner with her future self by its side. He was brawny, mighty and handsome, and his clean white mane fluttered in the breeze like falling snow.

Her friends stopped bickering.

Arriette approached the animal in admiration and he bowed his head to her. She gave his smooth coat a firm pat. "Is that a—" She broke off to examine a spiralling silver horn protruding between the horse's eyes.

"*A unicorn!*" said Casper.

"We've searched these parts several times over," said

Future Arriette. "We believe he could be the only one left of his kind," she said. "We don't know where he originates or how he came to be with us. As far as we understand, he's trapped in this loop for our benefit."

"But that's so sad," Arriette told herself. "Why have we not done more to free him?"

Casper gasped. "I imagine he's extremely powerful and could easily free himself if he wanted to, *if* the legends are true."

"Are they?" Baby A asked the future Arriette, casting a cautious side-eye to the unicorn beside her.

"I've tried everything to convince him to use whatever power he has to end this cycle. He's closely linked with the water element, so we went out to see if the ocean would initiate something."

"Did he show any interest?" Baby A asked.

"No, but afterwards he saved my life. He identified poison in my water; knocked the canteen right out of my hand. I'd be dead now if not for him." Future Arriette stroked the unicorn, sad to let him go. She handed the reins over. "He's been a trusting friend. Grounding. Please take care of him for me. Return him, as I have, when the time comes. I believe that it's his destiny."

"But where did he come from?" Tobias asked.

"He was gifted to me, too, by my future self. Hopefully, he will continue to help my line. He'll be loyal. He'll follow Arriette anywhere, including into this battle."

Baby A turned to Casper. "I read something once about unicorns—a myth, I think. It said they are born from tears, and and will spend eternity searching for a maiden to protect."

"*You* read a book?" asked Tobias.

Offended, Baby A folder her arms. "The book said to

call a unicorn, a young woman must be seated in the forest, alone with an offering. The unicorn will be drawn to that offering and if acceptable, it will lay its head in her lap to prolong the maiden's life."

The unicorn stomped its hoof and nudged Arriette, almost knocking her down.

"I hate to disappoint you," Arriette told the animal, "but I won't be sitting alone in forests. You probably know my track record with vampyrs, and retainers, and ex-boyfriends, and orcs. I have nothing to offer you, either, except perhaps a bit of excitement the next time our lives are in danger."

"That's not going to happen," Baby A said.

She flung an arm across the meadow. "I beg to differ."

Tobias cleared his throat. "Shouldn't we ask if this unicorn has a name?"

"Yes," said Future Arriette, "I call him *Ira Wilda*, which means 'the watchful and untamed', and he lives up to that name, I promise."

TWENTY—SEVEN

Arriette hated having thousands of pairs of eyes on her; each of them expecting her to negotiate a way out of this nightmare. Even with Ira Wilda at her side, Arriette's stomach fluttered and she couldn't help but shake all over. Future Arriette had already insisted getting too involved in this past would mess with her present, so she backed off, allowing Ira to lead her forward.

The Recruit hadn't really built an army, but their formation still worried her. She'd never been to war and any orders she gave would be instinctive, not based on past experience, tactics or strategy. She had relied upon Paulei and Pouki to organise her infantry and give advice based on the experiences of those they'd read. Anyone with memories of fighting in the past, wielding weapons or even sparring were pulled out to manage smaller groups.

Archers formed a thin line between the infantry and the enemy, and in the land awaiting their battle, beautiful wild flowers swayed in the breeze, beckoning them to clash and spill blood. Her people were skilled, but ammunition was low. The archers hadn't had enough time to make any more arrows, but Reiko thought if they could take out enough of the orcs from a distance, those on foot would have fewer to slay up close. His days living with the tribe he was born with in the mountains helped as they covertly hunted larger packs of animals in order to eat.

Besides attacking with hand-held weapons and arrows, Arriette was hoping the supes amongst them would quickly identify how their own powers might be beneficial. After all, Zïnnyi had assigned them to protect the innocent in scenarios like this, and she trusted His designs. Dreamers could use their telekinesis to fell trees, throw rocks, and retrieve anyone's discarded weapons. They were imaginative enough to work around each unusual threat and to retaliate in kind. Demons were rarely seen above the surface and nobody really knew what to expect. If advised by telepaths, dreamers would be able to prevent attacks based on the enemy's plans (providing, of course, they were of the orc or werewolf species) too.

Space, rather than time-travel, would allow some of her people to hop swiftly between each foe, leaving them bewildered long enough for the invisible Jet Carter to sneak up behind them. If supported by everlasts using their pendants to communicate with others near-by, and to share the retainers' collective knowledge of historical battles and the enemy's biology, wiccans and sorcerers amongst them could pass through unharmed to plant various potions. Sebastian and Reiko had brewed some explosives designed to blind, disorientate and disarm even the angriest of demons, but they left behind a strange-coloured, nasty smelling fog. Demons would be used to such an atmosphere in the Underworld, unlike the Recruit, so setting off these chemicals would require great care and skill. Thankfully, they had Ruby's expertise to guide them.

Finally, for those injured or suddenly without a weapon, an angel's wings were powerful enough to lift them to safety. Arriette's wingspan alone could block an orc's path and swat them aside. Dion had agreed to use her ability to shift shape to mirror this form if necessary. The followers were now used to her face, and Arriette hoped if they saw that blazing red hair approaching, they would accept her as an ally.

Everyone, including the humans among them, were capable in their own way.

Arriette smiled, regaining her faith in their creator.

Close behind the archers, Arriette and her friends sat on horseback. Rihaana and Charles were on Arriette's left, followed by Reiko, Pouki, Tabitha and Baby A. To her right were Tobias, Paulei, Sebastian, Joy and Jet. All were staring at the restless line of evil at the other side of the meadow.

Tobias pulled out a pair of binoculars to study the enemy's line of orcs as Arriette patted Ira Wilda's back. It had been a while since she'd last rode a horse and her confidence was shaken. She remembered the pounding of the black stallion's hooves as Dean Constable chased her through Manaia Forest and into the deathly clutches of Angelo and Roberta.

"They're starting to creep forward. If we don't despatch our people soon, they'll have us surrounded," he said. "If we want to leave this town in anything other than body bags, I suggest we strike now."

Arriette glanced back at her people. "We need to use magic."

"And the personal gain?"

"Self-defence," she told Baby A.

"We can't use magic to strike, only to defend. It would be too risky," Baby A said.

Arriette scoffed. "This entire ordeal is an attempt to defend a town filled with innocent supes. If you need to, use magic. Zïnnyi will understand."

The calling of her name drew Arriette away from the conversation. *Better to ask for forgiveness anyway*, she thought.

She searched her infantry and the empty meadow behind them. Four women, all similar in appearance but unique in ability, were jogging toward her and Ira Wilda.

It was the Elite Four: Di, Saph, Jade and Ruby. They raised their hands in greeting, then fell into line with those capable of spell-casting and potion-mixing.

Seeing them, Tobias had a burst of inspiration. He grinned and pointed at the Four Saviours, shaking his arm with excitement.

"We can hit them with a wave!"

"Pouki and Paulei arranged us this way for that purpose, Tobias."

"No!" he said, rolling his eyes. "I mean, use the Elite Four's elements to fight off as many as possible before we involve the infantry and their individual magic. The fewer using it to strike, the less risk of punishment for personal gain. We can literally hit them with a wave."

Arriette grimaced. "I don't think that's how it works."

"Look, I'll show you," he said.

They dismounted. In the dirt, Tobias had Arriette draw a diagram with the ceremonial sword's tip which represented their formation. She circled herself and drew a line direct to the leader of their opponents—a wide, ugly looking spirit demon on a midnight stallion. Arriette would ride Ira Wilda behind the Elite Four's wave of magic and lead the Recruit steadily forward, hoping she'd correctly identified him. The spirit demon was flitting between his own soldiers and looked to be giving orders and striking the weakest orcs by what would have been his feet, if he had any. She used the binoculars to scope out the creatures lingering at the back. She could see black and brown horses branded with an inverted cross, ridden by a mixture of spirit demons, smaller horned beasts, and the occasional vampyr. She was pleased the Recruit's stable hand had remembered to paint the Indalo symbol on the rears of their own horses in red so Arriette's followers knew who not to fire at.

Arriette spotted the leader advancing. Before she'd had chance to show Tobias through the binoculars or for him to explain how the wave would work, the orders to charge had been given.

Arriette and Tobias mounted their rides, and the Elite Four stepped forward.

"What exactly *is* that thing leading them?" she asked Casper as Pouki and Paulei directed the Four Saviours how, where and when to attack.

"He's a shade, but he's larger than most. A demon in its spirit form and one higher up. An older, more powerful one. Falkon's connections must run deeper through the Underworld than we originally thought."

"Are they hard to kill?" Tobias asked.

"If you can find somebody who claims to have killed one, perhaps they can tell you."

Arriette gave Ira Wilda a nudge and steadied herself before letting go of the reins to direct the front rows of archers. They released their silver-tipped arrows, firing low at a forty-five-degree angle. They rocketed toward the enemy's front line. Orcs squealed and clutched their wounds in despair as they fell to the ground. Some tried to rip the arrows from their flesh. Others lay limp and lifeless but another line of orcs quickly replaced them. Troops behind just ignored and trampled over them.

Ira Wilda raised up on his hind legs and shook his mane frantically. Arriette almost fell and, unable to find the reins quick enough, reached for his horn instead. It was sharp and solid, drawing blood from Arriette's palm. She screamed as the horn sliced deeper, dripping blood into her lap.

Baby A pointed across the meadow. "We're running out of time! Pouki, Paulei... are they ready?"

The Elite Four joined hands. "We have to do this now," said Saph.

"A wave," Tobias called to her. "We need to wash this land clean."

Saph understood. "Baby A, give the next orders *only* when we have finished our part. Arriette, you're up."

She quickly removed her white ceremonial dress with n o time for privacy or embarrassment, and donned her battle leathers. They were tight and uncomfortable, but thicker and would protect her human frame.

Baby A stared after Arriette as she galloped ahead with Ira Wilda, overtaking the archers and effectively placing herself in their line of fire. They retreated, passing her on the battlefield, to avoid what the Four Saviours were about to send their way.

Di, Saph, Jade and Ruby began to chant. "We call upon the elements of four. On the solid Earth and the soaring wind, the depths of the ocean and the heat of the flame. *Forendo ze de'va demetran zen, ze tran, ze aeir, ze flam, en ze walne.*"

There was a blinding flash of light initiated by Di. The closest orcs were forced to an abrupt stop and Arriette cowered, her eyes tingling from the radiance. She lay forward on Ira Wilda's saddle and buried her face in his mane. Flicking her wrists, still half-blinded, Arriette swept many of the smaller orcs off their feet with her telekinesis. They couldn't see her approaching, but the larger, horned demons were more difficult to deter. Years beneath the ground had creased their skin, darkened their compassion and ringed their eyes with ash and dried blood, making them ugly and fat, and in some cases, *blind*.

The Elite Four produced a second round; the first wave of their magic was over, but they were not done yet.

Now through the remaining orcs and safely between them and the next formation of demons, Arriette and Ira Wilda came to a skidding halt. She squinted, shocked to see a vibrant blue and white tidal wave crashing above them, likely created by Saph following Tobias's suggestion. It twirled and danced in patterns, temporarily blocking out the sunlight and casting beautiful mosaics of colour beneath their feet. Confident in Ira Wilda's connection with the element, Arriette covered her head as the wave crashed down, raining over the enemy and soaking her through. She clung to Ira Wilda, wrapping her arms around his thick neck, unable to watch as the wave drowned hundreds of those she had been unable to move herself. Ira Wilda was unphased by the volume of water beneath him, and he swam until the meadow drained, leaving behind soggy, water-logged bogs interspersed with bodies.

They stumbled between demonic corpses until they were only a mile from the next tree line. Ira Wilda refused to continue, shaking his head in the direction of a luminous red and orange vortex cast by Ruby, which ignited the trees in a smooth burst. A forest fire erupted and smoke blew across the meadow, restricting everyone's vision and disorientating Arriette. She coughed and spluttered as the smoke filled her lungs, but up ahead she could also hear the wheezing of orcs. Ira Wilda wanted to retreat back to the flooded fields where he knew he could protect her, but Arriette insisted they wait a while longer, watching burning leaves flutter all around them like fireflies.

Ira Wilda shifted to dodge a demon on fire. It screeched and flailed, rocketing into the trees where it fell with a thud. There was a disgusting crunch of bones, followed by an eerie silence. Arriette hoped, through her hatred of their kind, that one of his own had ended his misery.

They crept along for a while as the battlefield quieted, still unable to see clearly through the lingering smoke and ash. Arriette drew the ceremonial sword and let it rest against her thigh as they searched the grey atmosphere for signs of life. A chill crept down her back and lifted her hair. She shuddered and skulked lower into the saddle.

Ira Wilda stopped again when the ground beneath his hooves began to quake. *It must be Jade's turn.* She braced herself, expecting a stampede of huge horned demons to trample them. Instead, Arriette began to notice small cones of smoke, swirling steadily at first but growing larger and spinning out of control. They whipped like tornadoes, sweeping up the smoke and starving the forest fire of oxygen, allowing Arriette and Ira Wilda to see the destruction left behind. There were demonic remains strewn everywhere. They had to volt over piles of orcs several feet high to progress.

The whirlwinds avoided Arriette and Ira, programmed to offer them shelter from charging horned demons. Safely behind these unusual shields, Arriette watched as they sucked a few shades up and spat them out in random directions. She couldn't see where or how they landed, but she knew they would be lucky to get back up.

In the distance, Arriette heard a roar of voices as Baby A finally gave the orders for the infantry to follow, slashing the throats of any injured orcs they passed and picking off the weaker of the infantry. She and the Four Saviours' magic were now far enough ahead for her followers to have a chance.

The Elite Four continued to chant, helping Arriette through the worst of it, until their final attack.

Jade threw up walls of thorn-coated vines, which began to sprout and grow like beanstalks, creating a demon-free path for her and Ira Wilda to follow. The growth of the grass accelerated, so anything not entangled or strangled by the vines disappeared amongst the weeds. They pushed forward, shielded by a natural tunnel made of weeds, vines, flowers and shrubs, and Arriette began to wonder if the desolation on the outside of her shelter would ever end. By the time what remained of the enemy and Arriette's infantry crashed together, she and Ira Wilda were picking off stragglers at the far side, searching for the shade leading them.

She barely had a chance to catch her breath when a group of vampyrs surrounded Ira Wilda. They were dressed head to toe in black and their faces were covered, leaving only their luminous eyes and blood-smothered mouths visible.

Fresh blood meant a fresh victim.

Arriette's memory flashed back to that day in Manaia Forest when she'd fled from Kalvin and Dean Constable. She wouldn't let these vampyrs do to her what Roberta and Angelo did. She sheathed the sword and reached for the bow and arrow Tobias had given her in the hospital, ready with their silver tips. Wooden ones would kill a vampyr for sure, but if she missed their hearts, silver would hurt more.

And she wanted it to hurt.

Arriette kicked out at any who got too confident, then fired off a few arrows in quick succession, hitting the first two in their shoulders but killing over the third with a bullseye strike. The others hissed while the body of their comrade began to flake and dissipate in the wind, sending them into a frenzy. Their deaths had all been violent, and they told Arriette a brutal story through their mangled limbs, missing fingers, caved-in skulls and protruding bones. Each of these creatures were created following a nasty, twisted end. At the time, they probably hadn't deserved it. But now?

Arriette was about to jump down and take on the closest with her sword when from behind, she heard the thundering hooves of her friends' horses.

Susan and Dion were equally matched to their ideal opponents, so Arriette retreated and made haste for where she'd last seen the shade. She found him much faster than she'd expected, but he hadn't been trying to hide. Flanking him were horned demons and orcs, and fear rattled her limbs as she neared their embankment.

Hidden amongst torn black rags of clothing and beneath a pointed hood, the gnarling shade demon watched she and Ira Wilda with tiny red eyes. The stench of rotting flesh wafted between them as though his physical form had been dead for years, leaving only the tarnished soul behind.

She raised her sword for close range combat.

Ira Wilda charged, hoping to catch the demons off guard and lowered his head, using his horn as a spear.

They crashed into the side of one, sending him careening into the other. Arriette's followers were swiftly on them, carving the demons apart to allow her merely seconds to get to their master.

Ira Wilda jumped at the chance, but Arriette halted him, thinking *let him make a move first*. She cocked her leg over Ira Wilda's head and held the reins tight with one hand whilst preparing to fight with the other. She hoisted her body out far enough to protect Ira Wilda if the shade's first swing missed its intended target. It did, and he propelled passed, missing them both.

Arriette ducked to avoid some arrows that followed from foolish orcs who were trying to help their leader. She deflected a few using telekinesis and fired them back, killing two or three with a lucky shot. She considered dismounting and fighting them off with her sword, but her ankle wouldn't withstand the weight for long, particularly if she had to run, and her hand still stung from the wound Ira's horn had opened.

She caught the lingering scent of smoke from the now extinguished fire and had an idea. Dreaming up a fireball, Arriette pitched it and set the shade's robes alight from a few meters away. His entire covering went up in brilliant orange flames. Flummoxed and in pain, he fluttered about the battlefield, then seemed to implode, leaving a dusting of ash where his shadow had been.

Arriette let out a sigh of relief, knowing now that shades were easier to kill than they seemed. But it wasn't over yet—the enemy had already received their orders, and ending their leader would only anger them. The orc formations were crumbling though, leaving the Recruit to pick off their weakest and unprotected.

Arriette set off to help her friends.

***

Tabitha Hope and Baby A slashed the feet of a horned demon. Ira Wilda cantered alongside, and Arriette conjured a rope, casting it out with her mind to whip it around the demon's feet. She yanked at full speed, bring the creature to his knees so Baby A and Tabitha could clamber on top of its greasy body and plunge their weapons deep.

Baby A quickly travelled across the field to help Jet whose invisibility was flickering from the adrenaline in his veins. He appeared behind a gnarly-looking demon and slit its throat, then kicked it aside to work on the next. Baby A acted as his spotter, so Jet could turn on his invisibility only at the last moment to confuse his prey.

Both outnumbered, Tobias and Reiko had decided to regroup. Arriette sped up and headed them off. Between Reiko's powerful sword swings and the dreamers' combined abilities, they bashed a few orc heads together with telekinesis and grinned as the rest began to retreat. So Ira Wilda picked up the pace and leapt between those too cowardly to fight. Arriette kicked out, knocking them down, and Reiko finished them off.

Not far from their position, Sebastian threw a corked glass bottle which smashed at the feet of three horned demons, rendering them unconscious. Foetid blue and yellow puffs of smog drifted their way, and through it Arriette could almost see Joy struggling beneath her shield as an orc hammered on the other side.

The Recruit were scattered all over the meadow and unable to find Casper or Pouki, Arriette decided she had to fight through the lingering effects of the potion, her pain, and finish this once and for all on foot. Dead or alive, she needed to know her friends' positions.

She squashed an orc beneath her boots, rescuing an injured, heavily bleeding young retainer in the process. Through gritted teeth she hoisted him on to Ira Wilda's back, praying they would make it safely back to the town without her, and gave Ira's read a tap.

Another orc was on her before she could reach for the dagger in her boot, grabbing her by the shoulders. The blade was knocked free and they watched it spin through the air and land, hilt up, in the grass.

Angered and unable to fight at close range with her bow or her sword, Arriette lunged at the orc and wrapped her bare hands around his throat, smearing her bloodied palm across its neck until its eyes began to roll. She headbutted the orc, then scrambled for her blade and plunged it into its abdomen.

The creature raised a hand and tried to speak.

Arriette fell back.

Its features shifted shape, revealing a familiar face.

"C-Coyote? What have I done?"

Allowing the chaos to continue around them, Arriette laid her friend out on the sodden grass, wiping the blade clean. She drowned out the hissing of vampyrs, clanging of weapons, and piercing of flesh.

"I didn't know, I'm so sorry, Coyote!"

Ira Wilda was returning from his first trip to Town Hall. If Arriette could get Coyote there too, perhaps one of the retainers could save his life. She tried to hold him steady across her shoulders but couldn't. It was on her second try that she practically threw him onto Ira Wilda's saddle, using the thrust of her wings to lift his weight. Now panicking and running out of time, the three of them rode back to where the women and children were applying first aid at the town hall.

Arriette saw her future self had stayed to help with the injured too. There were bleeding men and women scattered across the street, and young boys and girls delivering medicine and bandages to their parents. She applied a cool towel on Coyote's forehead and tried to stop the bleeding with pressure to the wound until Future Arriette saw her and came running.

Arriette began to cry. "I didn't know it was him. He can't die. Not because of me."

"He's going to forgive you," she said, reaching out to take hold of her hand, "and eventually, you *will* forgive yourself."

TWENTY—EIGHT

Three hours later...

The meadow's vibrancy had been replaced by a corpse-ridden, blood-smeared, smoky wasteland. All that remained were bodies of fallen townspeople, remnants of orcs and demons, scattered weapons, and the occasional tumbleweed made of vampyr ash, strewn between fires and burning trees. Arriette was beginning to think the Elite Four had actually done *more* damage to the lair than the enemy, but their strategy to use the majority of their magic in one initial strike—as a *wave*—worked.

They won.

They were still alive.

Whilst sitting on the steps of Town Hall wiping her face and hands clean of blood (despite being unable to tell if it was her own) Arriette was approached by the Shou clan's Alpha, werewolf Master Kid Kyle. Behind him the Tri and Shoku clan leaders, werewolves Kaleb Solumn and Izzy Charter, stood at either side with their arms folded. Furious with the clans' involvement, Arriette drew her dagger.

"We mean you no harm," said Kid, raising his hands.

After seeing so many of her people slaughtered she was more than willing to take three more lives for the greater good. From the Indalo store, Tobias started toward her and until Kid bowed his head to show Arriette he wasn't lying, Tobias was ready to slay them. He stopped to see how she would react to their surrender, proud when she refused to lower her weapon.

"As I understand it, Pandora's box wasn't found," said Kid. He dare not look Arriette in the eye. "My wolves also tell me Falkon Lou is missing."

Through gritted teeth, Arriette said, "He's not missing, he's imprisoned. I told him the box wasn't here but he wouldn't listen. *Now* look what he's done! What you have *all* done!"

Kid shook his head. "We took no part in the plunder and chose not to fight the Recruit. I pulled our ranks before the attack. An outsider warned us of Falkon's intentions."

Arriette tentatively lowered her dagger. "Nazar?"

Kid turned to the other Masters. "She knows him?"

"I saved his life," Arriette corrected. "We may not have been able to defend the lair had you not stepped down. Perhaps the Recruit owe you and Nazar thanks, then?" She tucked the blade back into her boot.

Kid glanced up. "We may not have fought against the Recruit, but we didn't fight for you, either."

Arriette scowled. "If not to gain my thanks or my people's forgiveness, why *are* you here, Master Kyle?"

"To ask that our species be protected during the Recruit's initiative to increase the human population. In exchange, the clans will carry out Falkon's original plan to exterminate the orc species, should you wish."

"I do not."

"But we were under the impression you had approved the temporary exchange of powers. Now your enemies are dead, we hope to live in peace with those remaining."

Arriette raised an eyebrow. It seemed to her that whoever offered the clans protection had their loyalty until a better offer passed their council. Now that Falkon was out of the way, the logical choice was the Recruit.

"We killed many of the Underworld's creatures today but by no means enough for a peaceful existence. With Falkon Lou in custody, there will be no meddling with powers, no mass murdering of a species and *certainly* no power-happy everlast rulers to dictate Haeylo's future. You need not worry, Masters, it will be decades before we see a decrease to the supe population, and we are yet to find Pandora's box."

"For you to be so calm you must have eyes upon it; it *is* what birthed evil," Kid said.

"The box did not produce evil, Master Kyle, it produced eight entities acting as a gateway for it to enter this world. *People* birthed evil. *We* birthed evil. We're still going to find and secure the box, and attempt to put those eight entities back. Better to be safe, but you know, we *could* use some help around here."

The Alphas nodded and backed away, contemplating Arriette's offer to help them on their journey to Enzo, though she hadn't yet disclosed the details of their next quest. Arriette wasn't in the mood to hear them argue over a plan they couldn't control. She left them to ponder the implications and returned to Town Hall to find her friends and check on their recoveries.

There were injured followers in corridors and dead or mutilated bodies either laid out on tables or propped up in chairs. The morgue was overflowing with innocent people who shouldn't have died but gave their lives to protect friends and family anyway. The overpowering stench of death followed Arriette through the town hall. Each wall she brushed resulted in a fresh stain to her clothing or hair.

She entered a room where some of the lesser injured people were being treated. The rest of them had been relocated to the canteen where there was fresh, running water, first aid supplies, and a Retaining surgeon. Arriette would learn later that the surgeon on duty had actually saved her life too in Haeylo's infirmary. His presence there was courtesy of the everlast Charles Melovich and his daughter, Rihaana, who had also survived the battle.

Sat in the far corner of the room was Casper. He held a damp towel to a gash on his head and was waiting for stitches to a slash across his thigh that had gone through his robe, but he covered it up with what remained of them when Arriette entered.

"Were you knocked unconscious?" she asked, taking over so he could lower his aching wrist.

"I ran into someone's shield," he said, embarrassed. "The enemy must have thought I was dead because thankfully they left me alone."

"And the leg?"

"That happened before."

"Well I'm glad that happened to you because I thought you were dead. It's a relief you didn't see more of that hell. I came to find you but Coyote—"

"Yes I heard, but you handled yourself well." He smiled, then placed an arm around her shoulder. "I'm too old for this now. I think we ought to arrange your ceremony properly once we're patched up and back to some normality. I'll speak with Pouki."

"No, Casper, I'm done killing."

"I'm ready now," he said, "and so are you."

"Neither of us are ready! You said so yourself. You asked for more time."

"So I could say goodbye to those I've protected all these years. After today, I think I can pass that responsibility down."

"But that means I have to kill you."

"That's true," he said, cutting her off. "Once I'm gone, all this will be yours."

"I can't yet, Casper. How can I replace Susan as the box's guardian *and* lead the Recruit? Before we came here I might have agreed with you, but after Falkon?"

"I believe in you but if you don't commit, you will never know how capable you really are."

Frustrated and exhausted, Arriette handed Casper's care over to a near-by retainer and left without saying goodbye. On her way she examined a few who had been bitten and drained to within an inch of their sanity. All were covered in a sour-smelling inky blue substance, which Arriette recognised as demonic blood from her run-in with Coyote at Drakonta. It wouldn't be long before those injured followers died; all humans did when bitten by a vampyr.

All except her.

Further down the corridor, Arriette came across a woman in her early twenties. It was retainer Melanie Starr, Charles Melovich's city receptionist, who had followed him to the lair to fight alongside her boss. She had been poisoned by a shade like the one Arriette killed, caused by a deep puncture direct into her bloodstream.

Melanie's stomach was beginning to turn violet and wrinkled around the entry wound. There was a blonde-haired everlast taking care of her, but Arriette knew she didn't have long to live.

"Can I do anything to help?"

The everlast shook his head apologetically. He

lowered his voice, but Melanie was in and out of consciousness anyway.

"It's too late. Tabitha Hope said she thinks the poison has spread to her heart. Do you know her?"

Arriette nodded. "She's... my friend."

He propped Melanie's head up with a pillow. "I'll make her as comfortable as I can. It shouldn't be long now, but you'll want to leave before then. It'll be... unpleasant."

She gave Melanie's hand a squeeze then did as the everlast had suggested.

Mentally scarred by the image of what that venom was doing to her, Arriette stumbled through the building unable to register most of the other injuries until she found Dion sitting on a table in the canteen. The vampyr had been beaten and slashed with a silver blade, but she was by no means in critical condition. A retainer was in the process of moving her to the room where she'd seen Casper.

"Those lesions look deep," Arriette said.

"Am fine. Someone mistook me for one of 'em."

Dion's face was scratched in diagonal lines where a dagger had sliced her skin. She'd raised her hands in defence, so both were now shredded and sore. Whilst her lower body seemed unharmed, she'd taken a few strikes to the head and was feeling dizzy, which apparently was possible even for a vampyr if they hadn't eaten in a while.

"Can you stand?"

"With 'elp," she said. "What's up, Arriette?"

Her bottom lip quivered. "Melanie Starr is dead."

Dion's eyes widened. "Are ya hurt at all?"

"I sliced open my hand, but I'll live," she said.

Dion pointed to her bandage. "How?"

"Ira Wilda kicked. I caught his horn."

"Well, 'ave ya seen Casper?" she asked. "He's injured too, ya know."

"Yes but I can't talk to him yet because he's already planning the ceremony and I'll say something I'll regret. Did the same thing happen to Susan?"

Dion scrunched her nose and shook her head. "She asked me to tell ya not to worry, but some of the men decided to clear the meadow. She offered to 'elp drag orc remains to a mass grave out by the trees." She paused, waiting for Arriette to protest but her mind was elsewhere. "I heard 'bout Coyote. It's not ya fault."

"They won't let me visit him. I understand. *I* wouldn't want to see me either."

"He's goin' to live an' then forgive ya. *Ya made a mistake.* Ya weren't to know."

"Can you forgive those who tried to kill *you*? They made an honest mistake, too, though most people round here are familiar with you now, so maybe I should—"

"I blended in," Dion said and shrugged. "Difference is, *they're* not ma friends. There's no history between us. It'll take a while. Leave him be... for now."

TWENTY—NINE

The next day...

Although they were exhausted, Arriette had gathered her friends outside Town Hall to plan a hurried, uneventful journey to Enzo, because Finding Pandora's box now could mean fewer pre-arranged orc patrols to intercept them, plus some much-needed help from the werewolf clans without Falkon Lou's influence or protest.

On their return, Arriette and Casper would have to talk to Falkon in depth and negotiate a way forward; one thing had been decided for him already—the Recruit couldn't allow him to return to the city and resume his place amongst the governing everlasts, but they weren't going to kill him, either. Imprisonment was their only option.

Power was Falkon's sickness.

The Recruit would be his cure.

Before they set off blind, Arriette wanted to learn as much as possible about the dragon guarding Pandora's box. She needed an alternate route out of the Drakontan mountain range, a decent stock of weapons, and some strong horses to carry their gear. Although Arriette disclosed everything about what it would entail, the overall response to her suggestion they go only twenty-four hours after the bottle was exactly as she expected.

Disappointment overwhelmed her nevertheless.

The Recruit were on their own—none of the townspeople would volunteer to help them.

Overall in agreement that the journey was necessary, her friends hauled their supplies to Town Hall. They were groaning and cursing the early morning start. Many had to re-dress or bind their wounds first, including Casper and Dion, and everyone had bathed and changed out of their leathers and armour. Arriette missed the support of her leathers, but not the chafing when she began to sweat in them.

Tabitha Hope wanted to help make their journey less of a chore, so she spent her morning in the library researching dragon legends. The more knowledge she could cram and store, the more likely to defeat the beast and return safely home they would be.

At the stable with Ira Wilda, Arriette was approached by sorcerer Sebastian Sky to confirm he had finished reinforcing the lair's magical barriers. He and a select few sorcerers had replaced the wards that wiccan Harriet Foley left behind, so Arriette knew the lair would be safe until Pandora's box was located. It didn't stop her worrying, but she thanked him anyway. Alone, Sky might have been working for days to build new wards against evil, but together, they had made light work of it.

Baby A suggested they take the wormhole she opened also that morning instead of trying to navigate horses through the beach's underground passage, and the Recruit themselves were too tired to carry their supplies by hand. Arriette didn't argue with her logic. By using the wormhole, the Recruit could assess how useful it might be in future and how safe it actually was if Baby A could figure out how to turn it into a two-way passage.

"Future Arriette slipped away in the night," Tobias said as he saddled up his horse. "She stayed longer than she should have. Baby A's worried it will affect what she returns to. You should talk to her."

"I already did," Arriette said, doing the same with Ira. "*And?*"

"It's a bit late now. It's good she was here to save Coyote's life. Without Ira Wilda, I'd be dead too, exactly as she said. Funny how things work out."

"Do you think she made it back safely?"

Arriette shrugged. "Time will tell."

They set off at nightfall.

Baby A led the way through the lair's forest to the wormhole's location by candlelight with Arriette close behind. The others moved in a line, allowing the horses to follow a natural path through the trees. Tobias and Reiko, occasionally shifting the loads on their horses for comfort, walked side-by-side and behind them Casper, Paulei, Jet, Sebastian, Joy and the two vampyrs, Susan and Dion, kept a close watch of the shadows surrounding them. Falkon was in a cell back at Town Hall, but they were still under threat from his lingering followers and orcs that had fled their masters towards the end of the fight.

"Should be evening outside now," Sebastian told Dion.

At the clearing Casper gestured for the Arriette and Baby A to go ahead and activate the wormhole. The Recruit were in no hurry to risk their lives again; there would be plenty of time for that later, so everyone moved aside and found somewhere to sit for a few minutes. Susan and Dion each found barren tree stumps—two of the many left to rot after the malfunction all those years ago. They were surprised to see it had manifested as an intricate spiral carved in the back of a lone tree and Baby A had to really push on it with her power to activate the twirling portal. Arriette mimicked her movements to speed things up and together they widened it, stretching the pattern by tearing back their hands and locking it in place as though pushing a huge button. The wormhole began to spin too fast for the naked eye. The ground shook a little, indicating it was working normally.

The group fell silent as one by one, following Baby A and Arriette's successful passage, they hopped through the wormhole and out the other side, keeping a tight hold of their horse's reins. Arriette was pleased for the peace and quiet during this process as she had a lot on her mind. Her friends seemed to all enjoy the unusual experience; something she too found fun and fascinating. And this type of wormhole was new. She'd witnessed Baby A opening one mid-air before, but never through a physical item like this tree. It seemed unnatural to run and jump into something that only moments ago had been solid.

"You go first," Tobias suggested, and Arriette obeyed.

He and Reiko were carrying most of the supplies and weight in their packs, so they were the last to brave the vortex. When they were all through and waiting patiently at the edge of Manaia Forest, Baby A closed the portal behind them. Arriette could see that already the group were slowing, so she called to Casper for a break to allow everyone a slurp of cool water. She hummed as it trickled down her burning throat and passed her canteen down the row of thirsty females behind. Her ankle didn't ache so much after offloading some of her gear, but her head pounded from dehydration and stress.

Baby A, Tabitha and Joy took a mouth full, then Joy

offered the canteen to both vampyrs who, although grateful for the offer, explained that they rarely needed such replenishments, being dead and all. Blood sustained their hunger and thirst.

A lighter mood seemed to catch like wildfire, spreading through their group until they were smiling and rested enough to continue. Joy asked that they pass the water back to Sebastian, Jet, Tobias, Paulei and Reiko, all of whom were pleased for the pause to catch their breath.

It was late outside the lair, but the day's heat lingered until they were sweating and sticky from the humidity. They paused for another two rest stops on the main road into Enzo to change bandages and shift loads.

Eventually, though, they made it to the village.

"Where do we go from here?" asked Sebastian, rummaging in his pack for a handkerchief to wipe his forehead. "I'm assuming up?"

"Keep heading for the temple at the top of the hill. There's a well and a fork in the path. We turn left," Susan told him, keeping a watchful eye for the elderly Enzoian woman they had encountered before. This late in the evening, there were few other souls roaming the streets.

Arriette mounted Ira Wilda and trotted ahead to check the pathway was clear. She gestured for the others to follow with a wave of her arm. The hike was tiresome and lengthy but the view along the path was quite beautiful. Beneath the overhanging trees it was cooler. Flowers were fragrant and blooming even without the blaring sunshine. Sweet, floral scents filled the air, raising smiles from everyone in the group.

Tabitha moved to the front and handed Arriette some sheets of parchment detailing all that she'd memorised about the dragon species and their habitats. She'd noted a description of the typical appearance first. They had a serpentine tail, armed with scales and spikes for armour strong enough to shred a tree trunk in one swift smack. The teeth, depending on the dragon's size, measured up to eight inches in length with even thicker, razor-sharp talons. Waxy, bat-like wings in varying shades of green and brown acted as a camouflage against their natural habitat and, of course, they were enormous and chunky, so therefore difficult to slay without help.

She hadn't stopped there. Tabitha also noted a dragon's strengths and weaknesses; how and where to strike the armour. Brewing in the dragon's belly would be liquid lava, capable of being blown through its mouth and nostrils to melt an enemy in just a few seconds. Indicators were a yellow glow beneath the beast, snorting, and the quick exhalation of smoke in the moments before an attack.

Arriette skipped ahead to read about their vulnerabilities. Removing the dragon's sight or piercing its belly were top of the list but beneath the limbs there were fewer scales, therefore ideal targets for arrows. One lucky shot to an armpit or the back of a knee could bring it down. She thanked Tabitha for copying it down, then tucked the parchment into her pack.

They dumped their bags at the base of the well and sat to share a meal before they ventured into the mountainside. Thirsty from the heat, Arriette passed out their canteens again and the group gulped through their water supply without thinking. After the battle, being in possession of Pandora's box would give them leverage with the Enzoian locals if the well was dry, so they could ask for some more before heading home.

Susan began to fidget, watching the others eat. "All

we have to do now is kill the box's guardian."

"I'm not sure it'll be so easy," said Casper. He turned to Arriette. "You remember the story your mother told us in Drakonta?"

She nodded, recalling the horrifying tale of a disfigured spirit in the streets of Drakonta, wailing and warning anyone out late at night of a fire-breathing beast. Such tales were common amongst her mother's friends.

"That's a myth, isn't it?"

"I have never seen the ghost personally, but I'm sure it's warnings are quite real."

"We may not have to slay it the guardian," Tobias argued. "If we can distract the dragon long enough, Arriette can *steal* the box."

"She can't steal what's already hers," Susan said. "Falkon wasn't lying about that. She's the rightful protector—the next Pandora. If we steal it, the dragon will be angry."

"So you know how this works then?" Tobias asked. "Will the beast stand down if it sees Arriette and recognises who she is?"

Susan shrugged. "We can't assume it will respect her authority. A creature like that will strike first and question later."

"Then we should prepare for a fight," Joy said.

"We know where it sleeps. We've seen the cave. The box *has* to be close. It wouldn't leave such a treasure alone for too long," Arriette said.

"But none of us are in peak physical condition." Paulei gestured at Arriette's ankle, Casper's head wound. and Dion's scratched face. "How can we fight off something so monstrous with daggers, arrows, and longswords? Seems to me that we need claws and teeth of our own."

"Good job there are dreamers and Shifters amongst us," Reiko said, grinning. "We did just fine with the demons back at the lair. Zïnnyi allowed the use of magic during the battle. He'll allow it under these circumstances, too."

"I agree with Reiko," Arriette said. "And if not, we have two vampyrs on our side."

"It's easy for them," Paulei said, sighing. "How can you be afraid of dying when you're already dead?"

Dion stood abruptly, her fangs suddenly bright in the moonlight. "I feel fear. Ya forget on the inside am *human,* Paulei; am at a disadvantage," she said.

Paulei lowered his head. "I didn't mean—"

"Sure you did," Susan said, standing up beside Dion, "but it doesn't matter. You *do* need us and we're wasting time sitting here. Dion and I will have to sleep and hunt if you're relying on us to *save the day.*"

"If we hunt now we can regain some strength," Dion added. "Everyone else is eatin'. We should too."

"I thought you were vegetarian?" Joy asked with her mouth full. "Do you hunt for sport?"

Dion stopped at the tree line and smiled. "I don't eat humans, just animals. To *me,* that's vegetarian."

"It's by no means a steak dinner, though," Susan said, laughing. "We'll be back soon. Be ready."

The hunt didn't go well. The vampyrs were disappointed with their two rabbits and a squirrel, but leaving their horses tied up at the well, the group began walking single file through the left tunnel anyway.

When they were constrained enough to hunch, Arriette reported they were getting closer.

Dion played with the tips of her fangs, no doubt

thinking of food instead of concentrating on her friends up ahead. Arriette listened to the echoing voices of amazement and when they paused to study more wall paintings similar to the mural in the temple.

Dion slammed into the back of her. "Looks just like ya, Arriette," she gasped.

Jet Carter raised a brow. "Whoever painted that, they've seen you before."

"A coincidence," she replied, shuddering. "We should keep moving, it's not safe to linger here."

"It's not safe in there, either," Joy replied.

One by one they squeezed through the opening and gathered at the entrance to the cave. Arriette placed a finger to her lips and crept along a narrow walkway. In the bowl-shaped cave beneath sat a sleeping beast, which was almost perfectly camouflaged against the moss-covered rocks behind it. They were standing on the outer rim of what felt like a canyon, and the height made Arriette unsteady. At its centre was the box's guardian, exactly as the paintings depicted. It resembled Tabitha's description too except with spikes on his wings and spine. Behind the humongous lime-coloured tail was a tiny passage, wide enough for one petite person to shimmy through.

If she sprinted, she could make it.

Arriette was about to nudge her friends and point at it when one of the dragon's beady yellow eyes opened and glared at them. Billows of smoke began to rise from its widening nostrils. Arriette unsheathed Kalvin's scimitar and her friends all followed suit, one-by-one retrieving their weapons and fanning out.

"Uhm, should we run now?" asked Sebastian Sky.

Arriette quickly examined the thickness and strength of the walkway leading to the bottom of the cave. There were chunks of rock missing where it had eroded, leaving bright grey patches in the charred path, but there were slippery areas of moss and slime, too.

The dragon yawned and stretched as if it had all the time in the world against their measly army, then threw its head back and roared. The walls shook.

Baby A covered her ears. "This is impossible!"

"Keep him occupied. Fire from up here and if you have to, use your magic. Watch your step, for Zïnnyi's sake!"

Arriette unhooked her bow and arrows from a strap across her back and threw them to Baby A. At this height, she could make better use of them. Arriette hadn't had time to practice her aim, especially when running.

The dragon swished its tail, smacking its full weight against the wall beneath them and knocking everyone to their knees. Arriette stumbled and hugged the wall, hoping the dragon wouldn't notice her if the others made enough noise. Each thundering roar caused an earthquake, throwing Arriette against something hard or sharp. Down her left side she'd have fresh, tender bruises decorating her pale skin in the days following. Though she escaped the battlefield uninjured compared to her friends, she had a terrible feeling about this next challenge.

She struggled like that for twenty minutes and was almost at the passageway when there was a piercing scream from above. Tabitha's legs were dangling over the edge. Baby A was already spreading her wings and sprinting along the walkway to grab her, showering the beast with arrow after arrow whilst avoiding any wet, green smudges she could slide on. The arrows barely pierced the dragon's armour at that angle, though. Where Tabitha scrambled and kicked, the rock beneath began to disintegrate.

The dragon pulled back on its hind legs. Its rounded khaki belly was glowing an ominous orange and it coughed, preparing to smother Tabitha in molten lava. Arriette set off running back up the path to help.

Casper headed her off. "Go, Arriette!"

"I can't leave you here! She'll fall! You have to tell Baby A to aim for under the dragon's arms like Tabitha said."

The dragon's snout erupted, showering the cave with lava. Baby A swooped to snatch Tabitha from its path just in time and dropped her near the tunnel's exit. Unfortunately, she dropped the bow in the process, too, and beneath its gigantic claw the dragon crushed it. It snapped at Tabitha again but missed and Arriette sighed with both relief and defeat.

Susan dived left to avoid being crushed by its tail and crashed into Joy, sending her flying through the air and into the wall. Even from across the cave through the noise, Arriette could hear her wrist crunch. In floods of tears and holding her broken wrist in agony, Joy made a break for Tabitha and the exit, pulling the dragon's attention round in Arriette's direction. Casper ducked, but with a swipe of his giant claws, the dragon dug three deep grooves across Arriette's face, missing both her eyes by inches, but ripping open her top lip. Blood gushed down her forehead, temporarily blinding her. It clogged her throat, causing her to splutter.

She shouted for Casper to hide and fumbled to the edge of the bowl. Reluctant to leave her, he stumbled up the path and shifted his hands into claws, preparing to fight his way back to the others. There was nothing he could do for Arriette now' she was on her own.

Tobias lit two blue fireballs to get the dragon's attention. He pounded them in quick succession against its head until it roared and turned away from Arriette and Casper. She scrambled to her feet and between trying to wipe her mangled face and sheath her scimitar, she ran as fast as she could for the passageway, dodging debris and tumbling rocks, occasionally grazing the wall when blood congealed in her eyes.

Drowning out her friends' screams, Arriette dashed the final few feet across the cave. The gashes across her face were bleeding less heavily now with the natural morphine in her angelic blood, which numbed the pain a little, making each thumping step bearable.

Inside, the passage was reinforced with wooden beams and hanging from them were several dimly lit oil lanterns. The dragon's tail thrashed for one last shot at her, missing her by millimetres as she ducked under and out of its sight, avoiding knocking any of the lanterns free. She shivered in the coolness of the cave and blinking through droplets of blood falling from the highest wound.

Arriette continued as the chaos became quieter and the tunnels narrower and darker. Soon she had to shimmy. When she couldn't hear or see anything, that's when a glimmer of hope called her forward to an incision in the rock, which led to a damp, dingy chamber. The walls were smooth there, and tall burning torches lined her path, taking the edge off. It smelled moist and stale—untouched for a hundred years.

High above her on an unreachable shelf sat a small, unimpressive looking box. Arriette scowled, unable to comprehend how powerless it looked against her surroundings. She paced the length of the chamber and reached up on her tiptoes to get a better look, then jumped from her skin when an unfamiliar voice echoed across the room.

It was female and gentle, courteous and curious.

Arriette released her grip on the shelf and span to inspect the chamber, flicking blood in a semi-circle around her.

"Arriette Monroe?"

A female in her early twenties appeared beneath one of the torches. Her body shimmered and sparkled like a shade, but she was beautiful, with oceanic blue eyes and glowing golden hair.

"Arriette Monroe?"

"Who are you?" Arriette asked.

"My name is Pandora. Are you... Arriette?"

Pandora had been created to amaze, to stun, but to be deadly, so Arriette forgave herself for staring in amazement. Using the back of her hand to wipe away more blood, Arriette jumped as her fingers discovered just how deep her wounds were.

I must look like a monster. How will I gain her trust?

"Yes, I'm Arriette."

"And you are here for my box?" Pandora asked.

She nodded. "Are you here to stop me?"

In the cave, the dragon could be heard in the distance. It was still trying to defend its treasure, but Pandora didn't seem to notice or think to call it off..

"You must have known I'd be coming here," Arriette said. "Susan is out there. She remembers."

Pandora smiled; her translucent, shining image moving gracefully closer to Arriette like the spirit of an angel more beautiful than Baby A. She seemed unmoved by Arriette's wounds or the chaos unfolding back in the tunnel as she looked her replacement up and down.

"Susan's body was a vessel. I am my own entity."

Arriette looked back at the dank cavern toward the continuing bedlam where Susan was fighting furiously to buy her more time.

"She has your memories," she said.

"For a time she and I shared one mind. Those memories are as much hers as they are mine," the spirit told her.

Arriette grunted, only partly understanding the concept. "You've been back here since Susan's death?"

Pandora turned away. "Zïnnyi assigned the beast when our souls were separated to protect me from the outside world, and to protect *them* from *me*. I failed Him. Waiting for *you* is my punishment."

There was a piercing scream from the cave, loud enough to draw Pandora's attention. For a moment Arriette thought she looked concerned or pained, then she turned her back again.

"Can you help them?"

"He is here to protect, not serve me," Pandora said. "I cannot control his actions, so your friends rule their own fate." She materialised into a partially human form enough to pace, barefoot, toward her box. Arriette watched her move effortlessly, feeling sorry for the lonely ghost as she floated up and retrieved the treasure with both hands.

Arriette stepped aside. "Why did you open it again if you knew the consequences? There has been so much death. So much... destruction."

"If you accept your fate as the box's new guardian, you too will feel the pull of curiosity one day," Pandora said. "Until you experience that influence, you are in no position to judge."

Angry, Arriette said, "You should have released

hope!"

"Hope was never trapped in my box," she sniggered. "It is what brought you here."

She danced toward Arriette like a child desperate for her mother's attention.

"You should have tried to fix your mistake, Pandora."

"Oh," she said, holding the box out, "that I did."

Arriette took it from her. She dusted it with a bloodied palm, revealing a pearl surface beneath with intricate designs and Haeyloian writing around the edges.

"If we do not make mistakes, we can never learn from them," Pandora said, gesturing for Arriette to lift the lid and look inside. "See for yourself." Arriette hesitated." There is nothing left inside to escape."

"I shouldn't, you said so yourself—"

"The evils within have already been released."

She could do no further harm to Haeylo. Pandora was right, so she carefully peeked inside. There was nothing but dirt and cobwebs. A disturbed spider crawled over Arriette's fingers and fell to the floor, but still struggling to see and distracted by her wounds, she didn't notice.

Pandora's spirit began to fade, forming a light strand of silver smoke. Arriette shuffled away as it purposefully encircled her. Gentle whispers filled the air, but they were peaceful and calming, meant to relax her.

Pandora didn't appear to mean her any harm despite her obvious dislike to being replaced, so Arriette allowed the exploration of her body and mind.

Maybe this is how I inherit the box? She must willingly give it over to me.

"Do you think I deserve another chance?" she asked.

Arriette's heart pounded. "If your intentions are pure."

Half of Pandora's spirit broke from the silver smoke and entered the box, pulling the thick lid closed behind it. The rest consumed Arriette's upper body, temporarily cutting off her air supply and causing all her wounds to sting.

She gasped. "What a-are you doing to me?" In the distance, another sharp scream. "P-Pandora!"

The blending of their souls caused the box to illuminate. It vibrated between her fingers. All around her appeared a vision of the box's evil; a projection of the world's sickness, deaths, turmoil, strife, jealousy, hatred, famine and passion in all their forms. She saw the city's plague of bugs, saw its people thirsty, saw heavy flooding. She sank to her knees and curled around the box, hoping it would shut off this hideous reflection of Haeylo's current truth.

The pictures disintegrated and swarmed the cavern like flies. Panicked and suddenly claustrophobic, Arriette hastened to regain her sense of direction and realised they had in fact been made of tiny, now scattering, butterflies. Their multi-coloured wings and showered her, disorientating her already damaged vision, whirling and swirling in all directions.

Inside her head like a telepathic blessing, a tiny voice told her, *'get up, do not be afraid; witness my miracle'*.

Pandora fast-forwarded Haeylo's history of violence and destruction and, sensing Arriette's unique power and influence over the HPS, she rejoiced, forgiving herself for being its cause. Finally, they could reverse Pandora's one hundred-year-old mistake together. Here was a supe capable of healing their planet—a worthy replacement.

A new leader needs a new beginning.

A vile, sour taste filled Arriette's mouth. She flinched

and dropped the box, watching it bounce along the wooden decking as the walls began to crumble and the planks above her clattered to the ground. The butterflies froze mid-air when the voice faded, and Arriette saw her opportunity. She snatched up the box then ran at full speed down the passageway, knocking the insects from the air as she forged a path through, forcing herself not to look back.

After knocking and grazing her limbs in the labyrinth's darkness on the way out, she dived through the incision into the centre of the battle, but unable to slow in time, collided with the dragon's tail. It has been preparing to set fire to the cave, its belly glowing once again. The Recruit were at the exit, funnelling out one-by-one.

With no other known way to escape, Arriette charged up the walkway, screaming and waving at them to move faster. The cave was collapsing and rocks narrowly missed her as she struggled the final few feet. If they had to leave her behind, so be it, but if she didn't kill the dragon, he'd chase them through the village, bringing destruction and death to Enzo's innocent inhabitants.

For what she was about to do, Arriette needed both her hands. She slid the box down the tunnel after her friends, watching them disappear around a bend ahead and, still running, turned to bring down the cave's already crumbling ceiling with her telekinesis. The dragon's flames and a swarm of now glowing butterflies chased them as far as the wishing well, lighting up the passageway.

Arriette broke free and jumped aside in time to miss being barbecued. By her feet, the box began to glow; the panels rumbled and became too hot to hold. Arriette kicked it away, hoping if this was a defence mechanism that it would stop soon. She grabbed a blanket from Ira

Wilda's saddlebag and tried to wrap it around the box but she hadn't acted fast enough. The lid sprang open, and Pandora's soul inhaled. The box began to suck any loose items inwards including leaves, flowers, and some of their personal possessions.

From the tunnel came a deafening scream as the dragon was crushed beneath Arriette's final stand, but she was too mesmerised by the box to turn.

"What's happening?" Jet yelled.

Everyone collapsed to their knees and fought against the sucking wind, gripping the edge of the well or their horse's saddles with all their might as the millions of butterflies surrounded them.

Arriette grabbed hold of Ira Wilda's reins. Butterflies caught in her hair and in Ira's mane. She squeezed her mouth shut to avoid accidentally swallowing one, and closed her eyes.

Suddenly, everything stopped.

The box's lid snapped violently.

Arriette coughed, pleased to hear her own voice. She waved her hands to clear the dusty air and mentally counted her friends to be sure they were all present and breathing. The only evidence the butterflies had been real were a few lying dead in the grass and in her hair.

"What *was* that, Arriette?" Jet asked, patting down his clothing to extinguish a few lingering dragon flames. "We were so close to being toast!"

She groaned. "In the cavern, the bugs formed images of the gateway evils," she explained, "and of the city's plagues. I think Pandora was accepting responsibility for it, sizing me up to see if I was worthy or something."

"And that wind?" Sebastian said, adjusting his hat.

"She was calling it all back—*reversing* it. I felt her

using my energy and my telekinesis. Conjoined, I think we're stronger."

Tobias said, "Is s-she... inside you?"

"I... think so. A part of her, maybe. She asked if I thought she deserved another chance."

Baby A scowled. "Wait, you agreed to this madness?"

"I said if her intentions were pure then she did."

"An open invitation, then." Susan shook her head. "That wasn't your best idea, Arry."

"What you're suggesting is impossible anyway. We can't erase evil." Casper coughed and rubbed his throat. "And I swallowed one of those critters."

"Me too," Dion said, picking a wing from her fangs.

Arriette struggled to her feet, using Ira Wilda as a hoist. "She didn't possess me, she just influenced my power. All Pandora released were gateways, and they're trapped now. But it doesn't solve the problems they created." She glanced up at a cloudless midnight sky and smiled. "We *finally* fixed her mistake... together."

THIRTY

Later that week...

In the days following their return, the lair's dreamers conjured an awe-inspiring banquet for the Recruit to share outside Town Hall. They feasted in the street to celebrate victory on the battlefield; dancing, playing music, singing songs and setting off multi-coloured fireworks, courtesy of sorcerer Sebastian Sky and his potions. Arriette had been too tired to dream anything of her own and after twenty-four hours of noise, she wished they would all go away for a while. Her body needed sleep and silence more than company.

She excused herself from the party and walked back to her bedroom, carrying Pandora's box with both hands as she had been doing since returning from the mountain. She hadn't yet found the strength or confidence to visit Falkon Lou's cell and taking the box to him was prohibited. Until the ceremony to become the Recruit's official leader was over, she'd let Falkon stew for a while. He deserved it.

She almost made it to the stairs when a group of children stopped her.

"Tell about the dragon! Tell us how it almost ate you!"

Arriette wished she could change her name. Although the claw wounds across her face were beginning to heal and her angelic blood had decreased the redness and swelling, she would *always* bear those emotional scars. But as not to be rude, Arriette crouched to their height and told the story again, still keeping a tight hold of the box. With so much going on elsewhere, the children soon lost interest and skipped off to join their friends.

Baby A held out a courteous arm and hauled her up, laughing. "You're getting old," she said.

Arriette grumbled, cringing as her healing lip cracked and stung. "I'm boring too, apparently."

"Children just want to hear what they can re-enact later with wooden sticks. Everything else is tedious."

"They don't want to hear about Pandora any more than I wanted to deal with her," Arriette said, smiling.

Baby A reached out to take the box.

Arriette flinched and moved away. "Not yet."

"I don't know what Pandora said, or *is* saying, to you, but it's alright to let it out of your sight for a while. You're not sleeping or eating and frankly, we're worried." She held out a piece of folded parchment. "Casper asked me to give you the plans for your ceremony, anyway. He said you have already been working on a speech."

"She hasn't said anything to me since the cave." Arriette accepted them and glanced, nervously, at the box. Her fingers were white and stiff and wrapped around its edges.

"Pandora told me it would tug on my curiosity. So far it's just preyed on my fear. If I let go of it, I might lose it. If I lose it—"

"You can give it to me. *I* won't lose it."

Arriette hesitated then released the box into Baby A's custody. Immediately she felt relieved and relaxed. For a while, the safety of her people wouldn't be her responsibility.

"Need anything else?" she asked.

Arriette struggled through a smile. "Just my pillow, darkness, and silence."

Baby A left her alone to get some rest and disappeared into the crowd. Arriette did nothing but sleep and read after that, which is exactly what she wanted.

Outside, the werewolf clan Masters had decided to offer their help. They were building a huge wooden platform with a round fire pit in the centre, re-purposing the silvery curtains as an elegant backdrop for the crowning ceremony. Arriette could see them from the library window, carrying torches back and forth, setting out benches and fixing a security perimeter, just in case.

On the morning of the ceremony, Arriette's eyes were fixated only on the coffee in her cup as it swirled in circles, courtesy of her boredom and telekinesis. She massaged her neck in agony when a sharp bolt of pain jolted up her spine and into her skull, where she feared her only form of pain relief—caffeine—would not be able to reach. Her wings didn't appear, but the shock was almost a reminder forced upon her that she would never be wholly in control of her life now.

On the odd chance she did manage to doze off before rehearsing the ceremony, the dragon's dying screams still haunted her.

A knock at the door broke Arriette from her painful trance. She jumped and almost spilled her coffee.

Baby A's usual cheery grin had been replaced by an anxious sapphire stare, and she didn't have the box.

"Aren't you going to bed?"

"Where's the box?"

"Did you hear what I asked?"

"Where. Is. The. Box?"

Baby A sat beside her. "Relax, Arriette. Tobias has it. You're worrying too much."

"I don't think I'm worrying enough." She placed her head on Baby A's shoulder and took a profound breath. "Casper said I should memorise every word of this Haeyloian ceremony. I can't let him down."

"Work isn't everything. Casper knows that better than anyone. He appreciates all you're doing. We *all* do. One mistake won't make a difference. You'll still have our respect."

Arriette rubbed her eyes and, glancing at the clock, was shocked to learn she only had a few hours until the ceremony began. She thanked Baby A for her counsel and hurried to bathe and get dressed for her big day.

In the square, the lair's inhabitants were gathering. The Elite Four sat in the first row but the werewolf clans were still loitering; a few were having trouble hanging flags atop the podium, branded with a beautiful TOL crest in the centre, named after the Tree of Life where Arriette had first mastered her telekinesis. In Haeyloian it was called the 'Brune ze Litte' and pronounced *Broon-zee-lit* although the tree hadn't been referred to in that language for centuries. Arriette had never seen the crest before but recognised it from a tapestry hanging in the library and from hundreds of books read in Mousique. Practical and inspiring, the crest held many meanings but was actually a symbol of unity and strength amongst all supernatural species. In the centre was a man holding what appeared to be a rainbow, which Arriette knew as *Indalo*. He was surrounded by a shield knot like that the Elite Four used during their projection, and looming over him was the Tree of Life. Red, green, blue and white dominated their own quarter.

Seeing Arriette for the first time since the street party, Jade and the other Elite Four women waved her over.

"Are you here for my ceremony?" Arriette asked.

"We wouldn't miss it." She handed Arriette a tiny golden pouch. "I've been looking for you. Casper asked me to give you this."

Arriette peaked inside but it was empty. She was beginning to feel he'd been avoiding her, sending Baby A and Jade to deliver messages to the library instead. Since their return, Arriette hadn't checked in with her mentor and was beginning to feel guilty.

"It's a gift. I think it was his mother's? It was empty when he left it in my care," Jade explained.

Arriette thanked them and watched as other followers began to take their seats. Baby A beckoned her up to stand in the centre of the podium but she shook her head, and lingered to talk with the locals for a while.

An hour later, the ceremony was upon them. Arriette no longer had a choice.

She watched as Casper emerged from Town Hall and walked between the two rows of benches, wearing the same white robes and sandals he always did. Arriette glanced down at her ceremonial dress, feeling over-dressed and embarrassed. He touched his forehead, heart and both shoulders before stepping up to address his people for the last time. Arriette's entire body quaked. In a few minutes, she would be a murderer. Her conscience would be tainted forever.

"After so many years apart we have been reunited. Now, I am sorry to be leaving you again," he said.

The crowd remained silent.

As instructed to do on the parchment, Arriette knelt

beside Casper as a mark of respect for the man who had trained her to take his place. When it was time, he offered to aid her to a stance. She knew if she took his hand she wouldn't be able to let go, so she used a near-by wooden beam instead and tried not to look him in the eye.

Casper continued regardless. "I have chosen Arriette Monroe to be your next leader."

Several thousand pairs of eyes awaited her speech. She swallowed hard and cleared her throat. Although Casper had written the official speech down for her to ease the pressure, Arriette wanted to memorise her own. But now, faced with her people and the man she thought of as a father, she had nothing meaningful to say.

So she pocketed the parchment, moving aside the golden pouch from the Elite Four.

"I have always wondered Haeylo's three moons were positioned in such a way," she began, looking out at the hopeful faces in the crowd. "The Tri moon in the north. The Shou moon in the south. The Choku moon in the west." The werewolf Masters fixed their gaze on her intently, wondering where she was going with this speech about their sacred moons. "We are lacking a fourth in the east. I read recently that a moon is said to strengthen hope, and allow the creatures inhabiting a planet to *dream*. Of course, the sun rises in the east, just as Andrew Kaines has shone so brightly, and literally raised us above evil for so long."

Baby A's eyes were wide and she mouthed, '*What are you doing?*', but Arriette had already decided to do this her own way and in her own time.

"I think we are lacking a moon in the east because Zïnnyi gave us Casper instead." She continued, fumbling with her dress. "In ancient tradition, dating back to Earth and our ancestors, the east was said to symbolise optimism. Not only this, but some believed it was symbolic of a triumph of light over dark, and good over evil. I tell you this as a lesson, and a promise of years to come. Throughout history, like we are without that moon, Haeylo has been without peace. Let this be a reminder of our recent victory—a victory we made possible through unity and community. A victory made possible because of this man."

Casper's head raised proudly and he glanced over at the Wolf Masters standing side-by-side beneath the largest flag. They threw back their heads and released a howl; their approval of Arriette's tribute, and their promise to stand loyally beside her.

"I have been so afraid of this ceremony," she admitted, "because I deemed it the end of something. But it's not. It's the beginning. A truly beautiful one."

Arriette gestured at her friends and one by one, they mounted the podium and took their place beside her. It was now time for her to choose her own Recruit members, replacing those Casper had trained and appointed before her.

On approach, each of her friends lit a torch from the fire pit and held it at arm's length. Her ceremony would begin with the announcement of each newly appointed Recruit power, after Arrette had recited a memorised Haeyloian word. She would extinguish each of their flames with sand to represent the role being passed from old to new. And at the end, she would eliminate the final torch held by Casper and, when ready, re-light her own.

Then, she would quote from a special poem.

The line consisted of:

Rachael Hardcastle

Everlast Joy Johnas
Sorcerer Sebastian Sky
Jet Carter with his invisibility
Dreamer Tobias Shallow
Angel and Time-Traveller Baby A
Human and Potions Master Reiko Port
Vampyr and Shape-Shifter Dion Delavious
Telepath Paulei Leigh
Retainer Tabitha Hope
Vampyr and Astro-Projector Susan Petter

She knew there would be uproar about selecting two vampyrs, but the women were unique for a reason, and Arriette appreciated how Zïnnyi had brought them together. *For a reason.* They were already breaking a hundred rules by shortening the ceremony and being unable to hold it in the presence of the previous Recruit members anyway. Harriet and Scarlett were dead and Casper didn't want the reminder. So Baby A cleared it in prayer with their creator. If He had a problem with the new plan to crown Arriette, He sent no signs or messages.

But even with such skilled supes on her team, Arriette was missing the wiccan power, without which, the Recruit would be... incomplete. There had to be eleven.

Her first word was *Alef,* the Haeyloian letter A, and she was relieved to have remembered it. She announced Joy's full name and power and sprinkled a hand full of sand over the flame. Joy thanked her and stepped back, so Arriette could move along the row to Sebastian Sky.

Her second word was *Reshe*, the Haeyloian letter R, followed by the same word once again for Jet's flame. They each patted her on an arm and gave her a few words of encouragement, then joined Joy in the shadows.

Next in line was Tobias and Arriette was so pleased to see him she almost leapt with excitement. They locked eyes for a moment and smiled at one another. Her fourth word was *Vodd*, Haeyloian for the letter I. He winked as she extinguished his torch and moved to face Baby A, whose word was *Hie*, representative of the letter E. They held hands and took a step back together. Rather than feeling jealous of their past relationship and the accident that led to Baby A's hospitalisation, Arriette now watched them cling to each other with pride and satisfaction.

She tried not to linger with each of her friends too long until she approached Reiko, whose word was *Tau* for the letter T. He was trembling, terrified to officially be part of such an important cause despite being a mere human.

"It's alright," she whispered. "You've got this."

She squeezed his hand until he smiled at her and took a step back to join his hunting buddy.

Her seventh word was the same, and Dion's fangs were glistening as Arriette approached her. The crowd gasped when Arriette hugged her, but she ignored their whispers of protest. Dion was crying for the first time since being made vampyr, finally feeling respected and appreciated for who, not what, she was. Where Arriette expected to see blood, she saw real, human tears, which she wiped away with the bottom of her fancy dress to show those against Dion's presence a thing or two about loyalty and respect.

Paulei's word was *Hee,* which ended a series of Haeyloian letters that when de-coded would spell her name: A.R.R.I.E.T.T. E.

She heaved a sigh, thrilled to have made it so far without stammering or forgetting the words, then prepared to announce the final two letters, which were the initials of the leader she would be replacing.

Tabitha Hope bit her lip in anticipation as Arriette once again said *Alef* and passed her by. Then she approached her tenth Recruit member, Susan Petter. Louder gasps from the elder retainers at the front distracted her, but didn't seem to phase the vampyr, who merely stood taller and flashed her fangs. During Arriette's time in the library, she had given thought to whether Susan would be willing to accept the wiccan role, too, to learn and master spells and sorcery just as Harriet Foley had. She hoped allocating this learned responsibility to Susan might also ease her followers' reaction to her.

"I offer our final power of wiccan to vampyr and astro-projector, Susan Petter." She paused and cringed in anticipation. "Do you accept?"

Susan mouthed a brief *'thank you'* and beamed with happiness. "I accept."

Relieved, Arriette said her final word, *Kaf*, the Haeyloian letter K, and extinguished Susan's flame.

A. K. for Andrew Kaines.

Only Casper's torch remained, burning brightly. Now she was to recite the poem they all knew so well, before putting out the final light and setting fire to her own torch.

"To see a world in a grain of sand," she uttered.

Casper replied, "And a heaven in a wild flower."

Arriette sprinkled sand on the eleventh and final torch, then reached out to take her own from him. He bowed his head as she made her way to the pit and set it alight, then fixed it to a base to brighten Casper's face.

He had already cleaned and prepared the ceremonial sword, which he now held out with both hands, *inviting* her. Shaking, she stared helplessly at her reflection in the polished steel.

She began to cry. "I have your pouch. I know what it's for; what it means. You've been my best friend, my father, and my mentor. I pray someday you'll be able to forgive me for this—for... *everything*."

Arriette raised the sword to the height of Casper's neck and pulled it back. There was only one thing left to do.

Casper closed his eyes. "I'm glad I found you, Arriette Monroe. We *will* be together again. I promise."

The blade came down.

The ceremony was over.

THIRTY—ONE

Falkon Lou sat alone in the locked, empty office, listening to the clack of Arriette's shoes as she approached the Retaining guard outside and asked to speak with her prisoner.

Town Hall was eerily quiet since the ceremony had ended and the wolves had packed everything away. The corridors had been abandoned, perhaps even the entire building. Those low on the HPS—human, wiccans and retainers especially—were too frightened to be anywhere near the power-crazed criminal.

What if he had it in for their species next?

When she opened the door, he was juddering his leg and biting his nails. Rather than looking up to acknowledge her, he turned his back, so didn't notice Arriette's ruffled dress smeared with Casper's blood. It distressed her and anyone she passed, but Arriette had chosen not to change her clothing yet, hoping her psychopathic appearance might intimidate Falkon enough to talk more about his plans for power-swapping and species extermination.

The ceremony's events sat heavily on her shoulders. Killing Casper had replaced the weight Pandora lifted only two days before, so that peace hadn't lasted very long. Now she was... angry. Mostly with Casper for making her do what she did to him, and in public, but also with her friends for supporting their mentor's death and encouraging her to become a murderer. Without his guidance, Arriette was lost, forgetful, emotional and as Falkon was about to find out, a lot less patient. However, she was twice as determined not to let Falkon get away with what he'd done.

"You're missing a treat," she said, turning her chair to sit backwards on it. Her wrists were crossed atop the wooden backrest and her dress draped flatteringly around her thighs. "I thought you appreciated the sight of blood, particularly of innocent people, of *humans*? But your battlefield no-show wasn't your choice, was it?" Arriette leant forward and lowered her voice. "How does it feel, Falkon, to be without hope? Your followers think you're a coward. They've deemed you a traitor."

"I'm not a traitor, Deary. I *wanted* to be there. I *tried* to be there," he said.

"They don't know that."

Arriette grinned until Falkon raised his head and glared directly at her.

His leg stopped juddering.

His teeth stopped gnawing.

His voice was flat when he asked, "Are they dead? Were my orcs defeated?"

"Some fled, others surrendered. That's the first time you've admitted ownership of them, though."

"They'll be back. My wolves—"

"Oh, they are working for me now. The Recruit's promise of protection and prosperity was, and remains, legitimate. Seems the Alphas saw through your plan. They never trusted you to fulfil your side of the deal so they refused to fight for either of us. Seeing what a massacre it was out there, they came to their senses."

"I would have honoured my promises," he said, almost growling. "If not for you, Deary."

"Even now when there's nowhere left to run, no-one else to influence, you're *still* lying. You said it yourself, Falkon, why keep a species around if they are of no further use to you? Why keep *any* of us around?"

"You should have let me increase their value!"

Falkon seemed placid despite the blood down Arriette's front, though he did steal a glance at Kalvin's scimitar, sheathed and attached to her belt. It stood out.

"So you could destroy the HPS and play God?" she asked, tutting. "*You* should know better."

"You're not as smart as I thought. I offered to rid this entire planet of orc filth, build you an unstoppable, powerful army, all with fangs and claws and wings and you *refused*?"

"I did."

"Had you accepted, your precious leader might still be here to see it. All you had to do was lead me to Pandora's box. In my possession, wondrous things could have been done."

"If I had, the orcs and werewolves wouldn't have been the only species fearing for their lives," she said. "Casper wasn't killed by your army. He gave his life voluntarily for our cause. I did what I had to do for my people and if you push me, I'll do it again."

"I have no doubt, Deary," Falkon said, chortling in a sadistic fashion Arriette hadn't seen before. "It's what he'd have wanted, I'm sure. Let me ask you how much easier winning would have been without the HPS to limit your infantry's abilities? Without my experiments, you're no closer to peace than Casper was."

Arriette sat upright and folded her arms. "You will address him as Andrew Kaines... as the God he is."

"*Was,*" Falkon spat.

"We're at peace now *because* of him. We're in possession of Pandora's box and thanks to the Recruit, she —*I*—called the gateways back. We did that without your experiments." Arriette scoffed.

"Called back the gateways?" he asked, frowning. "What does that mean? Is the Underworld empty; a wasteland now?"

"The world is settling as Zïnnyi wanted. We're one step closer to the utopia we've always wanted."

Falkon shook his head. "You're going to throw years of research away when demolishing the HPS and putting supes in power may still be possible. If you would listen —"

"Enough!" Arriette said, taking the everlast by surprise. "You're going to prison for a *very* long time and I'm betting most of those inmates don't like you much. Might be something to think about on the way there. Just saying."

Arriette winked and replaced her chair beneath the table. She knocked for the guard's attention. Falkon's grin disappeared, his lips pressed to a firm line and his brow furrowed.

"Why not just kill me like you killed your leader?"

"And let you die a martyr?" She spat at his feet and her top lip curled with fury. "You're not worthy. Casper's death was beautiful; meaningful. He's a saint! You'll rot in a prison cell for your eternity, Falkon."

The guard stepped aside, allowing Arriette to exit the room.

As she was about to close the door, Falkon called out.

"I've been meaning to ask how little Angelica is doing? How's that *unusual* power coming along?"

Arriette's head re-appeared around the office door. Instinctively, she reached down and touched Kalvin's scimitar, preparing to unsheathe and, if necessary, use it.

"I told you to stay away from her."

"I did as you asked, Deary. I've been in here, under your orders."

Arriette's eyes narrowed. She crept toward him, wondering if there was something else about the child he hadn't yet disclosed.

Secrets were Falkon's means to manipulate those he found useful; perhaps this was all a ploy so she'd keep him alive or close-by, sparing his prison sentence until he found a way to escape.

"And poor Susan! Being a vampyr is difficult enough I'd imagine without having astro-projection to master, too. What is she, a scale ten, *eleven*, perhaps?"

Arriette slammed her fist, still grasping the blade, down on the desk in front of him. Falkon's expression flinched but his body remained still and confident. Since meeting Angelica in the castle she'd wondered about her past, hearing her parents had been made vampyr. She'd been captured and imprisoned by Falkon. If he'd been telling the truth about how she came to be there, why he was so interested in the child and her powers?

"Did you lie to me about Angelica's power? She wasn't born with it, was she? Did you use my blood to create her astro-projection? You *stole* from me to create a power with *no* authority or understanding of the consequences?"

"Tut tut, Deary! A leader should know that astro-projection already existed as a scale eleven," he said, "so I did *not* create it, merely... tampered with it."

"To change what?"

Falkon sat back in his chair. "Such an unusual power should be higher on the HPS. Unfortunately, I instead weakened their gifts. Projectors like Susan don't usually have to sleep to duplicate, but oh, no bother!"

"That's a little girl's *life* you were playing with!"

"She's alive, isn't she? Oh, I'm disappointed. With two supes as high up the scale as you and that dreamer, I'd have expected a better *product*." He paused. "So, you agree my experimentations were a success, then?"

"A product? Whether she was born with it or not, Falkon, what you did to her is sick!"

Without thinking, Arriette lit a fireball and pitched it at the back of the room, setting a pair of cream curtains alight. Falkon's eyes widened and he rattled the handcuffs his guard had chained through the desk to a metal ring on the floor. The flames roared higher and louder, quickly turning the room into a bright furnace.

Arriette sheathed her scimitar and grabbed Falkon by the scruff of his neck.

He began to sweat. "Do you want to *burn* for this?"

She threw Falkon's chair backwards. Both he and the desk went over in one smooth motion.

She stormed out and locked the door. The guard peered through the door's little window as Falkon struggled to get free of his cuffs.

Arriette glared down at her trembling hands and tucked them under her pits, closing her eyes when Falkon began to plea for help. He screeched and wailed at the top of his voice.

After several minutes, Arriette snapped her fingers and put the fire out. She unlocked the door and handed the key to the guard without opening it.

"Is he—"

"No, I just wanted to frighten him. Show him the fire he's playing with. I wouldn't have let him burn," she said honestly. "You and your men are to escort him to everlast Charles Melovich in the city." She paused. "Tell him Arriette Monroe sends her love."

With that, she left the bewildered guard alone in the corridor to deal with what remained of Falkon Lou's ego.

THIRTY—TWO

Arriette left Town Hall with crimson cheeks and clenched fists. She had never felt so incapacitated or feeble. Casper had stressed the importance of protecting the human race and innocent low-level HPS supes from the likes of Falkon Lou and, only a few hours after his death, already she had failed him by purposefully terrifying someone in a helpless position.

Arriette began to cry.

Ignoring the lingering pain in her ankle and the sting of her salty tears in the healing gashes across her face, she ran to the stable to find Ira Wilda and together they walked through town, passing the Indalo store with the castle's tower on her right, headed straight into the lair's forest.

Plenty of townspeople saw her. None dared question her tears or where she was heading on her own.

The wards were holding strong and no-one had seen an orc or a demonic face since the battle ended. Those with limbs remaining had fled the lair, so she'd be safe in the forest alone for a while.

Good riddance to them. At least Sebastian Sky has done his *job right,* she thought.

They continued straight to the wormhole's site and Arriette dismounted, careful not to put too much weight on her foot. Beneath the trees the clearing was sheltered and cool; an ideal place for her to rest and clear her head.

How was she supposed to tell a woman she had already killed once that she was *also* responsible for her unusual, unpredictable scale eleven power? A vampyr, too. And why would Angelica ever forgive her for being party to the violation of her blood? Her parents left Angelica a harmless child. They would be so disappointed with the Recruit—with Arriette—for allowing an everlast to ruin her with unscreened blood from strangers.

Until I ask Angelica directly about her power, I can't be sure Falkon wasn't lying to provoke me, she thought. *And I let him!*

She slumped forward, resting her head in her hands and sobbed until there were only dry heaves left. Ira Wilda nudged her.

"If you could understand what I'm saying, you wouldn't have chosen me," she told the unicorn. "Casper was wrong. I'm weak. I always have been, right back to Mousique."

She gave his snout a firm pat.

A rustle in the trees caused Arriette to jump to her feet, jolting Ira Wilda back a few steps. He clomped his front hoof and snorted, shaking his mane until Arriette took hold of his reins.

"Who's there?" she called. "I'm armed!"

She removed Kalvin's scimitar from its sheath and held it at arms length. A ray of sunlight poking through the leaves above her shone a bright reflective beam into the eyes of her pursuer.

He blinked and raised his palm to block it. "What are you doing out here, Arriette? It's not safe. The wolves haven't yet given the all clear."

Arriette sighed and threw the blade so hard it lodged

deep into a near-by tree trunk. Tobias hopped out of the way and scowled at her recklessness, using his telekinesis to pull it free.

"What did *I* do?"

"Nothing," she said through gritted teeth, "nobody did anything."

Tobias crept closer, offering her the knife back by the hilt. She reached up and took it lazily, then stuck it blade-first in the prickly brown grass beside her.

"What prompted this?"

Arriette cracked her knuckles. "I made him think I was going to set him on fire, Tobias. I used magic to *intentionally* threaten harm to Falkon Lou. That's *not* what a leader does."

"I'm sure he deserved it."

"Oh, *he did*, but that doesn't excuse it."

Tobias gestured at a barren stump close to where Arriette had been perched. She nodded, inviting him to sit and began to fidget with the bandage which stuck out from her leather boot.

"He'd be disappointed in me," she said, sighing.

"Actually, he'd be proud," said Tobias, reaching out to squeeze her hand. Arriette let him. "Now he's gone, I guess I should probably tell you something, though I'm not supposed to even know."

Arriette glanced left at him. "Tell me *what*?"

"Casper met you long before that day in Manaia Forest. When we brought you back, you should have seen the look on his face. He was so *relieved!*"

Tobias smiled through his pain. She forgot how close the two of them had been, several years before Arriette came into their lives. But she'd already guessed he recognised her from elsewhere from past cryptic conversations and eavesdropping.

He sniffled. "You were unconscious. We were staring at him blankly, awaiting some kind of instruction as to what we should do with you. I mean, you killed a vampyr and survived another's bite so to us you were an unnatural freak of nature already."

Arriette smiled. "Thanks, I think."

Tobias shook his head. "We were all for ditching you somewhere. We're not proud. Don't tell Baby A I said so. People fear what they don't understand and you put us in an awkward position. Casper sat in his chair stroking that long, white beard in deep thought for at least an hour. All the while you were just laid there." Tobias's hands began to tremble. He interlocked his fingers to hide his guilt. "Baby A said you'd die if we didn't act soon. Casper just grinned and instructed us to save you. It's like he knew you weren't going to die no matter what he decided or how long it took."

Arriette began to bite her grotty fingernails, suddenly feeling uneasy about Tobias's secret.

"How could he know that?"

"I asked him later why he was smiling. He brushed back your hair and took this long inhalation. I almost walked away it took him so long to reply. Finally, he said, *'because she's my granddaughter'*."

They stared at one another, speechless.

Arriette's heart began to thump so hard in her chest she thought she might pass out. Her runes were suddenly itchy, particularly where Dagaz sat over her heart. She tightened her grip on Ira's reins and tensed. The unicorn knelt beside her and rested his head in her lap.

Her jaw dropped. Tobias reached out and closed it.

"I was sworn to secrecy but I know I should have told

you sooner. I didn't know how and Casper wouldn't have trusted me again. I can imagine Pouki and Paulei were, too, being what they are." After a short pause, he inhaled deeply. "I'm not going to ask for your forgiveness because I don't deserve it. Please, try to understand though, for his sake."

Arriette nodded, unable to offer a sane response.

"Beyond my teachings, what more do you know about dreaming?"

She swallowed hard. "Only what I've read in books. It seems the higher up the scale you go, the more mysterious you are."

"We're not so mysterious. Sometimes, though, when dreamers are in close proximity our collective powers expand. To most, it's barely noticeable. A burst of energy, perhaps, or enhanced senses. To me, it's an opportunity."

"That must be what Baby A tried to tell me when we first met," she said. "When I got my Dagaz tattoo, she said it meant *psyche;* that there's a spiritual side to dreaming. Is *that* how you know Casper wasn't lying?"

He scratched hid chin. "What else did she tell you?"

"Nothing. She said I should ask you, but I never got the chance."

Tobias seemed to exhale with relief. "Our power comes from the psyche but our imagination allows us to project onto and control our surroundings. I'm rarely in the presence of so many other dreamers but when we arrived here I was overwhelmed. Using our collective influence I bounced off the near-by signatures and accessed an ability I haven't practised in... a long time." Tobias stood and began to pace. His hands were still shaking. "I don't like to do it. Some dreamers call it Spying, others Mirroring, but I call it Jumping, whereby my psyche duplicates to temporarily see the world through another's eyes."

Arriette watched him kick away rocks and fidget as he explained this second gift to her, as though sharing a piece of forbidden fruit.

"Do you possess them or is it like what I think Pandora and me might have?" she asked. "She's a hitch-hiker."

"It's to observe only," he confirmed. "I have no influence over their body or thoughts. Casper complained of a headache after but I doubt he recognised the cause. It helps us to better understand our enemy before we attack them. Ours is an active, high-ranking power and one we should take responsibility for."

"Alright," she said, "so you inhabited his psyche to do what, read his mind?"

"Telepathy isn't in my skill set but his emotions were an open book. He *loved* you. He was a proud, grateful grandfather. I used my power for personal gain because I *had* to know if he was lying."

"I'm not sure I understand," she said, shaking her head. "I *can't* be his granddaughter because he's an Earthling and I'm—"

Arriette yanked the blade up from the grass and re-opened the incision in her palm as Tobias had once done for her. Tiny droplets of red began to drip steadily down her arm.

"My bloodline doesn't make sense," she said. "It never has."

"How so?" he asked, binding her hand with a rag.

"Well, at Pouki's cabin that day, he said I would one day avenge my father's death but I always thought he died of Cancer."

"You're in doubt?" Tobias asked.

"I think I should pay Ma a visit."

Tobias offered to help her stand. Weak at the knees, she was unsure she'd make it through the shock, but with Tobias to lean on, eventually her balance steadied. Arriette reached out and placed her clean hand on his shoulder. She leaned forward and kissed him, lingering longer than she should to appreciate the scent in his hair and the softness of his lips, then mounted Ira Wilda.

"You're right, you should have told me before," she asked, "but I appreciate your loyalty to Casper. I wish I had been that loyal from the beginning."

"I respected and trusted his judgement," Tobias said. "It requires a strong will to take such a secret to your grave."

She sighed. "Did he know I loved him too?"

Tobias smiled. On tip toes, he lifted her chin with his finger. "I'm sure he did. He just needed you to be focused. Don't you find it freeing?"

Arriette rolled her eyes. "Uhm, no! How could *any* of this be freeing?"

"His death, I mean." He paused and looked up as a ray of sunlight broke through the trees, illuminating his face. "Casper made a deal with Zïnnyi, Arriette. He promised never to find his family and to dedicate himself wholly to Haeylo's protection. They wouldn't have known each other if they crossed paths in the lair."

"Then why would Zïnnyi agree? It's cruel! Why wasn't Casper punished like Pandora for betrayal?"

"Think about it," Tobias said. "He never acknowledged you as anything but his student and friend. He *did* seek to find you and in doing so broke his promise because it was a trick! He kept a more important promise when he sacrificed his own happiness, perhaps even yours, for the greater good. It wasn't a contract but a test. One he passed. Now he's free, and has been rewarded. What would you call that if not loyalty?"

Arriette smiled. "I'd call it family."

Thirty—Three

Arriette and Tobias rode back to Town Hall. On the way, still protected by the forest, she told him about Falkon Lou's successful experimentations and how both Susan and Angelica's strange astro-projection powers were likely created from a combination of dreaming and travelling (if Falkon hadn't been lying to provoke her).

"How can a scale two and a scale four create a scale eleven?" Tobias asked. "It doesn't make sense."

"There's a lot we don't know about astro-projection anyway. Falkon admitted his changes were a product of luck, not planning," Arriette said. "From what I understand, if Susan splits her astral from her physical self, her body sleeps until they're reunited. That's not supposed to happen; she should be able to run two cognitive states. She can't be in two places at once now, which is a limitation, but she can move through walls and speak, which is a benefit. There are more weaknesses with the power than there are strengths even before Falkon's interference because it's untested. Naturally, a place on the HPS is awarded, hence the low number."

Tobias scratched his chin and dismounted Ira Wilda first, walking both he and Arriette through the town to the stable.

"Have you told either of them yet?"

Arriette dismounted. She gave Ira Wilda a pat and handed his reins to the stable hand, kissing his nose and giving him a firm pat.

They set off walking back to Town Hall.

"I was hoping we could tell them together. How will they take it?"

Tobias shrugged. Neither he nor Arriette initiated the creation of this power and they were both unconscious for the entire process. Had they not been fighting in the morgue that day, they wouldn't have been captured and imprisoned, leading to the theft of their blood. They also wouldn't have been able to free their friends. Susan's reaction would be based on her logic, though, not theirs.

"You should brace yourself to fight her," he said.

"I don't want to. She'll overpower us both, though maybe we deserve it. I just appointed her an official member of the Recruit; if she attacks me, what do I do?"

"What you need to. We're victims too," he reminded her. "Angelica is too young to understand. She hasn't received her rune yet—whatever that may be—suggesting she hasn't been using the power. If she was born with it, she won't know much about how to use the ability."

"Neither has Susan," Arriette argued, "but she used it in the castle like an expert! They're both dangerous because there's nobody to teach them like you all taught me. Perhaps I should stay here?"

"No, you need to visit your mother," Tobias said, halting her on the steps leading to the building. "You deserve closure. Ma needs to see you're alive and well. News travels quickly. She'll have heard about the battle."

Arriette sighed. "You're right. I need to leave while it's light out. It'll be safer. We should do this now."

They found Susan and Angelica at the far end of the

canteen. Angelica was trying to drink from her cup and Susan was moving it out of the way, sending them both into fits of laughter. Tobias and Arriette sat between them, wasting no time. She and Tobias told Susan as much as they could, hoping the story wouldn't frighten or worry the child sitting opposite her. Tobias interjected with his thoughts, memories and evidence from the castle, and after talking non-stop with no interruptions from either Angelica or Susan the entire time, they finally sat back and waited.

Susan was scowling throughout but she sat quietly and processed the information in a rational manner. She already knew or guessed the majority anyway. She couldn't astro-project before being turned, so it made sense that whatever happened to her after her death. Angelica seemed content, perhaps not fully understanding that half of who she now was, *supposedly*, had been created in a laboratory.

Still worried about Susan, Tobias gave Angelica a light tap on the shoulder and suggested they go for a walk, leaving Arriette and the vampyr alone to talk through all they'd learned since Falkon's imprisonment. Without anyone to lean on or look up to, Tobias feared Angelica wouldn't know how to grieve them.

After they were gone and the canteen doors were closed, leaving Susan and Arriette alone at the table, the vampyr leaned forward and clasped her hands together.

"How long have you known about this?"

"Not long," Arriette told her honestly.

"Falkon told you?" Susan raised a brow. "Is he alive?"

"Yes," she said, desperately trying to swallow how happy the fear in his eyes had made her. "I couldn't kill him. I'm sorry."

"I don't blame you," Susan said, taking Arriette by surprise. "You were both violated by that monster, too. How could *any* of us have known he created my power in a laboratory—at least—the weaker version of it. I assumed Dion and I were alike; unique in our own way somehow. A gift." She lowered her head. "Are you here to remove me from the Recruit or, do you have orders to kill me? Of course, I'd prefer banishment."

Arriette was stunned to silence. She hadn't chosen Susan because of her powers, but for her friendship, loyalty, trust and personality. The Recruit were there to support one another; she needed people she could rely on, and Susan had the experience of Pandora's influence. It didn't matter if they were first or last on the HPS so long as they believed in the cause.

"I don't take orders anymore, remember? I'm just here to admit my involvement. How could you think that?"

"Because I'm an abomination," she said, cutting Arriette off. "As the Recruit's leader and the new Pandora, I thought you'd do what was necessary for the good of your people and planet."

"Your death isn't a necessity, Susan. Why would I make you the wiccan in training if I thought you couldn't handle your responsibilities? You're strong-willed and quick to learn. You'll master this like you do all your dilemmas, but if you *do* want to forfeit—"

"I don't want to forfeit learning wicca," Susan said, "Sebastian is excited to teach me. I'm not accusing you of trying to justify my existence, I'm trying to justify my own."

Arriette could understand the vampyr's longing for identity. Susan was trying to be so many people and so many things at once.

"I need to know if Pandora ever told you why she chose me as your replacement."

Surprised by the change of topic, Susan shook her head and sat upright. Pandora had taken refuge in Arriette's body during the retrieval of the box but so far hadn't spoken to her or influenced her actions.

"What does that have to do with my power?"

"You're struggling to recognise your own worth. I'm having a similar problem and I learned something in the forest today."

Susan tutted. "You were in the forest *alone*?"

Arriette shook her head. "Tobias was with me. I needed to clear my mind but he told me something I should investigate further. It's about my bloodline; my history and my ancestry. It's also about Casper."

"Pandora never spoke to me directly," Susan said. "I just *knew* things ordinary people didn't. I'm sorry, but if I can help—"

"I think this is something I need to do on my own."

They smiled awkwardly at one another, then Arriette left the canteen feeling no better than she did entering it.

Tobias was waiting outside with Angelica. She ran back through the doors excitedly to find Susan when Arriette came out.

"How did it go?"

"As well as can be expected," said Arriette. "She offered to help me in Drakonta but I said I needed to be alone."

"I'm not sure that's a good idea. I can come with you to Ma's, if you want?" Tobias wrapped his arms around her. "I'll get my things and meet you at the stable in an hour."

"Maybe I shouldn't go alone. Are you sure?"

Tobias winked. "Ma likes me. If she won't tell you the truth, maybe my astonishing good looks and charm will convince her otherwise."

THIRTY—FOUR

They carried their provisions for a few days, storing canteens of water in Ira Wilda's saddlebag to lighten the weight on their shoulders. After using the wormhole to exit the lair, Arriette led Tobias down an alternate route, through Manaia Forest in the opposite direction to Enzo, working their way around the base of the mountain instead of over or through it. In the west, the sun was beginning to set. Tobias set off to find firewood, leaving Arriette to reflect on all she'd learned. Without the threat of demonic forces looming over her, she was able to relax and let her guard down, though not entirely, and appreciate the forest for its peaceful beauty.

The final light of sunset sent a magical glow through the vibrant green canopy, showering her with warmth. Supporting her back was a humongous tree with giant diamond-shaped leaves and rustling somewhere above her was a foraging squirrel. Arriette was so engrossed in watching him that she hadn't noticed Tobias return with the firewood, or that the sun had finally gone down.

He offered her a cup of warm vegetable soup.

"There's more water in that than vegetables," he admitted, "but I'm sure Ma will feed us in Drakonta. We should arrive by tomorrow afternoon."

"Tastes good to me." She paused after taking a sip,

then said, "Didn't Casper tell you *anything* else about my family tree?"

He shook his head. "Are you worried?"

"A little. Pouki said I'd have revenge one day. Revenge for what, though? Ma told me my father died of Cancer; I was young and easily impressionable but I never thought she'd lie to me about something so important. We're at the end of one adventure and I'm not sure I can survive another."

Tobias flattened the grass with his boot and sat his own cup down, then he opened his pack and began to rummage for their loaf of bread, looking up at her every few seconds to reassure her he was listening.

"Why keep it a secret for so long?" she continued. "I can take it. I can handle whatever Ma has to say."

"Sometimes we don't lie to protect the people we love, we lie to protect ourselves," Tobias said. "It sounds selfish but it's actually just a defence mechanism."

"Then what could have traumatised her so badly?"

They fell silent, listening to the birds tweeting and rattling of the leaves, loosening a few and knocking them down into the clearing.

When Tobias had fallen asleep, Arriette focused on their fire and pitched a few harmless yellow fireballs of her own to keep it going. She much preferred a wood-fed flame. There was an unusual, spicy smell whenever she used magic. Despite feeling safer in the forest than she had in a long time, she chose not to wander off alone to find more firewood. The crackling flames were comforting and reassuring and they kept her company, filling the pitch black void of the night with its glow.

Ira Wilda knelt stood her, offering some protection in this unknown area. She threw him an apple from Tobias's pack and grinned, feeling devious for stealing his favourite fruit.

As Tobias snored loudly, scaring the squirrel away, Arriette tried to work out the mathematics behind her family's history. *How* could Casper be her grandfather?

Her mother and her sister—Arriette's unnamed aunt —would have to be Casper's twin daughters Eme and Mya Kaines, making her grandmother Christine. The children were very young when Earth fell according to what she'd learned since meeting Casper, and of course he promised never to seek them on Haeylo; he would miss watching them grow up, meeting any grandchildren or great-grandchildren. Or so he thought.

In the dirt beside her she wrote 2140AD with her finger, Haeylo's estimated year of creation (or exact if Casper was to be believed). She drew a line, writing 9280AD at the other end, leaving over 7,000 years between.

She laughed. Unless her entire family were everlasts, which they weren't, Casper couldn't be a blood relative unless by 'granddaughter' he meant a great-granddaughter or descendant. But Arriette remembered Casper had suffered through many lives on Haeylo, being reborn into the same role over and over again by Zïnnyi as per their agreement. During that time as he searched for the Recruit and, strangely, for her, it was likely he met a new partner and had a child... Arriette's mother.

It was feasible and made far more sense than her everlast theory, but how, then, had Ma not recognised her own father when they encountered Coyote in Drakonta?

No, she decided, Casper wasn't the type to abandon a pregnant woman, nor was he capable of purposefully and permanently removing their memory. Although it made the most sense, Arriette simply could not believe he would be so cruel. There *had* to be another explanation.

Arriette didn't sleep much that night but the next day she snoozed on Ira Wilda's back for a few hours until they were two miles from the main road into Drakonta. Tobias shook her awake and she hopped down, noticing her ankle was feeling stronger and more reliable.

"So," she said, yawning, "you're a loud snorer."

Tobias laughed and waved off the accusation. "You're over-exaggerating".

"You scared off that squirrel," she said. "Almost puffed out our fire, too, I had to relight it with a fireball."

"Does it make you love me any less?" He grinned.

Arriette beamed at him. After everything they'd been through, snoring was the least of her worries.

Drakonta was bustling when they arrived. The travelling tradesman was packing up, ready to move on. Arriette bought a bale of apples from him to replace the one she'd taken from Tobias and to keep Ira Wilda well stocked for their journey home.

Ma was pleased, if a little confused, to see their smiling faces and for a while they only talked pleasantries between admiring the new kitchen, drinking lemon tea and talking about their victory on the battlefield.

Tobias excused himself to check on Ira Wilda.

He kissed Arriette's cheek on the way out.

"He's a real gentleman," said Ma, touching Arriette's face with the palm of her hand, seeing through her wounds. "What is he again?"

"A dreamer, Ma."

"And how about your other friends, the angel and the old man with the beard? Are they well? Are they here too?"

Flooded with happy memories, Arriette's eyes began to fill with water and she shook her head. Ma offered a comforting hand and with the other passed Arriette a tissue.

"Baby A's fine. She's back at the lair, but Casper passed away, Ma. He lived a happy life but we all really miss him."

She remembered seeing Casper in her vision, drinking tea at the table. Zïnnyi warned her then about the consequences of her actions but seemed to reinforce the importance of ending his life too, just as her friends had done. She wondered if, in that alternate future, he had volunteered to come with Arriette instead of Tobias. Although she missed her mentor terribly, he was at peace now and the universe almost requested it. She was beginning to agree with them.

"I came to ask you about my father," she said, taking her mother by surprise. "Casper told Tobias that he was my grandfather. I need to know if that's true."

"Oh," she said, "I'm not sure I'm ready to talk about all that. Suddenly, I don't feel so well."

Arriette sighed and squeezed her mother's hand a little harder. Ma's eyes lowered and she shuffled on her chair, trying to think of a way to avoid telling her daughter the truth.

"Ma, *please.* It's important."

After a few awkward moments of silence, Ma let out a long, exasperated breath and nodded. Arriette released her hand and poured them both some more tea.

"Alright," she said. "It's true, but you should know that none of this was your father's fault. He was a brave man and he saved my life. He would *never* have approved of such secrecy and he loved you dearly."

"I'm sure he did," Arriette said, pleased to hear it direct from her mother. "So what happened? It wasn't Cancer?"

"Yes, but I should start from the beginning. My mother and your grandmother, Christine, wanted my sister and me to find my father when we arrived here on Haeylo. There were a lot of uncertainties on Earth. Chaos had erupted. We were frightened we'd lose one another, so she gave us a red apple on the night it happened. She and my eldest sister Harriet dabbled in witchcraft, though not openly. The government didn't approve and Harriet was estranged at the time. They had a reputation and an image to uphold on Earth, but they were skilled nevertheless. When we bit the apple we fell under a spell."

"What *kind* of spell?" Arriette asked, brows raised.

"It was a potion that helped us to sleep through the journey to Haeylo, but when we woke we were *different*. We didn't age like the other children and after a while we stopped celebrating our birthdays completely. We searched for years to find our father. My sister Eme said we would never see him again. We've been like that ever since. I changed my name—I haven't been Mya in... forever it feels like."

Arriette scowled, looking her mother up and down. She seemed perfectly normal. In fact, she looked like she always had since Arriette was a baby.

"Like what, Ma?"

"Time moved slowly for us. Friends grew up, married, had children of their own and were buried before we'd celebrated our next birthday. People accepted us but were ultimately afraid of us. Our family were on pause and it terrified those we once knew and loved into submission. Mother became a powerful queen, dominating our city which balanced atop a steep cliff face somewhere in the north-east; she was untouchable, everlasting. She knew and saw everything, renaming her city *the Edge*. Soon the children began to call her—"

"*Ze Entit Sehde Eyeh*," Arriette said.

Ma nodded. "You've heard her story, then?"

"Yes. So you're not everlasts?"

"Not exactly. I hear you are, though."

Arriette shuddered at the thought of how and why that pendant had chosen her in the Indalo store. Or, why and how *she* had chosen *it*.

"It was about fifty years ago I met your father. He was a guardsman at the city gate. He showered me with flowers and we walked together some nights, holding hands. He was sweet and kind to Mya but he never liked Harriet. He found her to be devious and ill-tempered. Mother didn't approve because she said he was beneath me, being human. She wanted to pair me with an everlast. She wouldn't bless the marriage of a royal to a peasant either, so we decided to run away together."

"He didn't care that you would outlive him?"

Ma smiled. "He said any time with me, no matter how short, would be an adventure."

Arriette exhaled, loving her father more and more with every word. He sounded romantic and charming, exactly as Tobias was around her.

"That must make you their *princess*? Oh my, my mother is royalty!"

"Yes, which makes you a rightful heir to the Edge, too," she said, "but at the time status meant nothing to me so to pay for food and shelter on the way, we stole two tapestries from the throne room and left the city that night. We sold them at the gate and with the money, we survived for miles. We spent our final night together at an inn a few miles south of the Edge near an old mine. The next morning we were picked up by my mother's soldiers. They separated us and—"

Arriette handed back the tissue when Ma began to cry, reliving the loss of someone she loved dearly. Arriette sipped her tea, emotional but excited to hear how she came to exist, and empathetic given her own situation.

"He was executed that night, right in front of me, but he gave me a gift your grandmother could *never* take away," she said, placing a hand across her stomach and smiling. "He gave me you. What I hadn't expected, though, was for the pregnancy to last so long. It seemed your development was cursed, too, so I hid the pregnancy well for twenty-two years. I knew when my mother found out she would take you away so I fled once again. A small group of supes attacked hoping to deal with my hideous mother, and I took the opportunity to distance myself, leaving both my sisters to fend for themselves."

"They *attacked* you?"

"My mother said so, but in honesty I think they were trying to gain control of her. She'd become, *unhinged*."

"The Recruit. They told me they'd had dealings with Ze Entit Sehde Eyeh in the past. She wore a mask, and Casper never came face-to-face with her. Do you regret leaving your family behind?"

She shook her head. "*You* were my priority. I had to protect you; it's what your father would have wanted. That mask may have concealed her real identity, but not her hatred and need for revenge for my father leaving us. I escaped and landed here in Drakonta." Ma paused. She took a few sips, rearranged her bottom in the chair, then continued. "A few months later I met your step-father,

Johnas Monroe. He never knew of my past and when I was finally showing, he asked me about my pregnancy. I never said who your real father was. You were young when he died of Cancer, Arriette, but he loved you very much. I kept his name to honour his decency."

When she'd finished her story, Ma began to clear the table in silence.

"That's why the everlast pendant chose me. I'm already... cursed?" Arriette sat with her fingers entwined, deep in thought. Somewhere out there, she had a complete —if a little crazy and irrational—family. A grandmother, aunt, and, no doubt, cousins. She could easily infiltrate their city and perhaps even meet them without being recognised if she went about it the right way.

"You look younger than you are, Arriette, and always have. I think the effects of your curse are minor, though, and now you're an everlast... young and beautiful forever." Ma beamed at her.

"For your age, you *are* a bit... baby-faced," Tobias interjected, then winked when she rolled her eyes.

Arriette joined her mother at the sink. "Did you recognise Casper when I brought him here, Ma?"

"Oh no, he was *much* younger when we parted ways, as was I, and if he recognised me he certainly never said anything."

"You were a child. Why would he?"

"Exactly, so I'm not angry. Father was bound by Zïnnyi's contract so I imagine he found out about you some other way. Don't dwell too hard on it, my dear. Time heals wounds and breaks bonds." She gave Arriette's shoulder a pat, leaving a wet handprint behind.

"So that's it, then? You're not hurt that Christine murdered my father or cursed us?"

"Of course!" she said, throwing water up in the air, "What can I do about it now, though? I'm too old for revenge. I bent down yesterday to pick up a spoon and couldn't get back up for over twenty minutes." She shook her head. "I'm sorry, Arriette, but we cannot change the past despite what your time-travelling friend believes. Death is a part of life and what you've achieved will eradicate much of the evil I experienced, paving a better future for your own children. You're a Kaines at heart like Casper, not a Monroe. Focus on that. Do you feel better now?"

"No I don't feel better!"

Arriette stormed toward the door, infuriated by her mother's lack of motivation.

"Wait, where are you going?"

She turned to face her mother with her head held high. How could she allow such treacherous behaviour to go unpunished?

"I'm going to the Edge. I'll claim my bloodline, my revenge, and my *throne,*" she said, as if she couldn't believe people actually referred to her evil grandmother as a beloved 'Queen of the Edge'. "And Mother, if *Christine* is a Kaines then I can *never* be who I truly am. Casper would understand that."

"But a Kaines is who you are, Arriette."

Arriette inhaled deeply and smiled at her wonderful memories of Casper—her grandfather.

"So be it, but for the records should I not return, and if Christine should take my life, my name is Arriette Monroe. Bury me beneath the lair's wild flowers. *Remember me.*"

The HPS

THE HAEYLOIAN POWER SCALE

1: Everlast - There are three classes of everlast, all with the power of everlasting life and the ability to communicate with other everlasts through an assigned pendant (*Mirror of the Soul*).

2: Dreamer - Power of telekinesis and power to turn imagination into reality. When in large groups, dreamers can mirror another's reality for observation purposes. This is referred to as Mirroring, Jumping or Spying.

3: Sorcerer/Rulecast - Power of wizardry through the use of magical items, potions and spells. Rulecasts specifically work with/for an everlast and have a higher level of experience.

4: Time-Traveller - The power of travel in time and space by opening and using wormholes.

5: Invisibility - The power to turn themselves and their sensory footprint invisible.

6: Angel - Possesses wings and has the power to communicate with the creator.

7: Shape-Shifter - The power to change physical shape. They can temporarily inherit the power/s of their chosen form.

8: Demon/Werewolf/Vampyr -
- *Vampyr* – power to change physical shape. Power of eternal life. Weakened by silver, sunlight and sharp wooden objects. Drinks human blood — their bite is fatal.
- *Werewolf* – there are blood born, bite born and shifter born breeds of werewolf. They form packs or clans. They can change their physical shape to that of a wolf. The three most powerful clans are the Shoku, Tri and Shou, named after the moon/s they worship.
- *Demon* – there are two species of demon, the spirit and the horned. A spirit or shade demon's claws are poisonous. Horned demons have increased strength and armour.

9: Telepathy - The power to read minds and emotions. They can read human minds clearly and most supernatural minds. From the demonic family they can only read orc minds. Vampyric minds can be accessed but only until the end of their human memories.

10: Retainer - The power to control their eidetic memory.

11: Astro-Projection - The power to separate their spiritual and physical forms. Most are able to control both forms and duplicate their existence—one as a spirit, the other as a shell. Due to experimentation, some are forced to use only their spiritual forms whilst their physical shells sleep.

12: Wiccan - The power of witchcraft using basic spells and potions. The power can be taught.

13: Orc - A demonic slave with no supernatural power.

14: Human - No supernatural power, however, most Potion Masters are human, which is a skill that can be studied.

ABOUT RACHAEL

I'm an Amazon international #1 bestselling author from the UK, and I write (mostly) fantasy and adventure books for young adults and teens.

I believe in entertaining readers by offering them a temporary escape from reality. My stories are fun, fast-paced and addictive—the ideal vacation companion, and I aim for relatable characters who embark on meaningful journeys, get into tons of trouble, but overall discover the depths of what it is to be human.

Through my emotive *Noah Finn* novellas, I also hope to encourage you to look within; to find *your* story.

Through books, I believe we can face our darkest fears, explore infinite new worlds, and realise our true purpose.

Creative writing helps me to understand what that purpose is.

Since starting my self-publishing experience in 2010, I have worked with many individuals to help make their dreams of publishing a book reality, including school children! My imprint, *Curious Cat Books (CCB)*, has been responsible for producing gorgeous children's books, memoirs and more since 2017.

***

Scan to visit Rachael's website or visit www.rachaelhardcastle.com for more information.

If you enjoyed reading this title, please consider leaving a short review and/or star rating on your favourite retailer website, as book reviews will help Rachael to reach more readers.

Thank you.

PRAISE FOR THE PREVIOUS EDITION OF *THE CHRONICLES OF PANDORA* WRITTEN AS *FINDING PANDORA* BY READERS FAVORITE

"The world of Finding Pandora is interesting on its own, comprising a mirroring history and an assortment of creatures that will make for consuming contemplation sessions.... This is testament to E. Rachael Hardcastle's ability to choose carefully what to show and what to suggest... It is with this skill that E. Rachael Hardcastle delivers a light-pierced sombre story with a compact, multifaceted plot." - **Book One**

"There is a spiritual, moral and instructive quality to this book, asking us to look at ourselves as a civilization, our values and our actions. That is where its strength lies and that is something very commendable." - **Book Two**

"Finding Pandora beats at a pace that keeps the reader's attention and interest. The story flows remarkably. The imagination, planning and execution of E. Rachael Hardcastle's work is the strongest I have ever seen it... Finding Pandora is rich with societies, environments and cultures that are bustling with life, history and tradition... But perhaps the strongest feature of the book is found in its insightful themes and discussions on evil, morality, purpose and humanity." - **Book Three**

"It is all action, anguish, emotion, twists, blood, and light. It is laced with feelings of triumph and defeat, anguish and happiness, closure and continuance. The lean economical style of E. Rachael Hardcastle accelerates the tense, quick pace... However, this isn't at the expense of depth... One thing is clear at the end, the Finding Pandora series is about sacrifice, the demands of living a purposeful life, and hope in the face of calamity. It is these poignant themes that make the series the moral force it is. As we close this chapter, we are reminded that this may not be the last time we see Arriette and the Recruit, and that should bring some excitement to fans because this story has more to offer." - **Book Four**

A NOTE FROM THE AUTHOR

Dear Reader,

If you've made it this far, thank you wholeheartedly. I wanted to give you a brief overview of the story's origins, as the path I took to share it with you is deeply important to me.

I started writing Arriette's adventures in 2010, when the series was titled *The Recruit Adventure* and was self-published in four parts: *World, Heaven, Infinity* and *Eternity* to reflect the poem it was inspired by: William Blake's *Auguries of Innocence*. A short snippet of the poem briefly features in the series in its honour—it brought me here, and continues to inspire me almost 14 years later. If you haven't read the full poem, I highly recommend the experience.

As with most indie titles, I've re-written and re-released the book a few times, most recently as *Finding Pandora* in 2018, which existed as a paperback collection of all four novels, or individual e-books. Whilst the production of that book was successful and beautiful, with *World* reaching #1 on Amazon's bestseller list, I always felt something was missing. I so desperately wanted to return to the adventure's origins to re-capture the magic I experienced all those years ago.

Writing a book is a thrilling, fun experience, but it's also hard work and takes dedication and time. Since 2010, many have supported my efforts in too many ways to fit on this page. I can't thank them all individually, but they know who they are and they know why they deserve a mention—that's what matters. Please know I am blessed and so grateful, whether we simply crossed paths or we are still in each other's lives today.

Finally, a note on my change of name. In 2010, I wanted to separate two sides of myself, so people I knew wouldn't necessarily associate me with my work, and I could write without fear of embarrassment. Since, I have accepted and embraced that being a writer is *awesome*; I'm ever so proud of it. I think about being E. R. Hardcastle fondly, as I will someday think about E. Rachael Hardcastle in the same way. But for now, I'm happy just to be Rachael. I've earned it.

And I'm so very pleased to meet you.

www.ingramcontent.com/pod-product-compliance
Lightning Source LLC
Chambersburg PA
CBHW030805210726
48290CB00002B/428